Road Kill

Texas Horror by Texas Writers

Volume 2

Edited by

E. R. BILLS

&

Bret McCORMICK

EAKIN PRESS Fort Worth, Texas
www.EakinPress.com

Published By Eakin Press
An Imprint of Wild Horse Media Group
P.O. Box 331779
Fort Worth, Texas 76163
1-817-344-7036
www.EakinPress.com

1 2 3 4 5 6 7 8 9
ISBN-10: 1-68179-099-8
ISBN-13: 978-1-68179-099-2

Contents

Foreword

2016 was a good year for Horror fiction in Texas. I met E.R. Bills at the North Texas Book Festival and *Road Kill: Texas Horror by Texas Writers (Vol 1)* came into being. Co-editing *RK1* was a task that brought me a great deal of enjoyment. The anthology got a warm reception from reviewers and readers, prompting us to keep mining that vein. *Road Kill Volume 2* presented an infinitely easier task. First, we had a full year to pull it together. Second, the press and word-of-mouth following the release of *RK1* flushed a lot of great writers out of the brush.

If there was any one criticism of our first effort, it was that it wasn't "scary enough" for serious horror fans. Thanks to this year's crop of talented writers, I'd say we've surmounted that obstacle. Every tale in ***RK2*** is an example of dark conjuring that will haunt readers and linger. A few examples that spring instantly to mind include "The Tree Servant" from Jeremy Hepler, "The Black Thumb" by Bonnie Jo Stufflebeam, "A Whistle in the Dark," from Mario E. Martinez and Ralph Robert Moore's "The Pond Behind the Trailer." I could easily express kudos for every story in the collection. They all belong here. And every last one of them will refuse to leave once you've allowed them entry into your mind.

Bret McCormick

Acknowledgments

Special thanks to our families and friends for nurturing and putting up with the acute symptoms and actual manifestations of our wayward and unconventional minds.

Southern Hospitality

By Jacklyn Baker

He can taste it on his tongue, the promise of electricity.

A spring thunderstorm is coming. He has some time—the clouds are only just starting to darken and swell. But the potential torrential rain isn't nearly as threatening to him as sundown. David Briggs figures he's got less than an hour of daylight left and very few options.

State Highway 19 stretches out in both directions. The last town he knows for certain is at least ten miles back. The next town could be half or twice as far. He can't get a GPS signal (or cell for that matter) to check and he certainly doesn't have a paper map. He's got no guarantee that if he starts walking he'll make it to a populated area before dark.

David contemplates this as he leans over the innards of his automobile. His only real option is spending the night in his car and trying to find civilization or a cell signal in the morning.

A coyote howls and two more answer the twilight call. He swears he sees something move out of the corner of his eye, but when he scans the line of trees, there's nothing there.

It would serve him right if he got eaten by a pack of coyotes. He figures that's what he gets for coming out here in the first place. He should have stayed in Big D, but something in his stupid brain told him it would be just swell to go on a one-man road trip through the great Lone Star state so he could "get some distance" from everything. He should have just stayed home and drank away his broken heart like a normal person.

He's tired, he's hungry, and he's just about ready to let the coyotes eat him, when the sound of tires crunching over the road reaches his ears.

He turns to see a Ford pickup truck, not in terrible condition but not new by any means, pulling up next to him.

"Hey there, partner," the driver says through the lowered passenger window. "You look like you could use a lift."

"Hi," David says. "Yeah. But what I could really use is a tow."

The man nods his white whiskered chin in the direction of the malfunctioning vehicle. "What seems to be the trouble?"

"I'm not really sure. I think I might've blown out the engine somehow," David says.

"Ah," the man says. "Yep, that'll do it. Welp. I can get you to town and Rick can take you back out with the tow. Won't be 'til morning, of course."

"Of course," David says. "How far is town exactly?"

"'Bout ten miles. Place called Montalba."

David winces at the distance. He's glad he didn't try walking.

"Also, ain't no place to stay in Montalba. But my daughter can probably put you up for a night. 'S it just you?"

It seems like a practical enough question, still his sense of self-preservation bristles. But it's not like he can hide the fact that he's alone. "Uh, yeah. Just me."

"She's got a bed that'll suit you then," the man says.

"I really couldn't impose on the two of you like that."

"Naw, ain't no trouble, boy." He pauses to spit slick, dark tobacco out of the driver's side window. David wrinkles his nose.

The man turns back. "Some of us still believe in that old Southern hospitality," he adds.

David doesn't move toward the vehicle.

"You coming or not?"

Climbing into a stranger's truck isn't a great idea, but neither is spending the night in his car, hungry, stranded, and surrounded by prowling coyotes—

A deep rumble comes from above.

—in a Texas thunderstorm.

"Yes, please," David says.

"Go on. Grab your stuff and throw it in the back."

David hurries to do just that. Then, he climbs into the cab and buckles himself in.

The man puts the vehicle into drive. "Got a name?"

"David. David Briggs."

"I'm Paul Till. Nice to meetcha, David."

"Thank you for picking me up, Paul. Really. I don't know what I would have done if you hadn't. I couldn't get a signal to call AAA."

"Yeah, not much of any kind of signal out here. It's not great in town either. But we still have those little old things called land-lines, so you can call whoever you need to."

"Great," David says. He gives a self-deprecating laugh. "I guess I wasn't prepared for this. At all. I'm realizing what an idiot I am now."

"Not from around here, I take it?"

"No, I'm from Dallas. I'm on a road trip."

Paul frowns. "Road trip. By yourself?"

"Yeah. It was supposed to clear my head or something. I don't think it's working."

"Huh. City types don't usually do too well out here." Paul doesn't say it in judgment; he merely states it as fact.

David still feels incredibly stupid. "Yeah," he says. "Thanks again."

"Sure thing," Paul says and keeps his eyes on the road.

David takes a moment to study Paul and the interior of the truck. Paul seems genuine enough. Weathered skin and worn hands. He looks like the kind of hard-working laborer common in small towns. There's nothing about him or the truck that screams "axe-murderer." David thinks he'd come out on top in a physical confrontation anyway. Paul looks to be well into his sixties and the hands that grip the steering wheel are marred by liver spots. David reaches down checking that his pocket knife is still in its place all the same.

When they step out of the truck at Paul's daughter's place, the sun is touching the horizon and the storm has turned into a full-grown monster. The clouds hang thick and dark above them, a solid wall of gray-black. The air is thick and too still, as if the sky is pressing in on them from all sides.

The one-story ranch house is sturdy despite its obvious age. There's no driveway or sidewalk to speak of, just trodden paths in the grass. The face of the house is a peeling white and the windows are dusty enough not to see through too well. Aside from that it seems well-maintained.

A black woman comes out, late twenties and fiddling with the sleeves of her flannel shirt. She stops on the porch with her hands on her hips and says, "What have you brought me now, Daddy?"

David double-takes. He can't have heard that right.

Paul comes around the truck, and David notices a slight limp in his left leg.

"Sheila," Paul says. "This is David Briggs. Car broke down. He's in need of a roof over his head for the night. Think you can accommodate him?"

"Well, sure." Her eyes travel over his body, scrutinizing. She must decide he measures up, because she beams at him before asking, "Engine quit on ya?"

"Yeah," David answers, unsure how she guessed that.

"We get a lot of that around here. Happens more than you'd think considering how few people pass through." she informs him. She tromps down the steps in heavy boots and extends a hand. "Sheila Till. Nice to meet you."

David shakes her hand out of habit, but his eyes are wider than they should be as he looks her in the face. "You're . . . Paul's daughter?"

She cocks an eyebrow. "Yeah. Something wrong with that?"

"No, no!" David assures her. "I just . . ."

"Expected her to be white," Paul says. "Ain't never heard of adoption?"

"I . . . Of course, I have," David says.

Paul's stare is unflinching. "Then there ain't nothing to talk about."

"I'm sorry, I didn't mean—"

Fortunately, Sheila interrupts before he says something else stupid. "Oh, Daddy, stop it. He's just giving you a hard time, David. Now come on."

Sheila ushers him inside and shows him where he'll be bunking. The room is small, but comfortable. The rusty bed frame creaks when David lays his suitcase down on top of the faded quilt that covers it. It's no Hotel ZaZa, but it will do for the night. David is just glad someone is willing to help him.

"Anybody you want to call tonight?" Sheila offers.

"No. The tow can wait until morning. I wouldn't want to go back out tonight anyway."

"Fair enough."

Paul stays for dinner and Sheila treats them to a meal of homemade beef stew and hot-from-the-oven Mrs. Baird's dinner rolls. Conversation is light and easy. They talk about what David does in Dallas and if he's got anyone special. Sheila meets Paul's eyes across the table when David informs them he just recently broke off an engagement.

"I just can't believe it," Sheila says, buttering a roll. "Someone leaving a good-looking thing like you?"

"Well, it's . . ." David stumbles over his words. "It's more complicated than that."

"I'm sure." A slow, lazy smile spreads across Sheila's face. She gazes at Paul and then David. "Still. Shame letting a man like you go to waste."

"Real shame," Paul says. His gaze is too intent on Sheila and it makes David uncomfortable.

Their relationship strikes David as odd and not because of the unusual racial pairing for the area. But he brushes it aside. It's none of his business. He doesn't bring it up. Instead he lets Sheila tell him about life on the ranch.

Thunder rolls again as David helps her clear the table.

"That certainly took long enough," Sheila says. "It's been threatening for hours."

"Won't rain for another hour still," Paul says, reaching into a tin he produces from his pocket. He places a pinch of tobacco in his mouth.

"Probably." Sheila wipes her hands on a checkered dish towel. "Bet there'll be a hell of a light show though."

She peels back the curtain above the sink to reveal the night sky. David looks over her shoulder. It's about sixty yards of nothing but grass between the house and the main strip they came in on. Several clouds spark at the same time and shadows dance between the rifts of light that spring in every direction and cast a searing purple glow on the empty field.

"What'd I say?" Sheila says, with a wide grin.

When the dishes are done, David excuses himself for the night and retreats to his bedroom. He hears the house creak around him and the sounds of Sheila and Paul saying good night. The screen door makes a distinctive clatter when it closes and David stares out the window to watch Paul's taillights drive down the dusty road until they disappear behind the trees.

A flash of lightning cracks the black sky like a fissure and illuminates the space outside his window. That empty field again. His window is on the same side as the kitchen's.

David gets ready for bed, but finds he can't sleep when he lays his head down.

Maybe it's his concern for his broken-down car or the ominous nature of the storm rising outside the window—or maybe it's just the old and creaky house itself—but David lies there with his eyes open for a long while, watching the lightning consume the room and listening to the thunder that follows. The intervals between the two get shorter and shorter.

The beams of a car's headlights break through the thin curtains and circle his room suddenly in a fleeting exchange of shadow and light across the wall. He blinks a few times, not sure who could be coming to the ranch house so late. Maybe Paul is back.

He sits up and peers out the window. He can't see much but the headlights at the other end of the field and then they blink out and he can't see anything at all.

"Odd," he mumbles to himself. Why would someone be parked all the way down there?

An electric flash illuminates the field and David sees the vehicle as clear as day.

It's his car.

David frowns, but there's no mistaking it. His car is parked on the other side of the field. He waits until the next quick-burst cluster of lightning strikes, just to be sure. But that's it. That's his car out there.

"What the hell?" he mutters.

He climbs out of bed and slips on his shoes. How in the world did his car get out here? The engine was busted.

He exits the house and begins stomping his way through the grassy field. He's not sure whether to be glad his car is working again or mad that someone drove it here without his permission.

He's only twenty yards from his car when the thought occurs to him that his keys are in his bag back at the room.

The storm is nearly on top of him. Lightning splashes through the area a beat before another rumble of thunder shakes David down to his bones.

That's when he sees the creature.

He can't think of any other way to describe the thing standing several feet behind his car. David watches in the glimpses between the light and dark as the creature unfolds from itself, like origami undone, spine shifting one vertebrae at a time. They move front to back over each other, pulling the creature's body up inch by inch. Its head doesn't follow until the last piece of its spinal column has straightened out. David can hear the grinding noise of each shifting joint, the sickening crack as each piece hits its mark. It turns fully toward David, the ribs snapping back into place like someone closed a pair of bi-fold shutters. It shuffles around on legs bent in awkward directions, the arms a similar design. It's tall, at least six feet, and it's thinner than most of the scraggly trees around there. Pale skin stretches tight across its angular bones and its eyes are enormous white spheres in its face. It stops moving and looks straight at David.

He freezes, his heart hammering in his chest. His pulse ratchets up another notch when he realizes that his pocket knife is back in his room.

The clearing fills with purple light again.

The creature is suddenly on the same side of the car as David.

David's feet move of their own accord. He takes off running for the house.

He glances back as another barrage of light goes off on all sides. The scene behind him flickers and he sees the creature, closer still, only twenty yards behind him, lumbering on all four of its stick legs and arms.

A cry for help escapes David's lips. He looks at the house, getting nearer and nearer, but not fast enough and screams for help again.

He can hear the creature's quick steps beating at the ground now, the chittering hiss of air that it emits as it closes in.

"Sheila! Paul!" The names leave his throat in a weak rasp. His lungs burn. He can see the porch steps in the gloom.

But he's knocked to the ground before he ever reaches them.

Sheila sits in the kitchen of the ranch house and cuts out recipes from a cooking magazine. The wind makes the sides of the house shudder and groan, and the thunder claps loud enough to sound like it's in the room with her.

In the intervals, she can hear the crunch of bone outside her back door.

Something squelches, wet and heavy. It's almost done.

Lightning rips through the room like machine gun fire. It overexposes the room, creating a negative space of bright white where black should be. When it fades, David Briggs stands in the doorway.

Sheila looks up.

David strides into the room and meets her heavy gaze.

"Well?" she says.

The first fat drops of rain start pounding on the roof.

David swipes a small tin off the counter and pops the lid. He brings a wad of tobacco to his mouth. He pops his jaw—once, twice—adjusting to the new skin before chewing.

"He fits."

"Good. Now get that car out of the field before somebody sees it."

He pushes open the screen door and steps out onto the porch. "Yeah, I'm going."

The screen door slams shut behind him.

Ansel & Stella

By Andrew Kozma

May 23, 2023

Dear Ansel,

The plague guns are firing again. Thud. Thud. *Like the steps of a blind giant wandering in the night. Five seconds after each thud, the sky lights up with too-beautiful greens and yellows, flowers against the stars.*

Tonight there are no screams. Either the city is empty, or a new plague is coming.

Oh, Ansel, I miss you so much. A rifle is a cold and silent companion. Useless, too. I can't remember the last time I saw one of them.

Tonight, I will eat the stew I've been saving to boost my spirits. The meat is unidentifiable.

~Stella

June 12, 2023

Dearest Stella,

Every time a postcard arrives, I cry. It is the only proof I have you're still alive.

Here in Houston, we're safe, far from the fighting on either coast. So don't worry. Don't! I know you want to, but the underwater fence off Galveston's shore is solid. They won't be able to get through.

Your sister is doing great—I know you were afraid to ask. The prostheses are perfect fits, but sometimes the loss overwhelms her. And it's impossible to blame her. She dreams of the front and can't stop. She asks where you are, how you are. Okay, I tell her. Again and again.

God help me, you better stay that way.

Love,
Love,
Love,

Ansel

June 29, 2023

Dear Ansel,

Today it was water worms. Yesterday, a fucking mob of rat bombs. Tomorrow, I'm expecting the sun itself to burn us from our holes like ants under a magnifying glass.

Every day, a hundred times, I find myself wishing you were here, and then I'm horrified. This is a place for no one, woman or man, or whatever they are.

At night, I want to dream of you, of sleeping in your wide bed, your arms around me, a grand meal of roasted vegetables and ground lamb over lemon couscous, but all I dream of are those I've killed, their half-faces melting as they die. The bodies they've taken dead long before.

I should feel better about that.

I don't.

~Stella

July 19, 2023

Dearest Stella,

Last week I sent you a care package of beef jerky (jalapeño flavored), dark chocolate and tampons. I hope it got there okay. I know supplies are hard to get on the front. I have to admit, it's getting harder to find them here, too.

Are you getting these postcards? I don't even know why I ask—the military will just edit out the parts they don't like.

God, now I'm hoping they actually do edit mail. This is too depressing.

Your mother's stopped talking to me, or to anyone.

At night, the air shields glow brilliantly when they intercept something. It could be a malsquito swarm or just a lost bird. The light fades, and I think of you.

Love
Love   Ansel
Love

August 1, 2023

Dear Ansel,

No package arrived. No one in my unit has received a package from home for weeks. It's the uppers, taking what's mailed in and dividing it between all of us. Hard to blame them.

Oh, Ansel, it's getting harder to breathe without you near me. I don't know how Cassie stood it for so long on the front without going mad, and I'm glad she's home now, even with the injuries.

The plague guns have been silent for days, but the plagues are here to stay. Every day another vaccination. Every morning, a mouth coated in dried glue, a stomach full of rotting meat.

Please smile for me when you get this. I can feel it from here.

~Stella

August 19, 2023

Dearest Stella,

Cassie is gone.

I know this isn't what you want to hear right now. What you want to hear is that we're all fine. That they aren't encroaching on Galveston. That gas and water aren't being rationed. That they aren't sending people door to door to "encourage" volunteering for local Houston defense. That your family is safe and sound. But I know you'd never forgive me if I didn't tell you about Cassie. She left no note. Your mom (your dad tells me) thinks she might've returned to the front.

I know what you're doing is necessary and important, but I don't care anymore. I don't. I need you here. You need to be here.

Please come home.

Love,

Ansel

August 22, 2023

Dearest Stella,

You will never read this.

Today I received your death notification. When the women knocked on the door, I opened it. I opened it. Then I slammed it in their faces.

They understood, and I know they'll be back, and I'll invite them in for coffee, and apologize, and they will tell me how you died, because I will ask, because even though I don't want to know, I have to know.

Then they will politely finish their coffee and politely leave.

I am writing this to you because there is nothing else I can do.

Cassie is still missing.

No one else here knows you're dead yet.

I'm sorry. I'm not strong enough to tell them.

Love,
Ansel

August 31, 2023

Dear Ansel,

For twelve whole hours there's been no fighting. No one knows why, but whenever there's a lull, there's talk of a truce. An end to the war.

Today, in the distance, I saw one of them, perched high on the remains of an office building. It was watching birds playing in the air. Jackie wanted to snipe it, but I stopped her. I'm still not sure why. Soon we'll be trying to kill each other again anyway.

Instead, I watched the birds, too. You would've been able to tell me what they were. Today, I honestly wished you were here with me, for this short peace.

You would've loved it.

~Stella

The Pond Behind the Trailer

by Ralph Robert Moore

The forest smelled like skunk.

Jonathan made his way deeper down the path. Wishing he had worn a long-sleeved shirt and heavier shoes. Bending forward to walk under low branches, lifting his knees to avoid tripping over exposed roots. Surprised at the woods' wetness.

Because he was so deep under the canopy, the air was not only cooler this time of day, but darker. Zebra and pink sunlight.

The day getting even darker, it occurred to him he might have to spend the night sleeping on the forest floor. Not a pleasant thought.

As the sun went down through the trees, the weight of the woods lowered onto his back. Animal cries around him increased. He made more and more faces to himself, drawing in his shoulders, then up ahead spotted a large clearing.

At the rear of the clearing, a quarter mile away, a trailer.

He recognized the trailer from his dreams.

Trotted towards it, across the clearing, exertions of his breaths in his ears, knapsack banging on his back.

As he came up on the trailer, its white metal door flung open.

A young woman lowered her sneakers down the three concrete steps, aiming a black handgun at his face. Long dark hair, the type that never stays in place.

She jerked up her chin, hand that held the gun shaking. "Is this your trailer?" Frightened young woman trying to act tough.

He threw up his hands. Lowered his head. Closed his eyes.

"No."

"Do you know who does own it?"

"No."

Hands up in the air, head still tilted down, he opened his eyes. "Can you get that gun out of my face, please?"

"It's not a real gun."

Still pointing the muzzle at his face, she squeezed the trigger.

A long line of water squirted out of the front of the gun, landing in his left eye.

He backed up, blinking, hands lowering.

Inside the trailer, knees bending sideways, he slipped off his knapsack.

The girl, not as nervous as before, placed her water pistol on the kitchen counter, by the sink. Smiled. "Do you know why we're here?"

"No."

Saw her twist her smile to one side of her mouth. Disappointed.

He took a better look at her. Half woman, half tall kid. Slender neck.

"Do you know?"

A shake of her long-haired head.

"I guess we sleep here tonight?"

She raised up on tip toes. "I get the bedroom, because I got here first." Gave him one of those firm stares kids think are unchallengeable.

But he was happy to sleep on the living room carpet. Better than sleeping in the forest.

Once that was settled, she opened up. "I didn't bring any food. Did you? There's a pond out back. There's two sets of snorkeling equipment under the kitchen sink. Masks, flippers. There's a bag of split peas in the cabinet. We could make split pea soup. There are instructions on the package."

"At least something here has instructions."

She didn't catch at first he was making a joke, but once she did, her young face split into a goofy grin. Somebody's kid sister. A lot of her tension getting released.

The pea soup was actually pretty good. Even though it didn't have the ham hocks you were supposed to cook with the peas.

The side of his metal spoon scraped up the curve of the bowl, scooping the last of the thickened soup.

Sitting across from him at the small kitchen table, she showed him the bottom of her bowl. "I still have some left. You want it?"

"No. You eat it."

"So it was pretty good? I never made a soup before. Like, ever."

"Yeah, it was."

Outside the window, animal cries.

"Did you lock the front door?"

She nodded.

He reached into his pants. "Mind if I smoke?"

"No! Can I have one too?"

He blew his smoke sideways, away from her, toward the trailer's stove. "I said the soup was 'pretty good', but actually, I really liked it. I just used 'pretty good' like most people do. My dad asked me a few weeks ago on the phone how my classes at SMU were going, and I said, 'pretty good.' He told me, Don't ever say 'pretty good.' 'Pretty good' isn't good enough. Everything in your life should be great. So yeah, your soup was great."

Her young face blushed. "Yeah, my parents keep trying to give me advice, too. I don't think they understand I'm really a lot more sophisticated for my age than they realize." She put her elbow on the kitchen table, carefully brought the cigarette to her lips, as if it were in an ivory holder. "I don't just read Harry Potter books. I read William S. Burroughs, too. Which would completely blow their minds if they knew."

"The truth is, college really is only pretty good, no matter what my dad says. But being here, in this trailer, out in the middle of nowhere, with you, not knowing what's going to happen, this is great. This is how life should be. Do you mind if I ask how old you are?"

She flung her long, black hair away from her face. "Wanna guess?"

Jonathan could see, behind her bravado and the tension in her eyes that she was just a kid. "Twenty?"

She snorted, relieved. In a low voice, looking away, cheeks red, she said, "Try fourteen."

"I never would have thought."

Proud, she smirked at him. "My mom said I developed early, like her." She avoided his eyes. "So, like, how old are you?"

"Nineteen."

If they had beer they would have gone through it, but since there wasn't any beer in the trailer, they smoked a few more cigarettes together at the kitchen table, then she went into the trailer's one bedroom. He lay down on the rough living room carpet, pulling a blanket Heather gave him over his shoulders.

The next morning he opened the door to the fridge, missing eggs. Nothing but wire racks and the glare of a small light bulb. Opened each cabinet door in the kitchen, nothing but pots and pans.

"There's snorkeling equipment under the kitchen sink. Maybe there's some fish in the pond?"

He made a face. "I don't think it would be a good idea to eat any fish from such a small pond."

"Oh. Well, yeah. I guess." Looked embarrassed.

He tried to turn it around. "When I was in the boy scouts, they taught us how to identify edible plants and roots and stuff. What if the two of us go foraging in the woods, and whatever we find, maybe we could turn it into a soup? But maybe you could be in charge of how the soup was made? Since your split pea soup turned out so great? I don't know anything about cooking."

That cheered her up. "Well, most guys don't. But I cook with my mom all the time. Not the dinners, but I help with breakfast. Usually I'm the one who makes the toast, and pours the orange juice."

He emptied his knapsack, so they could fill it with whatever they found.

And it was a lot of fun. It was nice going back into the woods, although not too far, not alone anymore but with her, knowing they had the trailer to return to, once they were done. And it was fun talking to Heather, telling her jokes, making her laugh. At one point, she laughed so hard she started to cry, waving her left hand at his face, pleading with him to stop. He waited until she looked at him again, then made another funny face. She punched his upper arm.

Once they were back in their trailer, he upended his knapsack over the kitchen table, pinching its bottom corners to shake out everything, all sorts of green, purple and pink forages.

"Okay. Bringing home the bacon. We got a lot of wild onion, plenty of mushrooms, some thyme, Indian Cucumber roots, and gooseberries. We can boil them all together to make a soup."

He selected a Dutch oven from the kitchen, took it outside to the pond, Heather following. Waded in, filled the Dutch oven with pond water.

He carried the Dutch oven back inside, holding the handles, water sloshing. Set it on the stove's widest burner. "Once we bring it to a boil, which will sterilize the water, we can add what we gathered, let it cook a while, and it becomes soup."

Heather got the bedroom to herself again. Jonathan slept on the carpet in the living room.

Around three in the morning, Jonathan woke. Took him a minute, limbs shifting, to realize where he was, deep in the east Texas woods, in a trailer. Fourteen-year-old girl sleeping in the bedroom.

He heard it again.

A noise from outside the trailer.

He sat up on the hard carpet. Ran his fingers through his hair. Raised his head, ear tilted.

Didn't hear anything.

Taking a flashlight, he opened the trailer's door. Went down the three concrete steps, out into the wet darkness and insect buzzes of the night.

Far off tree tops, barely visible in the starlight.

Jonathan listened, hair still sticking up from the way he slept.

And then he did heard it again.

Something rapid, start and stop.

He turned around and around, trying to locate the source.

Looked straight up.

Out here in the wilderness, away from any city, the black sky was full of stars.

The noise was coming from the sky.

Actually, two noises. One noise, then another.

A conversation.

Way up in the sky.

He couldn't make out any words. After about an hour, the back and forth hissing stopped.

The next morning, he was sitting at the kitchen table, counting how many cigarettes they had left, when Heather came out of the bedroom, barefoot, black hair even more mussed than usual.

Her eyes were red. Hands trembling.

"I just . . ." She burst into tears, hand against her hair.

Jonathan stood up from the table, putting his palms gently on her shoulders, guiding her over to a chair.

Once seated, she reached her fingers across the table, grabbing Jonathan's hands. "It was so awful!"

Jonathan squeezed back. "What did you dream?"

She kept her eyes down. "It was the worst nightmare I ever had in my life. Like when you're a kid, and you're paralyzed with fear?"

"What was it about?"

She swung her head. "I don't want to talk about it." Burst into new, hot tears. "I just want it to go away, but it won't go away. I can't get it out of my head."

Jonathan foraged on his own. Went back to the same patches they had visited the day before. On his way back, he killed a squirrel, swinging the hoe he had with him down at the ground.

So they'd have meat in their broth, tonight.

Heather was afraid to go to sleep because of the horrible nightmare she had. So instead of her going into the bedroom once it got dark, the two of them sat at the kitchen table, across from each other. If she fell asleep and her black eyebrows started pulling toward each other, he could wake her. Plus this way they could listen, kitchen window slid open, to see if the conversation in the sky came back.

He took off his wristwatch, placed it on the table.

At eleven-forty, a loud clapping. From outside.

Both of them, sitting at the kitchen table, heads nodding, fighting sleep, opened their eyes. Got up out of their chairs. Swung out the trailer's front door. Shuffled down the concrete steps.

A beautiful night. Constellations in the sky. Cool, moist air on their skin.

Heads tilted back, they walked around in little circles. The clapping was definitely coming from somewhere up above the clouds.

As they listened, the clapping, which had been machine-like, became rhythmic. It wasn't a rhythm Jonathan had ever heard before. But it was compelling.

Heather pointed up, at a slant. "Look!"

Something small dropped from the sky. They watched its fall, squinting to see what it was, but it was too small, its fall too rapid.

With a modest splash, it landed in the middle of the pond.

Heather looked at Jonathan.

Circles from the splash rippled outwards across the surface, in the banana moonlight, melting away.

Insect sounds started back up.

The pond's surface was still.

Jonathan walked around to the far side of the pond. Stepped up to its edge, sliding the yellow oval from his flashlight across the misty surface.

"See anything?"

He shook his head. Peered some more, gave up. "We can't do anything tonight. It's too dark."

"There's snorkeling equipment. Under the sink. For two people."

He walked back along the rim of the pond. "Maybe tomorrow, when it's light."

No food for breakfast.

He opened the panel doors under the kitchen sink.

The large, downward bulk of the sink's underside. Cartoon of white PVC pipes. A sponge blue on one side, orange on the other. Tall tangle of scuba diving equipment.

He pulled the black rubber shapes out onto the kitchen floor, stepping back, away, expecting cockroaches and mouse droppings, but nothing.

Like Heather said, two sets of equipment.

Two black rubber face masks, clear plastic visors. Two sets of black rubber flippers. Two snorkeling tubes, black rubber mouth piece at the bottom, white circular tube on the side of the mouth piece opening, like a wide white straw, at the top.

Jonathan untangled one set of the equipment. "I'll go in the pond."

Heather picked up the other set.

Outside, in the hot air, they stripped to their underwear.

He avoided looking at her body. Didn't want to make her or him self-conscious.

They strapped on the equipment.

Looking a little ridiculous.

Heather flip-flopped over. Just a head below his height. "I appreciate you doing this." Sincere blue eyes looking up at him.

She high-stepped her skinny legs, black flippers, to the edge of the pond. Her scared face turned back to Jonathan. "How about I go right, you go left, then we meet in the middle?"

Jonathan nodded. Fitted the black rubber mouthpiece between his lips.

He stepped his big black duck feet into the pond. The cold water slid around his ankles. Up his calves, and he was only a yard in. The underwater slope of the pond was more pitched than he expected. The middle was probably over his head. Maybe quite a bit over his head.

When the water was up to the waistband of his underpants, he looked down at the rippled surface. Mosquitos circling and dipping. He couldn't see underneath. The pond was too cloudy with tiny organisms, what you would expect with a stagnant body of water.

He brought his palms together, leaned forward. When his bare chest touched the cold surface, he lifted his flippers off the pond's floor.

He was floating horizontal. Waved his flippers up, down, behind him, just below the surface, to propel him toward the middle of the pond.

Face in the water, breathing through his snorkeling tube, breaths magnified in his ears, he could see, through his clear plastic face mask, several feet down.

Waving plants, surrounded by little silver bubbles.

Once he reached the middle, he lifted his face mask off the surface, with a slight suction, looking for Heather. Drops sliding across the front of the mask, he couldn't see her.

He took a big breath. Bent the front of his body downwards. His flippered feet rose in the air above the surface of the water. He dove straight down toward the shadow-waving bottom of the pond.

Standing in his flippered feet in the silt at the bottom, he twisted his face mask left, right, looking around for anything out of place.

Pushed off from the squishy bottom, hands pulling above his head to get him back to the surface.

Blew out the water in the snorkeling tube. Still got a mouthful of the brackish pond. Blew out again.

Swam across the surface another dozen feet, dived back down.

On his third dive, he saw a large, blurred figure swimming towards him.

The figure jerked to a stop, going vertical in the green water.

Came closer, cautiously.

Jonathan and Heather looked at each other's face masks from deep underwater.

She shrugged her shoulders.

Jonathan shrugged back.

Together, they pushed up to the surface, to sunlight.

Faces down in the water, they paddled back to the pond's grassy shore.

Jonathan stood up out of the water first, pulling the mask and tube off his face.

Hair plastered to his skull, he stepped the rest of the way out of the water, spitting.

Dropped his snorkeling mask on the grass.

Looked at Heather. "What did you just say?"

Heather, bent over, balancing on one foot, then the other, pulled off her black rubber flippers. "What?"

Behind her, in the center of the pond, bubbles broke on the surface. The bubbles grew bigger and whiter, spreading.

Jonathan and Heather backed away from the pond.

Something snaked across the surface of the water, toward them.

Stopped just before the edge of the pond.

Lifted its head out of the water.

Heather walked over to Jonathan's side, for protection. "Is that a turtle?"

The turtle, about ten inches long, raised most of its body out of the water. How could a turtle do that?

Dead-eyed face twisting left and right, like a machine that doesn't quite work right, spitting out sounds.

Jonathan's head flooded with black and red numbers. He lost his balance under the numbers' weight, falling. Lying on the grass, he tried adding up the numbers, sort them by color, but then more and more black and red numbers would pop up, to where he'd have to start again from zero.

Heather stepped back, frightened, uncertain, looking at Jonathan.

He jerked up onto his knees. His bare feet.

Red and black numbers enlarging, shrinking.

He walked forward on stiff knees.

Stepped into the pond, bending his body forward, until his face was right above the turtle.

The turtle pursed its lips. Sprayed pond water across Jonathan's face.

Jonathan obediently bent his face closer to the turtle's lips. The turtle rose further out of the water, licking its green tongue sideways across Jonathan's submissive forehead.

Heather's voice was high, thin. "Jonathan? What are you doing?"

He fell on the grass, eyes squeezed shut, moaning.

The turtle crawled out of the pond.

"Jonathan? You okay?"

She padded towards where he was rolling on the grass.

The turtle changed direction, heading her way.

She knelt down next to Jonathan, put her arm across his back. "You okay? Did it do something to you?"

She glanced at the turtle. Its progress across the grass toward her was taking a long while, leathery paws thumping slowly across the green blades. Plenty of time to drag Jonathan away.

Sitting him up on the grass, she got her arms through his armpits.

Heard a hiss.

Looked back at the turtle.

Its shell wobbled.

Life is normal, and then it isn't.

Pale toes unfurled from one side of the turtle's face, spreading apart like half a ruff.

Heather stayed on her knees, staring.

The toes wiggled. A long, naked male leg pushed out the side of the turtle's face.

Another male leg slid out the other side of the turtle's triumphant face.

Heather stood up.

A third male leg popped out at the back of the turtle's shell, on the left.

Heather looked down at Jonathan. Twisted around, to see how far away was the trailer.

A fourth male leg sprang out the back of the turtle's shell, on the right.

The four long, naked male legs flexed, lifting the turtle up in the air.

"Jonathan?"

The four legs swayed above the grass, twenty toes digging in.

She turned to run to the trailer.

The legs ran after her.

Faster than her.

Jonathan rolled over onto his back, desperately trying to solve the red and black computations, so he could get all those numbers out of his head.

He saw her getting dragged past him, toward the pond. The turtle's face above the four legs smirking.

Her small hands grasped at grass blades, getting yanked free, yanked free.

Her upside-down eyes pleaded with him to help her, to save her, and he wanted to, he really, really wanted to save her, but he couldn't solve the equations no matter how hard he tried.

She was dragged into the pond, into that awful water, crying like a kid, fighting with the energy of a kid, but once the turtle had her out over her head, in its element, her body was easily pulled under. Her flailing arms, her slender neck, her terrified kid's face.

Bubbles from her underwater struggle rose to the surface.

The red and black numbers left his mind.

He rolled over onto his back, free again.

The pond's surface was still.

He didn't go back into the trailer, because he didn't want to see the Dutch oven sitting on a stove burner, his blanket on the living room floor, her unmade bed.

He slept by the pond.

Woke up in the bed inside the trailer. All he remembered was his walk through the woods, to get here.

He was in the kitchen, flipping open cabinet doors, when he heard a noise outside.

A man walked across the clearing, toward him.

Jonathan pushed open the trailer's metal door, went down the three concrete steps.

The man stopped in his tracks, startled.

Jonathan lifted his jaw. "Is this your trailer?"

The Tree Servant

By Jeremy Hepler

I finally led Terry to the tree yesterday.

He arrived at my house for Saturday morning smokes and coffee just before 8 a.m. I was on the back porch in my rocking chair, watching the woods behind the house awaken. Treetop branches danced with the gentle autumn breeze. Most of the leaves had dropped, coloring the ground in smudges of gold and maroon and brown. Squirrels darted up and down the trunks, in and out of the leaves, their mouths fat with acorns.

When Terry's cane clacked on the porch, I turned my attention his way. His face was pale, eyes sunken in deep sockets. He'd lost a good fifty pounds in the past year, making his flannel shirt appear two sizes too big. The belt holding his jeans up had a fresh hole punched in the leather. "I didn't hear your truck," I said.

He made his way to the other rocker, leaned his cane against the table between us, sat down, and sighed in relief. "Doc Price says I should walk as much as possible when I have the strength."

I nodded. Terry's farmhouse was two miles south of mine. He was approaching eighty and had suffered three strokes in the past year and a half, the last one three months ago. Since then, his left arm and leg didn't work all that well. The left side of his face drooped some. And words traveled from his mind to his lips slower. Not that I was in better physical shape. We were both on the last leg of the race. In July, Doc Price had found an inoperable tumor in my brain. It was about the size of a golf ball, and "aggressive as a caged raccoon" in his words.

"How'd the leg hold up?" I asked.

Terry picked up the coffee mug I'd filled for him and took a sip. "As good as it can, I guess."

I nodded and offered him a cigarette. He lit up, and we smoked and watched the squirrels scurry for a minute or two before he said, "How are the headaches?"

"They come and go." I'd had a twelve hour banger the day before. "But mostly come."

He pressed his lips together and nodded. After sixty plus years of friendship, nods, head shakes, shrugs and smiles made up a large percentage of our conversations. And at our ages that was okay. Welcome even.

We sat and smoked in silence until we sipped our coffee cups dry. When I set my cup on the table, he looked my way. "I know you already walked a long way this morning," I said. "But are you up for a walk in the woods? For old time's sake?"

He smiled, mostly with the right side of his mouth, and nodded.

I smiled back.

The woods behind the house covered hundreds of acres of East Texas flatlands and rolling hills. As kids, Terry and I had spent countless hours exploring its depths. Shooting squirrels and birds with pellet guns. Building forts. Crafting spears and swords from sticks. Hiding from the Klepper brothers who often chased us after school, wanting to beat my ass for being black, Terry's for being the black guy's white friend. How we avoided coming upon the tree during those early years, I can't say. Probably simple luck. But when we were older and ventured into the woods to drink beer or hunt or something, I'd made sure Terry didn't come across the tree. Especially in the fall.

Terry and I didn't speak as I slowly led him through the woods. Birds marked our coming with paranoid tweets. Small animals scattered and hid. A light breeze stirred the leaves. When we were about ten yards from the tree, I stopped and waited for Terry to catch up.

"There's something I've wanted to tell you for a long time," I said.

He wiped the sweat off his forehead with his sleeve and nodded, probably assuming I was about to tell him something about the tumor or my burial wishes.

My mouth suddenly felt as dry as sheetrock. As though the secret I'd held for sixty plus years and wanted to set free was fighting its release. I cleared my throat, swished around what little spit I could muster, and managed, "I know what happened to Mark."

Terry's eyes perked up at hearing his brother's name. A name we hadn't spoken out loud in many years. Mark and Terry's father and mother had abandoned them when they were seven and five, respectively. Although they were adopted and loved by Lutheran Preacher Cal Parker and his wife Kathy, a middle-aged couple unable to have kids of their own, Mark had been the only family member Terry ever really connected with. His sole blood relative.

"What?"

"I lied about him not coming to my house the day he disappeared." A long pause. "I watched him die, Terry."

Leaning on his cane to support his tired leg, Terry just stared at me, confused. Baffled. His eyes never left mine as I told him about what had happened to Mark.

Mark died on a calm autumn day in 1953, two months after my thirteenth birthday.

Terry was sick with the flu that Saturday, so Mark walked to my house alone, hoping I would play catch with him. As a freshman, he was the Hudson high varsity backup quarterback. The night before, starter Jimmy Clawson had been injured, meaning Mark would take the helm the following Friday. When I answered the door, Mark asked if I would run some routes for him like Terry and I had done the previous summer. Help him hone his accuracy for the upcoming game. I said, "Sure."

We played catch in the clearing between the house and the dirt road for about ten or fifteen minutes before my grandpa stepped out onto the front porch and called us over.

I'd lived with my grandpa since I was three. My dad had died in the early 40s at the Mesa Tortilla Factory, drowning under tons of corn when a silo he was cleaning was accidentally filled. Afterward, my mom "lost her mind" according to Grandpa and ran off—a parental abandonment that Terry and I had in common. An abandonment that transcended race and culture. An abandonment that solidified our friendship shortly after we met in grade school.

"Louis, you boys meet me around back," Grandpa said as we approached. "I need your help finding Scooter."

Scooter was his dog. A small, raggedy gray poodle with a penchant for chasing squirrels deep into the woods.

Mark and I tossed the ball back and forth as we made our way around the side of the house to the back yard. Grandpa cut through the house and met us at the edge of the woods. He was only sixty, but looked closer to seventy-five or eighty. A lack of medical care combined with laboring in corn fields since he was eight years old had ruined his body. Chronic lower back pain caused him to walk with a pronounced slump. Tips of two of his fingers were missing, a couple of others crooked from breaks. Arthritis attacked his knees and knuckles. And piss yellow cataracts were progressively taking over his eyes.

"Did she chase a squirrel again?" I asked.

He nodded. "Ran to the west."

"You can stay here," I offered.

"Yeah," Mark added, pushing his sweatshirt sleeves up to his elbows. "We'll go get her, Mr. Jackson."

Grandpa shook his head, buttoned up his sweater. "Nah. I'll go, too. You boys just stay close and keep your eyes peeled."

Tossing the ball when space permitted, we sloshed through the fallen leaves, following Grandpa as he whistled and called out, "Scooter!" time and again. We crossed paths with a few squirrels and rabbits, even startled a bedded down fawn, but didn't see or hear any sign of Scooter.

About thirty minutes later, we were in a section of the woods I didn't recognize. Grandpa stopped beside a large cottonwood and leaned his shoulder on it, seemingly exhausted.

"You all right, Grandpa?"

"Just need to catch my breath."

"You want to head back?" I asked.

Mark ran his hand over his crew-cut and looked in the direction of the house. "Yeah," he added. "Maybe Scooter looped around and went back home."

Grandpa didn't answer. He moved away from the tree, squinting, eyeing something behind me. "Look there," he said, and pointed toward a large oak about twenty feet away.

I looked over my shoulder but saw nothing but trees and leaves and little patches of gray sky.

"What is it?"

"It's Scooter. She just ran behind that big tree. Go get her, boys."

Mark looked at me with the excitement of a hunt dancing in his eyes. "You go around the left," he said. "I'll take the right."

I nodded, and he darted toward the oak tree, cradling the football, dodging small trees and shrubbery as though they were lunging linebackers. I ran, too. When we rounded the tree we stopped and scanned the area but didn't see Scooter. I glanced at my Grandpa. He was leaning against the cottonwood again, his eyes aimed our direction.

"She's not here," I hollered.

"Sometimes she crawls up under the leaves. Hides behind big roots. Keep looking."

As Mark and I moved in opposite directions away from the oak tree, searching, the fallen leaves began to rustle, lifting off the ground in random spurts as if jumping for joy. At first I didn't think much of it. Gusts of wind whistled through the woods and jostled leaves all the time. A pile scattered. A new pile formed. No big deal. But when I realized all the leaves were moving toward Mark, thickening and quickening as they approached his back, my stomach turned to cement. I called his name, and he looked over his shoulder at me, smiling. I'll never forget that All-American smile. And how it disappeared when he noticed the leaves.

He dropped the football as they swarmed his feet. "What the hell?" he screamed, swatting at the leaves scurrying up his leg. "What's—"

He broke off as more leaves—hundreds of leaves—climbed, blanketing his legs and torso and arms and shoulders. Encasing his body. Rustling in apparent excitement. His desperate eyes met mine as the leaves crawled up his neck and face. When he opened his mouth to scream, they quickly covered the gap, some appearing to dive inside. In a matter of seconds, he was engulfed from head to toe, motionless, with his arms angled out to his sides. Like an autumn-colored scarecrow. A living work of art. Part of the forest.

I tried to run to him, to help, but I couldn't move. I looked down and realized I was covered up to my ankles in leaves. Moving leaves. Strong leaves. Leaves with legs. Leaves with mouths and teeth. Leaves working as one entity to anchor me to my spot. When I bent and tried to brush them away, they ran up my hands and arms. Before I was upright again, they'd covered my entire body except my face. And that's when I first heard their voices.

"Watch him die," they whispered.

My eyes bulged. "Ma—"

Three or four leaves crawled over my mouth and clamped it shut. The leaves on the ground in front of Mark piled on top of one another, forming a crude leaf rope that stretched to his chest. Then it pulled him to the ground. All the nearby leaves dog-piled his body. Muffled, terrified screams escaped the pile as it grew and moved and rustled.

My eyes filled with tears, and I cut them to my right, hoping to see Grandpa coming to help me. He wasn't. He was gone. He'd abandoned me. My heart hitched. I thought I was going to die. Knew I was. Every muscle in my body tightened, and I fought to free my arms and legs, fought to open my mouth, but I couldn't. I felt as if I'd been wrapped in iron. Tears trickled from my eyes as the pile of leaves housing Mark shifted and warped.

"Don't cry for him," the leaves whispered.

I closed my eyes. Leaves moved up my face and forced the lids open, held them tight.

"You must watch him die."

My eyes burned to blink. Ached to not see. Tears streamed down my cheeks. The pile shifted and shrank, as though dissolving into the ground. Eventually, after what seemed like an eternity, the leaves' movements lessened to light quivers and stopped, leaving the ground as it was before the attack—a benign, harmless, leaf-strewn forest floor. The only sign Mark had been there was the football he'd dropped. It was lying in front of the oak tree trunk.

My focus was on the ball when the leaves on my eyes and mouth released their grips and crawled away. I gasped and let out a soft cry for help.

"You are the help," the leaves whispered. "You're the Tree Servant now."

I didn't know what to say. What to do. What was real. "I . . . I'm…"

"Go back to your grandpa."

The leaves imprisoning my body fell to the ground as though they were metal and the magnet holding them in place had been turned off. I immediately ran to where Mark's body had fallen and combed my hands through the leaves, saying his name over and over. I patted my foot around, then stomped, but met only solid ground. I shook my head in disbelief. In terror. My hands and knees trembled. Mark was gone. Swallowed? Eaten? Evaporated? Buried? Taken? Where? Why?

The possibilities were horrifying.

I spun in frantic circles for a moment before running, stopping only to scoop up Mark's football as I passed the oak tree.

It felt like I ran for hours before I reached the edge of the woods. When I finally burst into my grandpa's back yard, I collapsed to the ground, crying, hugging the football.

When I finished the story, I could see the gears turning in Terry's head, grinding through the details, trying to make sense of it. He was a practical man. A down-to-earth man. An old school Texan who read the newspaper and enjoyed historical biographies. He didn't believe in aliens or demons or ghosts, and his natural tendency was to reject the absurd.

A long silence spooled out before he said, "I think that tumor has knocked you off your rocker."

I shook my head.

"Doc Price said you might start having problems with memory and stuff." He sounded as though he were trying to convince himself as much as me.

"It's a true story, Terry."

"I know you may think it's true but—"

"But nothing," I said harsher than I'd intended. "It's true. All of it."

"If it really happened, where's Mark's football?"

"Grandpa took it out of my room while I slept that night and buried it somewhere in the woods. He wouldn't tell me where."

"Your grandpa wouldn't do that."

"He took us to the tree on purpose, Terry. He knew what would happen."

Terry's eyes fell to his feet for a long moment, then rose and met mine.

"When I stopped crying and got up off the ground," I said. "I saw my grandpa sitting in his rocker on the back porch, smoking. Scooter was in his lap."

Terry's mouth slightly opened but he remained silent.

"I stopped dead in my tracks when I saw him sitting there rocking and smoking so calmly. Like nothing had happened. Like leaves hadn't just come alive and eaten Mark."

After a brief hesitation, Terry nodded for me to go on.

And I did.

Holding Mark's football close to my chest, I sat on the porch steps in front of Grandpa. He dropped his cigarette, smashed it under his shoe, then leaned forward and patted my shoulder.

"You okay? I know it's hard to watch the first time."

I lied with a nod, licked my dry lips, looked at the woods. So many questions were circling my head. I had no idea where to start. Everything I'd been taught about physics science in school, everything I thought I knew about my grandpa, everything I believed about the line between reality and fantasy, had all been shattered.

"I know it's hard to wrap your head around," Grandpa said. "It confused me when my Pa showed me, too."

I made eye contact with Grandpa. His yellow-stained eyes were slitted with sincerity and wisdom. "Why did you . . ." I couldn't manage to force the rest of the words out.

Grandpa nodded as though he understood the question, anyway. "Three of our family members were hung in that oak tree in autumn, 1913. Two men and one woman. Tobin. Jim. And Clara. A group of Hudson whites, some of whom had claimed to be their friends, accused them of stealing some livestock and feed. When they denied it, the mob dragged them out to the woods and strung them up. Ever since then, their souls are tied to that tree, and they can't move on until justice is served. Until all the descendants of their murderers are dead." The corners of his mouth turned down and he shook his head in disgust. "Since ours were not allowed to have families that could carry on their name, their murderers must not, either. That's where we come in. Whenever possible, the Tree Servant is to bring them one of the murderer's descendants within a week of when the leaves drop."

"How do you know all this?"

"My Pa told me, like I'm telling you. He was the first one to serve." He looked at the woods, back at me. "When he got too old to lure descendants out there, he passed the job to me. Now I'm passing it to you. I would've liked to have waited until you were older, but my body's falling apart. I don't know how much longer I have."

I shook my head. I didn't want the job. I didn't want to be the Tree Servant. I didn't want to lure people to their deaths. I wanted to be a professional baseball player like Jackie Robinson. "I don't want to be the Tree Servant."

"You don't have a choice. We're all they have. It's up to us to make sure they get justice."

My eyes welled up, and I shook my head again. "I can't watch anyone else die. Mark was my friend . . . Mark was . . . "

"I know it's hard, but it has to be done. The Tree Servant has to witness each death in order to balance everything out. What's fair is fair."

"What happens if I don't do it? What if I never bring anyone out there?"

Grandpa pushed a loud breath out his nose. "Then they'll be tied to that tree until the end of time, I guess. Angry. Sad. Hurt. Unfulfilled. Forgotten." He looked at the woods. "We can't do that to them. We can't forget what they endured. They're family." He met eyes with me. "And you do for family. Because when it comes down to it, family's all you got." A beat. "I guarantee they'd do the same for you."

We sat in silence for a long time before my thirteen-year-old curiosity and racing mind got the better of me and I blurted out, "How do the leaves talk? How are they so strong? How did Tobin and the others get inside the—"

Grandpa waved his hand in front of my face, cutting me off. "I don't know. My dad never told me. It just is."

"Leaves don't talk," Terry yelled with conviction. As though saying it with force would make it true. "Leaves don't kill people."

"Yes, they do." I took a step toward him. "After Mark, I watched it happen five more times. Heather Hill. Kathy and John Sanders. Paul and Mickey Washburn." I counted the names off on my fingers. "I led them all out here over the years." I pointed at the oak tree twenty feet to my left. "And the leaves took them."

Terry closed his eyes tight, lowered his head, wiped his hand over his face a couple of times, then snapped his head up and looked at me. His eyes were more alive than I'd seen in years. Alive with the revelation. "If Mark was a descendant that means my parents . . ." He was connecting the dots. Perhaps his parents hadn't abandoned him. Perhaps my grandpa had led them to their deaths. He tapped his own chest. "Then I'm . . ."

"I've put it off as long as I can," I said. The leaves close to the oak tree began to stir. To move. Come alive. "You're the last descendant."

He shook his head. "But you know I never . . . I don't have a racist bone in my body."

I nodded, hoping the sadness pressing down on my chest was evident in my eyes and tone. "I know. I told my grandpa the same thing on the porch that day when I realized I would have to lead you to the leaves, too. You want to know what he told me?"

Terry stared at me, and I held his gaze to keep him from noticing the leaves making their way toward him, clambering over one another, fighting to be the first to get at him.

"He said that a person's heritage always follows them," I continued. "Sometimes for the better. Sometimes for the worse." A pause. "I know it's not your fault who your ancestors are and what they did any more than it's mine who my family is and what some of them went through. But at least it ends with us. Here. Today. My relatives will be free to move on, and your ancestors' debt will be paid in full."

"Jesus Christ, Louis. You're fucking crazy."

The leaves were right behind him. A few feet away.

"What would you've done if I'd had kids? Killed them, too?"

I didn't respond. I'd actually come close to poisoning two of his girlfriends when they'd been late with their periods. I knew a lady in Hudson who made concoctions that forced miscarriages. I figured I'd slip it into their drinks if it came to that. Luckily, it didn't.

He looked down when the leaves climbed up his shoes and ran up his shins. As they swam up his thighs and wrapped around his waist, his eyes grew wide with betrayal and he yelled, "I thought you were my best friend." He threw his cane at me, and it hit me in the chest.

"I am," I said. "That's why I let you have a good long life." I gulped, trying to push down the lump that had materialized in my throat. "That's why I told you the truth about the leaves, about what happened to your brother. So you would know what was coming. So you wouldn't be surprised like the others."

He kept his eyes on mine until the leaves covered them. Seconds later, his entire body was shrouded in what looked like a colorful patchwork quilt. He never made a sound as the leaves formed the leaf rope and pulled him to the ground.

I stood perfectly still with my head slightly bowed, hands clasped behind my back, and watched until the leaves stopped stirring and the forest floor returned to normal. Then I picked up Terry's cane and slowly made my way back to the porch where I sat in my rocker—the same rocker my grandpa had been sitting in when he'd told me about the Tree Servant—with the cane on my lap.

My heart truly ached for the loss of my friend, but I was too old and tired and scarred to weep. As the sun set behind the woods, I rocked and smoked in silence.

Like Terry and I would've done had he been there.

Mama's Babies

By R.J. Joseph

When the dog jetted out between my legs as I opened the door, I knew Ray hadn't let him out that morning.

Figured.

Three kids and fifteen years later and he still threw tantrums when I left the house alone. If that was the only time he acted like a monkey, I'd be home free, because I rarely ever left the house without him or the kids. Unfortunately, that was only one thing that would set him to pouting.

I used to think those full lips were the sexiest thing ever, even in a childish pout. But everything got old after a while when it was tied to a one trick pony.

I glanced out the kitchen window to make sure Woof hadn't gone too far toward the river. He was nowhere to be found. I briefly debated going to find him, but I needed to check on the girls. If Ray hadn't let the dog go poop, he likely hadn't changed Evaline's diaper, either. I knew It was getting harder to get her out of her wheelchair to do that as she got older, but it had to be done.

A quick look at the kitchen counter told me he hadn't fed the kids, either.

Figured.

I was only gone for three hours that morning. The trip from Richmond into the outskirts of Houston took a long while, but I took extra time to relish my temporary freedom from doctors, a whining husband, and three little kids who needed me so desperately. I didn't mind the kids needing me—that's what Mamas are for. But Evaline's special needs were getting hard to juggle with a four- and seven-year-old to bounce on my hip, too. And that was without Ray adding to the burden.

I wouldn't have had to go find a pharmacy in the city that morning if he'd just done it on his way home from work the day before. The girls came home from school with some kind of virus, and it made their eyes look funny, like bleeding tears. Janey said she felt sick and I could only imagine that Evaline would have said the same thing if she could talk. I pleaded with Ray to go to the pharmacy right then, to see if he could get some ointment or something for their eyes, until he got paid again and I could take them to the doctor.

"I only get off work one day a week early," he complained, "and I'm not wasting my time going to no damned pharmacy. They'll be fine. You baby them too much."

"Really, Ray?" I said. "Look at them. You're not worried about this? They don't look good."

"They'll be fine. I'm going to the café to hang out tonight."

I smelled expensive cologne on him and knew he was probably lying. If he left, I couldn't even load up the kids and go to the pharmacy myself. "The café doesn't open until nine," I noted. "It's only four now."

"I got stuff to do, Zenobia. Get off my back about it."

He left out, slamming the screen door behind him.

I turned to my babies, lined up in the kitchen behind me, Evaline moaning more incessantly than usual. "Okay, Mama's babies, let's go put in a movie. Ray, Jr., it's your turn to pick."

My sweet-faced baby boy smiled at me with uncharacteristically tired eyes and ran into the living room. I unlocked Evaline's wheelchair and she and I followed Janey to the couch.

Two movies later, Evaline and Janey were burning with fever. I thought Ray Jr. felt warm, too, so I gave them all fever reducer before putting them to bed a little earlier than usual. After my shower, I sat in bed with a book, too preoccupied to really read it. Instead, I stood and went to the bedroom window. The room overlooked the back yard, which bordered the Brazos River.

I hated that old stinky river, hated the river critters even more. I was glad to only have to chase two kids out to the fence. Janey and Ray Jr. always wanted to take Evaline with them on adventures, and I was glad her wheelchair made them move too slowly to get completely away from me. They loved their sissy and I knew they'd take care of her when I passed on. We really couldn't count on their daddy to do much of anything.

After I finally fell asleep, Evaline cried out loudly. I stumbled into the girls' room. Her bed was full of diluted blood, still leaking from her eyes. The fever seemed to be breaking, but she thrashed around like she had severe gas pains. Janey tossed in her little bed, too, but she seemed to stay asleep. I changed Evaline's sheets and rocked her until she calmed. Then I lay her back down and pulled up the bed guard. Ray, Jr. slept peacefully in his room.

I didn't go back to sleep that night. It looked like I might have to take Evaline to the emergency room in Rosenberg if the bleeding didn't stop. I called Ray's cell phone and got his voice mail. He never did answer or return my calls, but finally showed up at the house at seven the next morning.

"I'm taking the girls to the ER," I said.

"No, you ain't. We don't have money for that."

"They're still sick. I have to try and get them to see a doctor or get some medicine or something."

He ignored me and walked up the stairs. I followed him.

"Ray, none of us hardly slept last night."

He went into the girls' room, at least having the decency to move quietly. He peered through Evaline's bed guard. "She's sleeping fine now." He looked at Janey's bed. "Her, too."

I didn't believe him, so I went to check my babies myself. They were sleeping peacefully and their brown, smooth skin was cool to the touch. Really, really, cool. The blood streaked tears had stopped, too, the remnants dried on the towels I'd placed underneath their heads.

"I still need to get some medicine," I said. "And since you clearly hadn't planned on going to work today, you can stay with the kids while I drive into Houston. The girls can't go to school like this." When he didn't have a ready retort, I knew he was hung over and had had such a busy night that he simply didn't have the energy to fight or argue with me.

I dressed in a hurry and made one last check in the kids' rooms. They hated for me to leave them behind, and I wanted to be gone and well on my way back before they were up for too long. I hated to be without them, too, but the walls of the house were closing in on me. We only had one vehicle and I was the one who was left without, day in and day out. The kids and I entertained each other well enough, but sometimes I wanted to be around other adults. Besides, with the girls gone to school all day, Ray, Jr. and I were left to play with Woof. In the fall, my baby boy would be gone to school, too, and I'd be left with only the dog all day.

I drove below the speed limit to extend the drive. On a whim, I stopped into a coffee shop before earnestly looking for a drugstore. I never felt more like a fish out of water. A young male barista complimented me on my locks and all I could do was stare at him, open-mouthed. He was probably my age, and wasn't asking me to marry him, or even go out on a date. I mumbled my thanks and escaped back to the truck with the coffee, my freedom now sullied. I had to get back home to my babies.

The pharmacist wasn't familiar with any of the symptoms I described in my girls, so she suggested I bring them in to the onsite clinic they had. I told her I would, but that I wanted to make them comfortable, first. I knew I wouldn't be able to bring them. I think she knew that, too. She kindly pointed me toward an eye ointment on the shelf and an additional fever reducer to alternate with the acetaminophen I was already giving them. I thanked her. For a brief moment, I was jealous of her, getting to spend hours on a job that paid her for her time.

I drove home just above the speed limit.

Forgetting Woof, I walked slowly up the stairs.

My brain struggled to decipher the sounds I was hearing. It sounded like the dog had found something to put in his mouth and chew and suck on. But it couldn't be Woof. He'd abandoned me. And I doubted Ray had let him back into the house.

The door to the girls' room was ajar, as usual. I could see the bottom wheel of Evaline's overturned wheelchair and I ran to the room. My heart pounded in my throat. I expected to find one or both of my girls trapped under the heavy chair that weighed more than each of them. The girls weren't under or in the chair. They were on the floor, next to their father.

Janey clawed into Ray's stomach, tiny purple hands scooping entrails to her small mouth. She slurped, like Woof with forbidden contraband. Evaline lay on her stomach, scooting close into Ray's neck, her limited head movement not hindering her meal of his throat cartilage. She'd never eaten anything orally, since birth, only fed with a g-tube. Now she chewed and smacked and gobbled.

My bowels tightened. *My babies.*

I backed away from the door slowly, toward Ray Jr.'s room. My baby boy wasn't there. I checked in my bedroom, keeping watch on the girls' room at the end of the hall. I ran down the stairs, two at a time. Ray Jr. met me in the living room. Blood streamed from his eyes.

"Mommy, I don't feel good." *My babies.*

His fat cheeks glistened with blood and pus. Dark purple bruising settled around one side of his face. I reached to pick him up, wanting to run, wanting to scream. But I instinctively knew I had a little time before he'd turn like the girls.

I ran my hand lovingly across his tight curls. "Mommy needs to go get some more medicine. And maybe some ice cream." My voice cracked and I couldn't breathe around the lump in my throat.

"Okay. Then I'll feel better?" He stepped closer to me and licked his lips.

"Yes, baby. Why don't you go into the living room and watch a movie?"

"Okay, Mommy." His short legs moved in a slow amble, in stark contrast to how he'd gone into the same room just yesterday.

I ran out to the yard and jumped into the truck. Then, I realized I'd left they keys in the house, upstairs in the girls' room. I threw myself out of the truck door and headed for the woods along the river. I jumped the fence and stumbled over Woof, his fur crusted with blood. He paddled his legs fruitlessly and tried to wag his tail. Had whatever that had gotten to him gotten to my babies?

I didn't turn around.

I kept running.

Freedom.

Bushes cut my legs and face as I tore through them, trying not to look back at the house.

Escape.

Trying not to look back at the house where my whole life was.

My babies.

I stumbled to a stop against a tree. I continued to run, but this time retracing my steps.

Back home.

I pushed the door open and Ray, Jr. stood in the kitchen, waiting for me.

"Mommy." He reached up with pudgy arms.

I lifted my baby boy and hugged him close to my heart. He nuzzled his wet, baby face into my neck. He would turn, like the girls, soon enough. Maybe his sisters would make it down the stairs by then, Janey helping Evaline drag along and down each step. Evaline might even walk.

I had to wait. I had to see them.

Until then, I would hold my sweet baby boy. Then, Mama would be with all her babies once again.

A Writer's Lot

By James H. Longmore

Hi, my name is Roy Fitznorman, and I'm an author.

I know, that sounds like some lame-assed, clichéd introduction to a support group meeting, Horror Writer's Anonymous, perhaps? But no, it's just me, and there is no such group that I am aware of.

Maybe there really ought to be.

I live in Palestine—not the Palestine with the Gaza strip and the wall and the dumb, endless war over whose God has the biggest dick—*Palestine, Texas*.

It's a small town out in the boonies, Southeast of Dallas and a stone's throw—Lone Star style—from that wonderful institution that is Huntsville State Penitentiary. Aside from my primary motive for taking up residence in Palestine, it was a simple, absolute delight to witness the shocked looks upon the faces of my clueless family and friends back in Blighty when I regaled them of my plans to relocate the eight thousand-odd miles to Palestine.

I'd upped sticks and moved here a bunch of years ago, all the way from merry old England in the true spirit of that intrepid yet indubitably pious Mayflower lot, hoping against hope that by simply dwelling in close proximity to my literary hero—and quite possibly the greatest living horror novelist on the planet—Guy Woods, I'd boost my own rather more modest writing career if by nothing other than pure osmosis.

The town itself is a small, unassuming place, also less than a blue jay's fart from Houston, that huge, bustling cosmopolitan metropolis, fourth-largest city in the Union and the first name to be spoken in outer space.

". . . we have a problem."

Palestine is far enough away from either of the big cities to be classed as entirely rural. It comprises a clutch of lovingly kept, single-story, white board houses surrounded by vast, sprawling ranches bought and inhabited by good ol' rootin,' tootin,' huntin' and shootin' Texas folk who'd made obscene amounts of money pumping black gold out of the very ground they'd been born on. The ranchers made for good neighbors, though, since the land they owned was so incredibly spacious that their monstrous houses the size of hotels sat miles away from us common townsfolk.

It was on one of those ranches that my idol lived (and worked), his faux-colonial style house just about visible from my more modest, modern two-bed affair, and by more than pure coincidence we just happened to share part of a driveway.

Once I'd become accustomed to the relentless Texas heat—temperatures above the mid-seventies in England are considered a killer heatwave—I grew to enjoy the place and in no time at all I considered it home.

Whilst I have enjoyed some success as a writer—enough at least to move my ass a continent away to be close to my biggest inspiration—it has been nowhere near the success enjoyed by Woods, his wealth close to a cool half-billion dollars and still climbing. Now, jealousy really isn't my thing; I sincerely wish the man well with his work and his limitless pots of money. He'd worked damned hard across the years to earn every single penny his horror tales have generated, and soon I discovered at what cost.

Guy Woods had been churning out bestseller after bestseller for near-on five decades. Everything the man wrote sold in the millions—movies were made, poorly-executed TV series commissioned and everything that came out of Woods' beautifully twisted mind was pure literary gold.

I'd grown up with Woods' stories, his books a welcome escape from the dull, pre-electronic days of my childhood. His were the tales that introduced me to an entirely new world, one of terror, death and depravity that plunged to humanity's darkest depths, where arguably no mind had a right to venture; a tangled web of beautifully crafted words that had the adolescent version of me reading with a sick knot in my stomach and a hard-on that could cut drywall.

What I have always loved about Woods' work is his occasional tug at the reader's mind, a gentle reminder that you are, in fact reading a story. Many critics hate this trademark, but I find the pull back to reality to be quite comforting, as if it were Woods' own safety mechanism deliberately woven into his work to safeguard his readers' sanity.

Guy Woods had been my inspiration to seek out my own fortune as a writer in the first instance, and although every single copy of every book I'd sold had been a long, hard slog, I did finally reach the point at which I could consider myself a reasonable success.

Yet that was never enough, I always wanted more. Hell, I felt in my gut that I could do more, if only my brain would allow it and quit with the ever increasing periods of writer's block that had plagued me from the very beginning. The creative mind—when active—can be the most wonderful thing in the world; but when it lapses into lethargy it's like staring at a road kill bird, flat and stale, with a solitary, dried out wing flapping against the warm draught of each passing vehicle. You know the creature will never up and fly but you stare at it nonetheless, a sad part of you willing the dead thing to take flight

And so, I was compelled to insinuate myself into Woods' famously secretive life and maybe steal just a little of the man's success.

Shortly after moving into my neat little house I began to take early evening walks, ostensibly to air the cloying, claustrophobic sensations that tended to cloud my brain after a hard day's writing, but mainly because that was when Guy Woods—*the Guy Woods*—would take his own evening constitutional along our long, winding shared driveway and a mile or so down the tree-lined lane that ran from the ranch land into town.

For the first couple of months or so, I failed in my mission to coordinate my early evening excursions with Woods, resigned to watching the back of my idol's head from a distance as he walked briskly along his well-trodden, verdant route. And all the while I'd run our planned first conversation through my mind in much the same way that I mentally recite my PIN upon approaching an ATM.

As the saying goes—the best laid plans of mice and men and all that; it worked out that my first encounter with Guy Woods was nothing at all as I'd planned.

It was a baking, humid dusk and the fat, black and white striped mosquitoes that reminded me so much of miniature, flying humbugs were out and in full force—buzzing and whining about my head in the soupy air as they sought their blood dinner. The setting sun was a gaudy salmon pink slouching over the horizon, the sparse smattering of clouds stained by its dying rays, the sky itself afire with a peach glow.

As I had every evening thus far, I turned left at the end of the driveway and headed slowly toward town, my hero nowhere to be seen.

Either my timing was off or Woods had been delayed that evening leaving his house, but I found myself taking my perambulation ahead of the man I so desperately wanted to engage. Now it was his turn to watch the back of my head as I sauntered along the leafy lane, planning out in my imagination our very first conversation.

Should I begin with just how much I adored *Vice Ring*? Or do I lead with how *Resurrection* inspired me to become a writer? Or perhaps I should launch straight into how I thought Hollywood had absolutely destroyed *'Possum's Walk* with the insertion of dumb action sequences and a sickly-sweet, schmaltzy ending?

Lost in my reverie, I sauntered by a dead armadillo that lay flattened at the edge of the thin lane, the sun-baked ropes of its entrails squished out of its rear end and its body being deftly picked apart by a small flock of ugly, scowling buzzards, each one the height of a small child—a somewhat ignominious end for the state mammal, I thought to myself.

The portly, shiny black birds refused to fly away at my approach, choosing instead to hop little more than a stride or so onto the overgrown grass verge. They stared hard at me with their dark, beady eyes, as if daring me to so much as think about stealing their fetid meal, as the stink of the armadillo's rotting carcass filled the damp air with its sickly-sweet bouquet.

"Stop!"

I froze.

"Don't move!"

I'd heard Guy Woods' voice before, of course. He was particularly active on social media and often popped up on TV—not to mention his many movie cameos—but this was the very first time I'd heard the great man speak in person.

And he was talking to me!

I wanted so badly to spin around and welcome his conversation, but didn't dare disobey the man I so idolized and thus appear rude. So I stood there, stock-still and listened as Guy Woods' light footsteps padded along the crumbling blacktop and he caught up with me.

"Hi, I'm—" I began when his shadow stood next to mine on the narrow road.

"Shhh," Woods replied with a sound that brought to mind the harsh hissing of escaped steam from some clunking monstrosity of Victorian machinery. "Don't speak, don't even blink," he whispered, his mouth so close now that I could feel the moist warmth of his breath upon my ear.

There then came a second noise. A dry, rasping that sounded to me like a velvet bag of small bones clattering together. I glanced down—daring only to move my eyes—and that's when I saw the rattler.

This was the first time since relocating to Texas that I'd encountered a real, live and terrifyingly wild rattlesnake. Of course, I'd seen the things at the annual Rattlesnake Round Up over in Sweetwater—I'd even eaten Rattler Burgers with all the fixins on more than one occasion—and of course I'd noticed plenty of the grotesque things mashed into the roads around my house. But seeing one so damn close to my foot had the sour stink of fear-sweat seeping from my pores in a heartbeat.

"Diamondback," Woods hissed in my ear, his sibilant voice the embodiment of the reptile that sat tightly coiled, incredibly pissed off and ready to strike less than twelve inches from my bare calf.

My racing brain took great delight in informing me that there are on average one to two snakebite deaths in Texas every year. I'd read many a drugstore pamphlet on the subject since my arrival. And I couldn't help but wonder if I was about to become part of that morbid statistic—this monster was a huge one, its taut, wound body thicker than my arm in its middle, the creature's fat, arrow-shaped head easily bigger than my fist.

I stared down at the snake and the snake stared right back at me, its unblinking eyes trained upon mine, lithe, pink tongue flicking from its mouth with a cold nonchalance I found to be most disturbing.

Woods stepped in front of me, his Nike-clad foot placed deliberately between the Diamondback and myself.

"What?" I stammered, thinking the man had lost his mind.

Woods ignored my protestations.

Like some crazy shaman, Woods waved a long, thin stick over the snake's head and whispered something quite indistinguishable beneath his breath. In an instant, the snake ceased its rattling and recoiled as if it had been struck. It then turned tail and slithered away into the long grass with what I imagined to be a look of abject terror etched upon its scaly face.

"Thank you," I said, and the breath I hadn't realized I'd been holding whooshed out of my chest in one hot, wheezing wave.

"You gotta watch out for those varmints around here," Woods stated the damned obvious with a broad grin. "They'll take a bite at ya as soon as look at ya," he added and his eyes darted to where the end of the snake's tail vanished into the rustling, tinder-dry grass.

"Thank you, Mr. Woods," I said again, my voice breathy and weak.

Woods let out a light chuckle, his eyes twinkling in the fading light. "Call me Guy," he said, momentarily forgetting himself and half-extending a gloved hand for me to shake.

Before he could retract the offer, I'd taken a firm hold of the writer's hand and was pumping it enthusiastically. His leather glove felt strange against the sweating skin of my palm, the soft leather dry and brittle like aged skin.

Woods pulled his hand away. "I'm sorry, I don't usually . . ." he said. I'd read about the writer's chronic germaphobia and his famous reluctance toward human contact, an affliction he shared with Howard Hughes. I'd always presumed that was the reason Guy Woods was rarely seen in public.

And so that's how I got to actually shake hands with my hero, having just watched him dismiss Texas' most lethal reptile with nothing more than a sycamore twig and the biggest balls I think I'd ever seen. In my dizzy state of adrenaline and hero-worship I didn't register it as being in the least bit odd that on a hot summer's night in deepest Texas, Guy Woods was wearing leather gloves, nor that the large, black gloves had seemed to be so very full.

"Let's go catch a beer," Woods said, planting his hand firmly in his pants pocket. "Sure looks like you could use one."

I loved how he said that—*catch a beer*—as if a cold, alcoholic beverage was some rare and ephemeral thing.

And so, we did just that.

Guy Woods and I continued our walk in the sticky heat of the dying day along the lane and into town. I soon found my tongue and all the way there I fired off the well-rehearsed questions I'd been dying to ask at the famous author, each one of which he fielded with patience and good grace, even though I guess he'd heard them all a thousand times before.

When, finally, we arrived at Palestine's one and only sports bar, we made ourselves at home at a wobbling table closest to the counter where we were served a pitcher of frothing, icy cold beer by a sweet young thing named Miranda.

The place was called Roxy's Dive Bar, which at the time of its naming was apparently meant to be ironic. Sadly, for a drinking establishment that was now so run down and reeking of stale cigarette smoke and body odor, the bar's given name pretty much hit the nail right on the head.

"Anything else I can get y'all, just holler," our waitress said as she scurried across the room to serve a corpulent, gray-haired man who sat all by his lonesome at a table next to the Seeburg jukebox. As Miranda walked, she surreptitiously tugged at her tight denim shorts that had ridden up into the alluring cleft of her ass and crotch, either not realizing that everyone in the bar could see what she was doing, or not particularly giving a damn.

"Ya know, Roy, there's nothing that says Texas sports bar quite like Daisy Dukes and camel-toe," Woods said with a chuckle, his eyes sparkling in the faint flickering of the fluorescent strip light above our table. I smiled and nodded my agreement and Woods and I chinked glasses and downed the first of our many beers of the night.

The fat guy by the battered old Seeburg waved a hand over his head and lifted an empty glass in a silent toast towards us, his ruddy face beaming ear to ear.

"You know him?" I asked. In hindsight, it was a dumb question really—you can't be the world's most famous horror writer and not know everyone in your small town. I'd seen the old guy in the bar before, and on occasion about the town, but mostly he tended to keep to himself.

"Delbert?" Woods replied. "He runs the mortuary, Roy, so it pays to buy him a beer or two by my reckoning—we all end up on Delbert's slab at some point or another." Woods took a long slurp of his beer and waved across at Miranda. "Another Shiner Bock for Mr. Mundy," he called over to the gal. Mundy nodded his thank you and returned his attention to the Astros game that was playing out on the flat screen above the fire exit. The Astros were having a bad time of it, as far as I could make out with my somewhat limited knowledge of the game—no points at all and well past half time really couldn't be good in anybody's book.

"I guess you're itching to know why I still do it?" Woods said between slurps of a beer that was vanishing at an alarming rate. "Or are ya gonna ask about my process? All writers do. It's usually the second thing out of their mouths after where do all your scary ideas come from?"

This amused Woods and he laughed awhile. I was pleased with myself for having decided upon not asking him the latter question, although I was intrigued as to how the man so convincingly got into the heads of the maniacs and otherworldly beings he conjured up.

"They all want to pick my brains to see if they can figure out my magic formula so they can emulate it." Woods frowned and he adopted a most serious countenance. "I'll tell you the secret for nothing, Roy," he said. "Friend to friend—*there is no magic formula!*"

He laughed again, this time a tad louder and Delbert Mundy shot us both a withering glance.

"So, go on. Ask me," Woods continued.

"Pardon me?" Woods' insistence took me completely by surprise, I'd pretty much exhausted the vacuous chit-chat on our post-Diamondback walk along the lane; I'd all but asked the poor man his favorite color (taupe, as it turned out) and what he'd had for dinner that evening.

"Why I still write," Woods replied with a wink. "They all do, although it's difficult for me to explain to a non-writer, of course."

I took this as a great compliment, the fact that Guy Woods considered me a fellow writer; I fought hard to repress the smug, satisfied grin that so desperately wanted to form on my lips. "I guess so," I said, trying to appear indifferent.

"I mean, I already have more money than any one individual could possibly spend in a hundred lifetimes, so why keep on hitting the keyboard day after day?" He took another swig of his beer, his sizable, gloved hands wrapped around the tall glass as if he feared its escape.

"I do often wonder how come you refuse to retire," I confessed. "You could be doing so many things instead of working."

"Like what?" Woods replied with a lop-sided smile. "Playing golf? Cruising the seven seas on a boat filled with geriatrics? Catching up on *Oprah* and *Jerry Springer*?" He laughed out loud at this, drawing more stares of disapproval from around the bar.

"Err—I guess so," I said, all of a sudden quite self-conscious.

Woods placed his near-empty beer glass upon the wobbling table with a solid thunk. He leaned toward me and spoke in a low, conspiratorial whisper. "For the self-same reason McCartney keeps on churning out songs that nobody wants to listen to, why Buffet still goes into his office every day of the week, why Van Gogh kept on painting through his insanity even though he sold the sum total of Jack-shit in his entire lifetime." There Woods paused, studying with intensity the tiny rivulets of condensation that raced each other down the sides of his glass. He prodded at one with a leather-clad finger and destroyed the tiny, tear-shaped droplet in one fell swoop.

"It's because we have to," Woods said with a derisory snort. "We have no choice."

"Yeah, my agent rides my ass pretty hard, too," I threw in. Although my agent, Katya De Santiago of Santiago and Associates, seemed more interested in her cosmetic surgery procedures of late than my plateaued literary career.

Woods leaned in yet further, his face uncomfortably close to mine as he grasped my hands in his. "It's not my agent," Woods offered, with a strained snicker. "Even that asshole thinks I should have retired after I finished *Letters from No Place,* but he doesn't understand, Roy, he doesn't see."

"See what, Guy?" I inched back in my seat, keen to be away from Woods' hot, beer-fumed breath and wild, distant eyes.

It was then that Guy Woods told me about what he had christened the River of Madness—his term for whatever the thing was that he claimed to see every waking moment of his ostensibly charmed life.

"You know those first few minutes of wakefulness that you experience coming out of a solid night's sleep?" Woods asked. "That disorienting, nebulous place between the dream world and the cold harshness of reality?"

I nodded. That was precisely the time of the day when I found my own creative mind to be at its most fertile—the sole reason why I slept with a notepad and Dictaphone on my nightstand.

"That's what it's like to write under the River's influence, day in, day out," Woods explained to me. "For those of us who have roots into the worlds beyond."

There he paused, his eyes searching mine, as if for signs of incredulity. "Although sometimes I feel that Mycelia of Madness may be a name that serves the thing better," he continued. "Since it creeps into the mind like some sticky, pernicious fungus."

The corners of Woods' mouth twitched. He was clearly very pleased with his analogy.

"Only a handful of us get to see it, although many more are influenced by its malevolence," Woods said as he unclasped my hands, the leather of his gloves somehow sweaty against my skin.

"Writers, artists, musicians—did you know that Brian Wilson actually hears complete tunes in his head long before he writes them down? He's one of the lucky ones. We writers of the dark and horrific see such deeply unpleasant things that lurk in the bleakest of places, Roy." Woods eased back in his chair a little, that haunted look glistening behind his eyes. "Have you ever wondered how come writing is one of the professions that enjoys the most longevity, and yet an inordinate number of us commit suicide?"

I shook my head in silence. Truth was, no—I had never wondered.

"For those of us who dare dip our toes into the River, we are but conduits for the malignancy that churns and froths within its unearthly waters. It's not inspiration, Roy, it's *compulsion*."

Woods was doing his very best to explain himself, his tongue loosened with beer; but I found myself increasingly distracted by that faraway look in the man's eyes—eyes that I had only just realized were the most striking shade of blue.

"And where is the river?" I figured I ought to contribute something to our increasingly one-sided conversation.

Woods swept an arm in a broad arc around his hunched body. "The damned thing is everywhere, Roy," he whispered, "absolutely fucking everywhere."

I glanced around the bar, half-expecting to see a slow, churning flow of darkness teeming with vulgar, otherworldly, Lovecraftian creatures slithering over one another's obscene, putrefying bodies to take their place in our earthly realm.

But, no.

Instead, I saw only the grubby sports bar and its motley smattering of clientele. "I see nothing," I said, disappointed. "I wish I could. I'd kill for some inspiration right now."

"Think yourself lucky," Woods replied, a most serious expression set across his face. "It would drive you quite mad, young sir," he skillfully emulated my accent.

Woods drained the dregs of the beer from his glass, and then topped it up with what remained in our pitcher.

"Its tributaries flow all the way through those of us whom it chooses," he went on. "It reaches deep into our souls to regurgitate its turpitude, giving us no other choice but to release the blackness out into the world as seemingly innocuous words."

"And you are one of these conduits?" I asked, enjoying the lively metaphor Woods was weaving.

A sage nod. "There are others who have been touched by the River, and many, many others who wish they could be—not knowing that it can be a pure, living hell."

"So, how do I find this River of Madness?" I pushed, ignoring the sinister tone in the writer's voice.

"You don't," Woods said, his bluntness dismissive and bordering on rude. "It finds you."

I guess I should really have expected an answer like that from Guy Woods, ever the master of ominous suspense. It was just the kind of rote answer a dark, shadowy character in one of his doorstop-thick novels would come out with.

"Did I tell you about my chair?" Woods leaned all the way back in his high-backed seat, his eyes twinkling as clumsily he changed the subject; clearly all talk of his nefarious, invisible river was over and done with, the intense moment duly passed.

Of course I'd read all about the famous chair in Woods' authorized biography, as any number one fan would. It was as well-known as the antique typewriter he'd bought eons ago at the garage sale of some old hoarder who'd died, upon which Woods had written the first draft of every one of his books since. According to the biography, Woods had spent the better part of six hundred dollars having the thing professionally restored. It was a quaint eccentricity, I know, but indirectly germane.

I nodded and sipped at my own beer, which by now was decidedly flat and warm.

"Used to belong to the Reverend Trevor Ravenscroft," Woods told me, as if I'd never read *Satan's Chair*, his second—and in my opinion Woods' at his very best—novel. "Legend has it that Ravenscroft used to perform human sacrifices on that very piece of furniture. If you look closely enough, you can still make out the marks the ropes made on its arms and legs."

Reverend Ravenscroft had a reputation for being one of the last century's most prolific Satanists, all the way up there with Crowley and LaVey. Having made the mistake of sacrificing the wrong virgin (the daughter of a powerful media magnate) to his Dark Lord, the Reverend had mysteriously disappeared slap-bang in the middle of his murder trial in 1973. He'd vanished without a trace from his heavily guarded cell beneath the courthouse and, of course, the majority consensus was that he'd been spirited away by a legion of winged demons. It was speculated by the more level-headed, however, that it was more likely he'd been sprung by a sympathizer on the inside and had lived out his days in a country that had no extradition treaty with the United States.

"I have it nailed to the wall in my office," Woods told me. "Because people who have sat in that chair over the years have met with untimely and particularly gruesome deaths." The sparkle shone bright in Woods' eyes, and for a moment I fancied I saw reflected there a roiling, bubbling, living thing that was impossibly black.

"Now, that I'd love to see," I gushed.

"That would be quite impossible," Woods uttered, cutting my enthusiasm down like a troublesome weed. "The house has become a complete mess since Ashlynne left with the kids.

A silence descended upon us.

Woods sipped at his beer, clutching at the glass with one large, gloved hand. I simply stared at my own glass, hopes of becoming bosom buddies with my lifelong hero and sole inspiration evaporating as surely as the dew on its side.

And that was pretty much that, my evening with the one and only Guy Woods, my fleeting insight into what drove the famous writer to keep on churning out hundreds and thousands of best-selling words year in, year out, and to what I sadly supposed was to be the end of our potentially beautiful friendship.

For it was the following evening, during his customary walk along the narrow, picture-postcard, dappled lane, that Guy Woods was mugged, beaten senseless and left for dead.

The town was abuzz with the news.

Nothing much happened in Palestine, Texas, so Guy Wood's brutal attack was a front-page story, or certainly would have been had the *Palestine Informer* not gone out of business back in '99.

I'd made my way down to Roxy's that evening, desperately wanting—*needing*—the company of others, my head reeling with the fact that only the night before I'd finally connected with Guy Woods and if I'd not been delayed leaving my house by taking a phone call from my increasingly absent agent, I would have been with Woods and may perchance have prevented the attack.

Either that or I'd be occupying the hospital bed next to him or quite possibly stiffening on Delbert Mundy's slab.

The air ambulance had flown Woods to the Memorial Hermann Hospital over in Downtown Houston; although, why the hell they'd taken him there instead of the much closer Parkland in Dallas was beyond me. Maybe somebody figured the great writer would like a panoramic view of the Houston Zoo from his hospital bed.

Delbert Mundy was in Roxy's when I arrived. By the looks of things, he'd been ensconced in the dim, smoky bar for quite some time. He sat at his usual table, nursing what appeared to be his fifth beer and stared vacantly up at the TV. There, a pretty young reporter from *Fox 26* was doing her rote piece to cameras outside the hospital, where—coincidentally or otherwise—Woods' attacker had also been taken the previous night, although his fate had been somewhat different.

"Jumped from the top of the JP Morgan Chase building," Mundy pre-empted the pretty reporter before taking a mighty slurp of his beer. Seeing that the glass was almost empty, I bought the fat old coroner another one and plonked myself down at his table.

"You know what happened?" I prompted. The reporter had not yet mentioned precisely where Woods' mugger had met with his untimely demise.

Mundy nodded sagely, his alcohol-glazed eyes brimming with tears. "Heard it from Chuck Hawkins, an old bowling buddy who works down at the City Morgue," he told me. "Used to be in the same league team before his diabetes kicked in and he lost one of his feet. Hell of a player." Mundy slurped at the beer I'd bought him, and I couldn't be all that sure he'd noticed that Miranda had swapped out his near-empty glass for the new one. "The bastard made his way to the top of the highest building in Houston in the middle of the night and took a two-step into mid-air—it's over a thousand feet, don't you know?"

"A thousand and two," I said with a wry smile. I'd recently researched the JP Morgan Chase office block for a novella I'd been planning to write sometime very soon. "Seventy-five floors, the guy wouldn't have stood much of a chance."

Mundy leaned his not inconsiderable bulk forward, the chair beneath him creaking its loud protest. "There's less violent ways to off yourself, sir," he said. "I'd say the guy either had a flair for the over-dramatic. . ." An odd silence settled over the aging coroner, and a spaced-out look filled his already distant eyes. He glanced up at the TV, which had already moved on to a new snarl-up on I-10.

"Or?" I took a swig of my beer, the chill liquid hurt my teeth and it tasted of nothing in particular.

"Or he wanted to make sure," Mundy's eyes met mine. "Ya know," he said, running a finger across his throat in that time-honored depiction of death. "And ya wanna know the damndest thing?" Mundy leaned even farther forward, his flabby man-tits resting on the rickety table. "My buddy said that the fall didn't actually kill the guy—he was dead before he hit Travis Street."

"Is that so?" I motioned for Miranda to furnish the man with yet another beer—three great, gulping chugs and the pint I'd provided was all but gone—to oil the wheels, as it were.

"Yup," Mundy replied with a stupid grin on his face. "There was absolutely no sign of the man hitting the building on the way down, and his neck was completely broken."

"Wouldn't that be consistent with a thousand-foot fall?" My guilty pleasure was watching reruns of procedural cops shows—I flatter myself that I've kind of picked up the lingo.

"Shattered bones are consistent with such a fall and the poor bastard had smashed up pretty much every one of those he had on the sidewalk. Not sure about his inner ear bones though, I must remember to ask Chuck about that next time I talk to him." Mundy paused just long enough to eye-hump Miranda's jiggling butt as she deposited his new beer and sashayed back to the bar. "This guy's neck had been twisted all the way around—at least twice—it's what we in the biz' call an *internal* decapitation."

I'd heard about this particular phenomenon, of course. It's what kills hanging victims if the job's done right; and while it's not quite so visually gruesome as an actual decapitation, the head is technically separated from the body, held on by little more than skin and sinew.

"Apparently, according to Chuck, it was as if somebody chased Woods' assailant all the way to the top of Houston's tallest, threw him off and then snapped his neck on the way down," Mundy said with a snort. "Like I said, damndest thing."

I sat back in my chair, more to escape Mundy's sour beer-breath than anything, and contemplated what he'd just told me. Could it have been more than pure coincidence that Woods' attacker had met his grisly death on the same night he'd relieved Woods of that evening's beer money on that picturesque, sun-dappled lane—less than a stone's throw from the hospital he'd put the writer into?

"And ya know something, son?" Mundy's beer-fueled unprofessionalism obviously knew no bounds. "I'd have pegged that writer buddy of yours for murdering the punk, if he'd not been laid up in Memorial pissing in a bag with his face smashed in." He then leaned all the way back in his chair, the wooden slats digging into his rolling folds of back fat. "Then again, who knows what people like Woods are capable of? All that creepy, nasty death stuff he writes about. Christ only knows who—or what—he convenes with?"

And with that, Delbert Mundy fell silent, lost in the swirling thoughts of his private, drunken reverie, glassy eyes firmly affixed upon the dancing light of the TV that sat high in the corner of the bar.

I was surprised that there was no security at the hospital. I'd have thought they'd at the very least have stationed an off-duty cop outside of Woods' private room. Surely a writer of his fame and fortune would be at risk from pestering, but well-wishing fans, if nothing else.

But no. I was allowed to walk straight on in, basket of fruit that would most likely be putrescent slop long before Woods was capable of eating it in one hand, bright yellow, Mylar balloon bobbing gaily upon a nylon string clasped firmly in the other. The balloon was a "Minion"; the little yellow character grinned inanely and clutched an oversized banana with *Get Well Soon* scrawled on it. I was positive I'd read in an article a long time ago that Guy Woods loved those little guys.

Nothing could have prepared me for the sight that greeted me in that hospital room. Seeing my all-time favorite hero laying there amidst the over-starched bed sheets, his body bandaged and his poor face looking like a sagging, month-old jack-o'-lantern. The mugger had really gone to town on Woods for just a few bucks. And at that moment I felt an immeasurable rage bubble up inside of me, the likes of which I'd never experienced before in my entire life. Ardent pacifist that I am, I'd still have merrily bought a beer for whomever had hounded that asshole to his well-deserved and somewhat fitting death.

"Hey," Woods said, as I wandered into the room. "Good to see ya." His voice was barely a low, gurgling whisper as his swollen lips struggled to form coherent words.

I placed the fruit basket on the bedside table, taking great care not to trip over or snag any of the myriad wires that connected Woods to the impressive array of flickering machinery that surrounded the bed. I looked down and saw that Delbert Mundy had indeed been correct in his assumption. There snaked a thick, transparent tube from beneath the bedclothes that emptied out into a half-filled piss bag that was hooked to the underside of the metal bed frame. I peered out through the window of Wood's room. "You can see the zoo from up here," I offered. My skills at making small talk had never really been all that hot.

"Yeah, if I really try hard, I can see the giraffes," Woods told me, shifting his body a fraction in the bed.

"That's neat," I replied, trying not to stare too hard at his swollen hands that were bandaged up tight; one of which had a cheap Paper Mate stuck to it with transparent surgical tape.

"Not really—can't stand giraffes," Woods replied with a snort. "Too much goddamned neck for my liking." He then let out a strange wheezing sound that I think was supposed to be laughter and screwed up his battered face at the pain that it elicited.

I gave Woods my very best lop-sided grin and tied the Minion balloon to the foot end of his bed.

It was then that I noticed that Woods' heavily bandaged hand—the one with the pen so crudely attached to it—was moving. Almost as if of its own volition. It skated slowly, deliberately over the surface of a fat legal notepad that lay next to Woods' hip. And in its wake, the pen left a thin, spidery scrawl.

"Should you really be working?" I inquired, with a kind smile. "You know, in your—"

"Condition?" Woods interrupted, his face cracking a pained grin.

"Yeah, that." I tried my best not to stare at the yellow paper, but found my eyes drawn to it.

"You're a writer, Roy. You know what it's like when the inspiration grabs you."

It's not inspiration, it's compulsion.

"I guess so," I said.

Of course, I knew full well that nagging, irritating itch when a great idea hatches out in a creative brain—and just how infuriating it can be if there's no way to birth it. Having said that, and judging by the disturbed look in Woods' bloodshot, blackened eyes, my experience at the hands of inspiration was not even in the same zip code as his.

"I can't stop," Woods whispered, an odd gurgle bubbling up in his words, as if attempting to drown them. "It won't let me, *they* won't let me." He glanced down at his hand, scrutinizing the thing as if it were something entirely alien to him.

"The River?" I ventured quietly, although no one else was in the room.

"Yes," Woods replied, his split lips working against the black threads that held the torn flesh together. "Won't even give me a damned break in here." He kind of shrugged his shoulders and let out a huge, gasping sigh that made his entire body tremble. And Guy Woods—*the Guy Woods*—looked so small and vulnerable lying there amidst the tubes and wires and crisp white sheets that I had to fight back tears.

"I'm sorry," I said. "Is there anything I can do?"

"Nope," Woods replied, "this is all on me." He stared at that bandaged hand, watching with transfixed fascination as it skittered across the legal pad. "I guess this will all make one hell of a story, though." He forced a wan smile and his body slumped against the mountain of fluffed pillows that propped him up.

"You're tired," I ventured, surprisingly keen to be away from the place and its sterile atmosphere. And to think that just two nights before, I'd have given anything to have remained in Wood's presence until the end of time itself.

"Yeah," Woods sighed. "Thanks for coming, Roy."

"Don't mention it, and get well soon." I took a step or two towards the door. Opened it. "We'll catch a beer or two when you get back home."

"I'd like that," Woods said and for a fleeting moment that familiar, haunted look in his eyes flickered away. "And Roy—"

"Huh?" I was halfway through the door, the stink of antiseptic from the hallway prickling at my nostrils.

"Thanks for the Minion," Woods nodded to the balloon that hung mid-air above his bed. "I love those little guys."

It was dark by the time I arrived back in Palestine—I'd taken my own sweet time on the long drive from Houston, even stopping in at a Buc-ee's for an extended restroom break and a hot dog. I'd also treated myself to a monster bag of Buc-ee's Beaver Nuggets for the remainder of my road trip—I think I love the name of the snack even more than whatever a beaver's nuggets are supposed to be.

I noticed the light at Woods' house as I traversed the shared part of our driveway. It shone a dull yellow through the window of which I had always assumed to be Woods' office, the very room in which he wove his tales of terror. This was nothing more than romantic conjecture on my part, as often I'd imagine the great writer slaving away at his next bestseller long into the devil's hour and beyond. For all I knew, the light came from the man's kitchen as he rooted out another cold beer from the refrigerator.

Normally, I would have thought nothing of it other than the fact that the house ought to have been empty that night, and I knew for a fact that Woods always switched off the lights whenever he left the house for his evening walk. Kinda stalky, I know.

But, being the good neighbor that I always strive to be, I decided it was my duty to ensure that no lowlife was taking advantage of Guy Wood's hospitalization with the view of the giraffes. And if I happened to grab a quick look-see into the great man's home in the process, then so be it.

The driveway was long and incredibly dark, the night sky blackened by an uncharacteristic smothering of thick, bulbous clouds that strangled the light from the crescent moon I knew lurked up there somewhere. The air was still hot, though, despite the impending storm, and almost as soon as I stepped out from the air-conditioned cocoon of my automobile, my shirt had stuck to my back and the tart stink of sweat offended my senses.

As I neared the sprawling facade of Woods' mansion, my ears pricked up at the faintest creaking noise, an irregular *click-clack-click*, like the sound of a solitary deathwatch beetle going about its nefarious business inside derelict timber. I slowed my pace and stepped onto the neatly manicured lawn in order to avoid giving myself away with the rhythmic crunching of my shoes on Woods' gravel driveway; and why I didn't think to call the cops, I'll never know.

Or, at least, that's what I tell myself.

The light from the small upstairs window cast a withered glow downwards, just enough for me to make out the thin shadow between the front door and its frame—the door was most certainly cracked open.

A light prickling of gooseflesh coursed the length and breadth of my body, despite the oppressive Texas heat that pressed down upon my scalp with stagnant, soupy air.

Against my better judgment (but intrigued by the faint tap-tap-tapping from above), I pushed open the heavy wooden door—oak, if memory serves me correctly—and stepped inside the dark, dank interior of Guy Woods' palatial home.

Almost immediately my nose wrinkled and my throat burned as the acrid stench that seeped out through the darkness reached out to caress me. My eyes watered up and memories of my childhood friend, Joe, and I letting off stink bombs in the food hall came flooding back; an innocuous schoolboy prank in those heady, innocent days long before the likes of Columbine.

Undeterred, I continued on, making my way into the deep, inky shadows that concealed the staircase, a huge, sweeping affair that spiraled upwards into the darkness of the upper floor. Slowly, my heart bouncing around in my chest like a thing possessed, I ascended those stairs, my sweat-dampened palm clamped tight onto the coolness of the bannister.

Upon reaching the second floor, I let out the breath that I'd been holding onto and I was startled to see the stale exhalation clouding before my face in the darkness. It was with great reluctance that I then took in a lungful of the fetid air that draped around me like some foul, stinking ghost. I ventured ever onward, my feet sinking into the thick pile of the carpet, whose luxurious depth I could only begin to imagine since my legs were cloaked in pitch-blackness.

Ahead, a narrow slit of light seeped out beneath one of the doors on the landing, a feeble, yellowed sliver that was all but swallowed up by the voracious dark.

Click-clack-click.

That sound again, the one I'd heard from outside. Only this time it was far louder, its repetitiveness resounding about my ears like a scolding schoolmarm, the tone at once accusing yet indescribably alluring.

One quaking step at a time, I made my way toward that door, forcing myself to breathe in the cold, rank air through my mouth. Even though it rasped at the back of my throat like some noxious wartime gas, I still found that preferable to smelling its foulness. The door beckoned to me, its outline shadowy and that tantalizing thread of greasy light a siren's call through the darkness.

My hand rested upon the chubby brass knob, as if daring me to demand that it twist the thing and reveal what my racing imagination simply knew awaited me in the room beyond, the room from which that titillating *clack-click-clack* emanated like the efforts of some diabolical rain bird.

I hesitated, my curiosity wrestling with the inherent horror that lingered in the most primal recesses of my brain and cajoling me to turn tail and run.

The door eased silently open upon well-oiled hinges and the jaundiced light oozed out to both embrace me and illuminate the horrors that skulked beyond the threshold.

"Ah, you came," Woods greeted me. "I'm so pleased that you did."

"I—*I thought you were . . .*"

My voice—as well as my wits—abandoned me.

"I decided to check myself out," Woods said, his swollen lips sticking together as he spoke. "I have so many stories to tell." And, so saying, he tapped away at the keys of his ancient Remington-Rand, the one he'd spent a king's ransom having restored.

I stood and I stared.

Guy Woods—*the Guy Woods*—was seated in a simple, wooden-backed chair, his battered body hunched over the ornate, mahogany desk before it like Hugo's protagonist. Above and to the left of the desk there was a triumvirate of ragged holes in the sheetrock, where the chair had been hastily ripped away from the wall. The chair itself was a dusty, faded old thing, and when I looked carefully, I could just about make out the rope marks in the timeworn, cracked wood of its arms and legs.

Woods had discarded the bandages that had smothered his hands, and they lay upon the desk like thin, bloodied strips of dry skin. His unfettered fingers bobbed up and down upon the typewriter—one finger for each one of the forty-eight round metal keys and his thumbs upon the space bar at the bottom, each digit melded to its corresponding key as if man and typewriter had become one and the same.

I could barely begin to comprehend what my eyes were telling me; not even in the wildest extrapolations of Woods' conjurings had I ever imagined such a thing possible. Each one of the writer's fingers was split at its base to give rise to a pair of thin, spindly digits, and from each of those there sprouted more fingers, each one complete with a brittle, broken nail and oozing with clear, watery blood. And as I watched, those hellish fingers pressed and manipulated that typewriter like a lover at his muse's body, creating a flowing prose that materialized upon the paper at the top of the machine as if by magic.

"What is this?" I managed to say, although my every sense screamed at me precisely what it was that I was witnessing.

"This is my process, Roy," Woods informed me, his tone most matter of fact. "This is where the River touches the surface." He glanced in my direction, his fingers not once breaking the rhythm of that incessant beat upon the Remington's keys, his eyes flicking downward.

I followed the writer's gaze and saw that far from being covered with the luxuriant, deep pile carpet of the ridiculously wealthy, the floor beneath my feet was constructed of solid, highly polished dark wood. My shoes were all but indistinguishable from the coagulated, swirling darkness into which they had sunk. It was a vile liquid mess teeming with slippery, writhing things that possessed narrow, squinting eyes, needle-sharp teeth and long, spindle fingers that themselves ended with tiny razor dentition; all of this swirling, bubbling and just beyond the grasp of my full comprehension.

Panicking, I attempted to lift a foot—my right, as it happens—but found myself hopelessly stuck, as if the slimy turbulence was holding me tight, reluctant to allow me to venture farther into the writer's realm, yet refusing to let me leave.

"You wanted to know, Roy," Woods said, returning his attention to the Remington-Rand, his hideous fingers undulating atop their respective keys, beating that relentless tattoo as strings of faded gray words unfolded upon the virgin paper. "And now you do—I think that you were always meant to."

And then the dark, shadowy tendrils made themselves visible, literally shimmering into being before my eyes.

Like vile, fleshy, headless snakes, the dark things coiled up from the bubbling blackness, their suppurating flesh sucking the dim light from the room, slithering lengths dotted with dark, glinting eyes, tiny, mewling mouths and what looked to me to be the twisted, tormented faces of innumerable tortured souls. And each one of those fiendish things was inserted into Woods—his arms, legs, the soft part of his belly, either side of his spine and with the biggest of all burrowed firmly into the back of the writer's skull.

And as I stood there, hopelessly transfixed with the slopping, swirling madness that clutched at my feet, those hellish tendrils eased themselves out of Woods's body with a wet, smacking, slurping sound, leaving in their wake wide, jagged holes that oozed with thin, weak blood. Woods sighed out loud as the things left him, a long, wheezing sound of profound relief. And, as the final, fat tendril extracted itself from the writer's head, dragging with it sharp splinters of pink-white bone, his eyes met mine.

I saw in that instant the same haunted, desperate look Woods had possessed on that first night we'd met—only three short days before, by what I'd innocently assumed to be pure happenstance—and the unmistakable reflection of the putrid rot that festered deep down in his soul.

At that moment, I understood.

I didn't so much as flinch when those creeping, reaching things approached me, nor did I resist as they burrowed their way inside my body and maneuvered me toward Woods' old chair, the one Reverend Trevor Ravenscroft had used for human sacrifices. I had to step over Woods' limp, spent corpse as I did so, but somehow the man's demise didn't upset me in the least. In passing on the baton to me, he had finally found his peace.

And those abysmal, wretched things that extended out to me from that River of Madness filled my creative mind with stories and promises of success and wealth beyond my wildest dreams, myriad thoughts and bright, vivid images that raced around my whirling brain like crazed dervishes—terrible, horrific creations of the infinitely cruel and wickedly depraved.

My fingers split apart as I sat upon that infernal chair. Wet, pointed shards of bone erupted from the soft pads at their tips, spatters of crimson showering the awaiting keys of that antiquated typewriter. And from each split there grew more fingers, and from them, yet more, and before I knew it, my hands resembled nothing more than bloodied, fleshy branches of some nightmarish tree as each one of those abominations rested upon its appointed key.

And then, as fingertips old and new fused with the cold metal of the machine, I began to write.

The stories that flowed up from the gurgling maelstrom spewed out from my frantic fingertips, and the metallic clacking of the old keys sounded like the most wonderful music, a fitting accompaniment to the horrific tales that appeared upon the paper before me.

I have to confess that I had never felt so incredibly alive, so creatively vibrant, even though I knew in my possessed heart that I was nothing more now than a simple channel for the murmuring undercurrent which was sourced from and coursed through the deepest, darkest corners of Hell. It seemed to me most fitting that this River should choose to bubble up so close to the surface of our existence in this hot, humid corner of Texas, its vile malignance flowing alongside—through—the thick, black primordial lakes that likewise drove the sanest of men into madness.

Yet none of that matters to me now. I exist as little more than a dreadnought of dark art, a bridge between the Hadean world and this, and while I do indeed receive my just earthly rewards, I know that true recompense awaits me deep down in the inky, swirling undercurrents and eddies of the River of Madness.

A Whistle in the Dark

By Mario E. Martinez

I.

Something broke in Domingo Halcon the day his son got lost in the monte. There was no great mystery, for the public or himself, who was to blame. The boy, Polo, hadn't wandered off. No one kidnapped him. The boy had been lost in the monte for six days because Domingo left him there.

All he'd wanted to do was teach his son a lesson. The boy had been a terror for hours, screaming and demanding all sorts of things. He kicked the back of Domingo's seat like he was stomping a colony of ants and cried like he was on fire. Domingo had told him to stop. His wife, Ana Cristina, threatened to spank him right on the highway. Still, the boy carried on, wailing and kicking.

"That's it," Domingo had said as he pulled the car over. "You're getting the belt, young man." He'd met eyes with his son through the rearview mirror and the boy looked terrified. Domingo often thought of that look in his boy's eyes, thinking how monstrous he must've looked to his son.

So terrifying was that look, it sent Polo scurrying out of the car. They'd pulled over beside one of the many ranches that lined the highway. The boy ran through the tall grass and reached a barbed wire fence. He climbed over it like a monkey and ran to the brush line, stopping just before going headlong into thorny mesquite and plate cactus.

The day had been so hot, Domingo remembered, and the heat made him angrier. He walked through the tall grass, undoing his belt. He whipped it around like a machete, swatting the grass around him. "You get over here this instant," he screamed. He reached the fence, mostly rust and jagged edges, and looked into the boy's eyes. "I've had it! You don't respect me, you don't respect your mother! You cry and whine like you're prince of the world. But, I'll show you, believe you me. You come out of there now."

"No," Polo had told him, seeing he didn't want to cross the fence.

"Polo, you get off that land now," Domingo seethed. "You are trespassing, young man. Do you know that? In Texas, little boys can be shot for trespassing. Now get out of there!"

Polo, he remembered along with the heat and terrified reaction, gave him a smug look, one that told his father that none of his threats or shouts meant a thing. There, Domingo was playing the boy's game, a game he'd played for too long. "I won't," Polo said, his squeal equally pathetic and defiant.

"Really?" Domingo told him. "Fine. I'll tell you what, little prince, why don't you stay here, then? Eh? You like it so goddamn much, stay.

"If you get tired of it," Domingo said, pointing with the belt still clenched in his hand, "the house is forty miles that way. See you at supper."

He walked halfway to the car before turning around and, seeing that Polo hadn't moved, waved. "See you, son," he'd yelled. Once in the car, he told his worried wife that the next turnaround was in a mile, that they'd only pretend to leave him. It would shock the boy, he'd told her.

When Domingo had to talk to the reporters, he asked them how he could've known that the turnaround had been closed or that it would take thirty minutes to get back, not the five he'd planned. How could he have known that the boy wouldn't stay still, frozen in fear? He'd looked in the monte for hours, shouting his son's name, telling him that he wasn't mad. He only wanted to know he was safe. With no sign of his son, he had been forced to get the nearby town involved, which alerted the media.

He was ashamed under the glare of the camera lights and the accusation-laced questions. But, he endured it because the more who knew, the more might come and help look for his son. For the days leading up to the boy's rescue, it was an ominous story, people waiting as time went by to hear of a little body being found. So, when the boy was found on the sixth day, the whole world seemed to be watching. And the weight of that attention was on the boy who'd survived, many said, despite his horribly irresponsible parents.

II.

For three days after being rescued, Polo didn't speak at all. He was examined by doctors and pathologists and psychiatrists but, surprisingly, there wasn't anything wrong with the boy other than having lost a pound or two. People thought it was a miracle that he survived the cold nights and the hot days in such unforgiving terrain. There were snakes and smugglers and wild dogs roaming the monte, any of which wouldn't have given much thought to hurting a child.

When Polo did finally speak, the whole world seemed to be listening. He said that he'd cried and ran into the monte, where he got lost. He followed a path, thinking it would get him back to the road, but all it did was lead him deeper into the brush. Scared, he'd wandered around until nightfall, where he slept under a tree. Somehow, he found a ranch house. The door was unlocked and though there was no food, there was a working faucet to drink from. Polo said he waited there until he heard the search teams.

The whole world was sympathetic to his horrible adventure and showed it with a shower of toys and clothes and scholarships. They gave these things, thinking that those trinkets and checks would somehow compensate the boy for having terrible parents. The same went for the reporters, praising Polo's bravery while wordlessly calling Domingo and Ana Cristina monsters.

Domingo said nothing. He understood.

He understood when news anchors and talk show hosts howled with rage that he and his wife weren't charged with any crime. They cried neglect and abuse and, some, attempted murder. They wanted Polo taken away like Domingo was at home waiting with a bullwhip, ready to beat the boy to death. For a week, he was the national example for what was wrong with modern parenting and the modern legal system. Petitions were passed around. Features on websites devoted to people like John Wayne Gacy and the Pig Man of Northfield, Vermont.

The world thought he was scum and every time he looked at his son, saw the way he acted after his week in the monte alone, Domingo understood why.

Polo wasn't the same hyper child. Before the monte, he was perpetually bored and aggressively sought out solitude. His parents annoyed him and he avoided them at all costs. But, after his return, Polo was never out of their sight. Wherever his mother went, he either positioned himself to be able to see her or outright followed her into rooms. Even when in the bathroom, Domingo and Ana Cristina could see the shadows of Polo's feet under the door. He watched them in silence whereas, only weeks before, any time around his parents was usually filled with obsessive questions or outright complaints.

For weeks, his father wanted to sit down and talk to him, not to try to explain himself or justify what he did, but just to listen. To try and help his boy to understand what happened, what he endured. But, as much desire as Domingo had for dialogue, he didn't have the strength to actually approach his son and speak.

The shame that came from his cowardice mingled with his guilt over leaving the boy and took a toll on Domingo. Soon, as if trying to atone by reliving the boy's suffering, he ate little and hardly slept. He'd stay up for hours, the television on though he wasn't really watching it. Ana Cristina kicked him out of the bedroom because the TV light gave her strange dreams.

Domingo spent his nights in the living room, eyes open and mind shut inward. On one such night, flipping through the channels, Domingo heard a whistling between the ebb and flow of programs. He followed the sound through the darkened house until he reached what he thought was the source. The whistling seemed to come from Polo's room. Domingo stood there a moment, knowing he should investigate, but was still too ashamed to brazenly approach his boy.

After a moment, he decided to open the door just enough to look inside. Domingo found Polo standing at his open window, looking out into the night and whistling a familiar tune—some theme song to one of his cartoons. But it wasn't the bored notes of a wandering mind. Polo made those sounds with a deliberateness that Domingo was not prepared to hear at that hour.

Domingo watched him a minute, the boy whistling half a tune and then waiting before starting again. "What are you doing, Son?" he asked. The suddenness and volume of his voice in the silent house made Domingo cringe, thinking he might frighten the boy again.

"I'm calling my friend, the bird lady," Polo said, not turning to look at his father.

"Who's the bird lady?" Domingo asked from the doorway.

"She's the one who kept me safe," Polo said, finally looking at his father. "She gave me back to you."

III.

The next morning, while the boy ate cereal and toast and jam, Ana Cristina questioned him about the bird lady. She too felt the guilt and tried to broach any subject calmly and without accusation. "She sounded nice," she added nervously. "I'd like to thank her for helping you."

Polo smiled, his mouth still full of cereal. "She was real nice," he said. "She let me stay with her until you found me."

"Why didn't she try to find us?" Domingo asked softly. "I'm sure you told her that we were looking for you."

Polo looked at his father with a stare that seemed to scrutinize him beyond what a boy of his age was capable of. "But, Dad, I didn't know you were looking for me."

Domingo had to look away for a second.

"When she heard all those people going through the monte, she told me to go to them," Polo told them. "I told her to come with me, but she told me it was real important that I didn't tell anyone that she helped me."

"You should've told us," Domingo said quickly, though he shrank away, expecting his son to recoil from his tone.

"I know, Dad," Polo said, the mention of Domingo's title working on the man like pleasant music. "But, she made me promise not to tell anyone. She made me swear."

Ana Cristina gave Domingo a look. "Why would she do that, honey?"

"She said she doesn't like people," Polo said. "She likes babies and kids but not people, that's why she only goes out at night."

"Did . . . did you find her house?" Ana Cristina asked. "Is that how you met her?"

"She found me," the boy said. "It was dark and I was cold and hungry."

Each of Polo's words made his parents feel as though weights were being lowered onto their necks. "And I was crying and it was dark," he continued. "Really dark. Then, she whistled. She whistled 'Dog Pound Detectives.' I heard it and yelled, but she didn't come. She whistled again so I whistled back. And then she came and got me and took me home."

"Did she tell you her name?" Ana Cristina inquired. "Mommy and Daddy—"

"She said names are secrets," Polo interjected.

"Well, uh, what did she look like?" Domingo asked, inwardly berating himself.

"A little . . . but . . ." Polo stopped to think a moment. "She looked like an old lady with feathers and they were—wait!" Polo scooted his chair out and went to his room.

Ana Cristina and Domingo huddled together, debating whether or not to press the boy. Whether or not to call the police.

"I drew a picture of her for when I see her again," the boy announced, bringing a colored sheet of computer paper to the table.

"See her again?" Ana Cristina asked, taking the picture. "When . . ."

"She said all I had to do was whistle and she'd hear me," the boy said, beaming, unaware that his mother's face had drained of color. "I hope she likes it."

Ana Cristina passed the drawing to Domingo and it nearly crushed his soul.

The drawing was childlike, but Domingo imagined seeing such a person emerge from the monte in the middle of the night. Her stark white hair fell all the way down past her waist and framed an emaciated face comprised of a hawkish nose and jutting cheekbones. Her eyes were too large for her face and, for some reason, Polo had colored them a golden yellow devoid of pupils. Her clothing seemed to be a jumble of feathers and filth, though Domingo told himself the ghastly features were due only to his son's lack of artistic talent.

"Do you think she'll like it?" Polo asked.

"She'll love it," Domingo said, only half paying attention as though something of himself was being lost in the crayon-yellow eyes.

IV.

Domingo told the police about what his son had told him, but, when they checked on the boy's story, the police said that no one lived on the property. It belonged to a development firm that was sitting on the piece of land until it was profitable to sell it. Any constructions on the land would've been destroyed and anyone living there would've been driven out a decade earlier. At first, the boy's parents weren't sure what to do with that information. But, soon, Domingo thought the story of the bird lady was only natural.

The boy had been alone, lost, surrounded by dirt and thorns. He'd been hungry and cold and delirious with fright. In times like that, Domingo felt he could understand the boy pretending there was some grandmotherly figure there to help him survive. But, with those thoughts, came the visions of his son huddled inches from snakes, without tears left to shed, whistling to himself just to hear anything other than the oppressive silence of the monte.

So, on those sleepless nights, Domingo excused the whistling. Each note, he felt, was like a sort of prayer to whatever powers allowed his son to survive. Some nights, Domingo stood outside of the boy's door, listening to the half-tunes the boy sent out his window. He listened to them as though there was something important in those songs, something to be memorized and cherished.

One such night, Domingo heard the whistling start up and he crept to the door to listen to it. The little songs started the same way they always did, a few bars followed by silence. He listened for a few minutes, but once the boy whistled for the sixth or seventh time, the boy stopped. After the silence, the boy said, "Yay! I knew you'd come, I just had to keep calling."

The words wounded Domingo, knowing that the boy's imagination had saved his tiny psyche, not his father. At that moment, Domingo was filled with such a profound paternal instinct, he lost all his fear and hesitation and wanted with his whole being to open the door and embrace his son.

"Claro, niño," a voice from inside the room said. *"Son amigos, no?"*

Domingo nearly fell when he heard the voice. The words couldn't've been made by his son, no matter how he altered his voice. The person who'd spoken sounded like an ancient woman, a speaker of a language the boy hardly knew. Domingo opened the door and was confronted by the maddening din of beating wings filling the room with a rush of discordant sounds. But, in an instant, there was silence.

He opened his eyes to see Polo standing at the window, scowling playfully. All around him, black and white feathers drifted to the floor like a light snowfall. "Dad," he complained playfully. "You scared her away."

Domingo wanted to ask who, but, landing at his feet, the crayon drawing with large yellow eyes told him the answer.

V.

The Halcons took their son back to the state psychologists to talk about the bird lady. But the doctors all said the same thing. The bird lady was a manifestation of the boy's imagination, a coping mechanism for the trauma of being left alone in the monte. When questioned about the strange voice, one doctor laughed and said, "The vocal cords are remarkable things. They can imitate all kinds of voices and children have a tendency of playing with voices during their cartoon phases."

None of them had answers for the feathers.

Domingo had collected them in a plastic bag and showed them to the doctors, some of whom, in their amateur opinions, didn't think they were the type found in pillows.

Polo maintained the same story. The feathers, the voice, they were all from the old woman who'd helped him in the monte. She'd only come to visit and see how he was doing now that he was back home. She'd heard him whistling.

"How does she get to your room?" Ana Cristina asked her son. "If she lives near the highway, does she drive?"

Polo thought the idea of the old woman driving was funny. "No, Mom, she flies. She's got big wings like a bird and flies to my window."

Hearing this, Ana Cristina smiled and told Polo to go and play. She looked at her husband and sighed. "It's all just in his head.

You heard him. Bird ladies flying to his window . . . It's like the doctors said."

"Then explain the feathers, Ana," Domingo told her.

"He could've picked them up out of the yard," Ana Cristina said. "The Cuevas' cat kills pigeons and crows all over the neighborhood."

Domingo listened to his wife's explanation and nodded, though he didn't believe a word of it. She hadn't been in the room. She hadn't heard the booming whoosh of titanic wings. But, he could find no explanation that could make sense of what he'd seen and, perhaps, all those sleepless nights and weeks of stress confused him. It had been the middle of the night and Domingo hadn't really seen anything.

Still, like the guilt of leaving the boy, the thought that all the doctors and his wife were wrong nagged him. Alone, the only light coming from the TV, Domingo couldn't resign himself to believe any of it—he'd been there. But, if it wasn't the boy's brain and his collection of feathers, if the boy told the truth, he'd been saved by an old woman with the wings of a bird.

Engrossed in this fantastic idea, Domingo heard his son whistling in his room. At once, he was filled with a mixture of dread and exhaustion. He laughed to himself and rubbed his face. Domingo went up to the boy's door, telling himself that it was how the boy survived. How he dealt with the memories of the elements and the dark. Memories of a shitty father too impatient to do the right thing. No more, he thought.

Domingo opened the door and found Polo at his open window. The boy did not seem surprised that his father was there. "Hey, son," Domingo said, walking up to the window. "You, uh, trying to call that lady again?"

"Uh-huh," Polo said, nodding. "You've just got to whistle. If she whistles back, you answer, and she'll come."

Domingo smiled to hide the pain that came with the image of his son listening to the dark for a friend that would never come.

"Can I do it too?" he asked.

"Sure," Polo said, excited. He pulled his father by the arm and set him at the open window. It looked out to their back yard with the cinderblock fence hidden in shadow and all the undeveloped land behind it. "Go on, Dad," the boy urged. "Whistle."

Domingo looked at the dark for a second before looking at his son again. "What should I whistle?"

"Anything you want," Polo said, smiling up at him.

"All right, let me think," Domingo said. Thinking of one, Domingo whistled the tune of an old radio commercial for a Chinese buffet. Hearing it made him smile a bit. After a moment of silence, Polo told him to do it again, saying that she never answers after the first time. Domingo whistled again, his ear trained to the night air. But there was nothing. A part of him, somehow, was disappointed. Yet, the majority of him told Domingo that it was proof that all this late-night whistling was nothing to worry about. There were stranger ways to cope.

As though in affirmation of this, Domingo whistled into the dark again and basked in the silence.

Faintly, he heard a bird song, a tune for a Chinese buffet closed for twenty years. Domingo froze at the sound. Again, logic tried to flood his mind, tried to tell him that it was nothing, a strange mingling of the boy's playful imaginings and Domingo's newfound relief.

Polo tugged at his father's arm. "You've got to answer, Dad," the boy told him.

Domingo hesitated. He let out some of the tune and the silence that followed it had a weight, a presence. It was herald to something, Domingo felt. He looked out at the dark yard, over at the dark sky, thinking he might see some hint of movement.

Nothing.

Within seconds, Domingo relaxed, thinking again, it was his son's imagination that affected his own. He trained his eyes on the dark to prove it once more to himself. Smiling, he looked down at his son and tussled his hair.

"Look, there she is!" Polo cried.

Domingo snapped his head up and the scream bubbling inside him was caught in his throat.

What came out of the shadows did not look human. Shaggy with feathers, it had a hunchback that hid its face in shadow and it lumbered forward as though it shouldered a great weight. Yet, it moved silently, its footfalls unseen beneath the shroud of black feathers. As if sensing Domingo's fright, the thing approaching them let glow its eyes, huge yellow discs that, even devoid of pupils, Domingo could feel focusing on him. Their light gave the thing's face deep contours and the wrinkled skin looked like tattoos carved by an uncaring hand.

Domingo got hold of his son, shut the window, and walked backward slowly, keeping his eyes on the dark outside. Never had the boy's room—or any room for that matter—felt so vast to him than in that moment. Still, Domingo didn't run, didn't shout. Somehow, he thought, doing so would spark an outrage within that figure creeping toward their home.

As his back bumped against the door, the figure appeared at the window. All dark hunchback and bright yellow eyes, the figure's face glowed against the glass. It smiled wide, revealing a toothless mouth. Up came its hand, its palm and fingers human, but the nails were the talons of a bird. The figure tapped on the window, calling, *"Niño, abra la ventana. Por favor, mijo."*

The boy tried to pull away from his father, but Domingo wouldn't let him go. "Dad," he whined. "She wants to come inside. She's my friend. Please, let her in—"

"Be quiet," Domingo hissed, grabbing the boy tighter. "Go to your mother. Tell her to call the police."

"But, Dad—"

"Don't argue with me!" Domingo barked. "Now, go."

The boy's struggles ceased and, deflated, he sighed and slowly went to the hall.

Alone in the boy's room, Domingo stared at the withered face, which still smiled with an unwavering consistency at him. Meeting eyes with it, Domingo had to fight to get even the fewest of words out. "L-l-leave," he told it. "This is my house. He is my son. Leave us alone."

The figure put a second claw against the glass, scratching at it slowly.

"Get away from here," Domingo shouted, the bluster in his voice sounding forced and pathetic. "You're not wanted here. You—"

"Me llamaste y yo le respondi," the figure whispered.

Stay away from us, Domingo wanted to say; but as the words formed on his tongue, the figure outside Polo's window crashed through the glass, filling the room with the sound of wings and cackling laughter.

Domingo shouted, throwing up his hands in a vain attempt to defend himself. Great wings battered his head and body and a maelstrom of motion confused and frightened him. He felt his fists connect against a feathered body of what felt like solid mesquite, but, despite the crunches of his fingers and knuckles, Domingo didn't dare relent.

In an instant, Domingo felt those taloned fingers hook into his shoulders, the wounds immediately searing with pain. His body locked as he screamed and, as suddenly as he'd been caught, Domingo was pulled off his feet with such a force he thought he'd been ripped in half. He was still intact, though no longer in his son's room.

Domingo was flying up into the night sky, blood dripping on the land rushing by below him, serenaded by the hacking laughter of an old woman with the wings of a bird.

VI.

The police arrived and searched the house. Domingo Halcon was gone. Polo's room was a mess of broken furniture and shards of glass and blood. Again, Domingo was in the news, except now he was missing. Search parties were formed, posters and flyers printed.

A week later, animal control was called. Vultures were picking at something large and stinking by the highway. What they found was a body, shattered and mangled, in a small crater of its own making. The coroner examined it—the wallet retrieved had Domingo Halcon's driver's license in it—and found that the injuries were consistent with a fall from over fifty feet, though there was no structure of that height within miles of the body and, as far as the police could tell, no planes passed over that area. The coroner noted that the eyes, the tongue and some teeth were missing, but they wrote it off as the result of vultures.

The Halloween in Me

By E. R. Bills

"Haunt" is such a harsh word. It's a word the dead do not use.

I didn't exactly understand that before, but now I do. Especially as I stand in the dark next to the pear tree in front of my house. I wait beside it now hoping to catch a glimpse of my children. But it's certainly not my intent to haunt them.

It all started a couple of years back. I distinctly recall the conversation.

"That doesn't make any sense," I sighed into the phone. "Mr. McShay died several months ago."

"No argument from me," Jackie replied from the other end of the line. "I just thought you should know."

"Ok," I said. "I'll see what I can find out."

Sheesh, I thought. Was someone else living there? Had they rummaged through Mr. McShay's attic? I thought he took the Halloween figures apart every year.

Ever since my wife Jackie and I had moved back to the old neighborhood, she had complained about the McShay place. "He puts a lot more effort into Halloween than he does Christmas," she'd say.

It frustrated me.

I loved my wife, but the free-spirited, open-minded coed I'd been smitten by at a Bad Mutha Goose concert in Austin in spring of 1987 seemed to fade a little more every year. She was becoming her parents. It was happening all around me. Friends, relatives, old teammates—wild as March hares back then, but now, middle-aged, reverting back to whatever default settings—political and/or religious—their parents had instilled in them when they were young. We had passionately rebelled against it in college, but now they were taking over. It was happening in slow motion. Jackie was even starting to make comments about me missing church.

Later that afternoon as I pulled into our driveway and stepped out of the car, the first, cool October wind hit me. I stopped and stared north.

Halloween was coming. The weather would change suddenly and then we'd have our night.

They'd have their night. The kiddos.

Or at least they used to have it.

We had Halloweens when I was a kid. Full-throated Halloweens. And Halloween had been my favorite holiday, bar none. It still was. But the thrill of it was much diminished. My wife preferred taking the kids to the Fall Festival *(They wouldn't even refer to it as a Halloween festival!?).* Held at a local church, it included an overnight lock-in for the teenagers in the gym. What teenager wanted to be locked up in a church gym on Halloween? *Wasn't the equivalent leaving them in a graveyard for Christmas?*

I was offended by this usurpation. Especially as a former teenager.

I took a deep breath of the October wind, turned and surveyed the McShay place four houses down on the other side of the street. Mr. McShay's oak trees were barely affected by the breeze, but, sure enough, a couple of Halloween figures were out in the yard.

"Shit," I said.

My best friend growing up had been Terrence McShay. Terry.

He'd lived in that house until he joined up for Operation Desert Storm. His dad was a Vietnam vet and a stint in the military seemed to be a point of family pride. Terry went to Kuwait and I went off to college.

Terry and I spent every Halloween together growing up and

his house was always the scariest in town.

Mr. McShay was an electrician, and early every October, he'd bring scrap metal conduit, fittings and boxes home and build figures in his yard. He'd pull out his 1/2" bender and construct skeletons out of EMT, creating striding legs and flailing arms. Then, we'd dress them in old clothes and whatever else was lying around.

The first year he only had one figure. He stood up an EMT skeleton for a mummy, driving the legs into the ground to keep it upright. Then, he padded the abdominal area, placed a Styrofoam wig head on top and wrapped the entire affair with athletic tape that was torn in half (all the way through the roll), giving it the proper width and a head start on fraying. It was startlingly realistic.

The next year he had two figures and the year after that, three or four. Sometimes they wore life preservers or brandished fake plastic knives or hatchets. Later, there were soldiers.

After a while, Mr. McShay would stand up 10-12 figures every Halloween, starting with a few in early October and increasing the number until All Hallow's Eve. One year they were all cowboys and Indians. Another year they were all soldiers. One even wore a flight suit. It was wickedly off-putting to pass the McShay place after McShay had added a figure or two. It always startled me.

The kids in our town loved the display and, before long, people from out of town were even dropping by. Mr. McShay started purchasing dry ice and placing ceramic casserole dishes of it around the front yard, covered with fallen leaves. It created an eerie Halloween ambiance. A couple of years after that, he added a strobe light.

The rag-tag, twisted figures leaned sometimes unnaturally and sometimes grotesquely in the breezes, and wisps of dry ice fog rose to make the whole yard look like a graveyard. The strobes made the figures look as if they were moving.

On Halloween night, the younger kids would stand on the

street curb and trade dares about going through the McShay yard or up to the house for candy. If you'd already mustered the courage to do it and been scared yourself, you'd hang back or sit on a curb across the street, a wily veteran, and watch the other kids as they worked up the nerve to risk the McShay place and earn their treat. It became a rite of passage.

Some of the newbies were so terrified their parents had to practically drag them up to the house. But we could tell grown-ups got the willies, too. They just hid it better.

In the early days, we helped Terry's dad bend the EMT conduit and build the figures. But as we got older, hit puberty, got interested in girls or baseball, we were less involved. Mr. McShay pressed on by himself, making monsters, "Halloweening" the yard as he'd put it. And though we might have developed other interests, we still made appearances come Halloween. The dry ice, the strobe light and the swaying figures—we acted too cool to admit it—but they were as scary as ever.

Terry was killed in Desert Storm. I was still in college. I missed that Halloween at the McShay place and several after when I lived in Austin a few years.

I didn't forget about Halloween, though. I just got busy with other things. When I'd talk to my parents they'd fill me in on what Mr. McShay was doing, how many figures he had up. As far as I could tell, Mr. McShay hadn't lost a step. Kids still came from all over.

The years flew and eventually my parents passed away, followed shortly by Mrs. McShay.

When I brought my wife and kids to live in a house in the neighborhood a couple years back, Mr. McShay was still around. He was thrilled to see me. He claimed he hardly knew any of the new residents on the street. He said he thought they didn't know what to make of him, especially on Halloween. But the kids still came around and that was all that mattered.

We talked about Terry and baseball. Mr. McShay loved our

visits, but sometimes his eyes would well up and he would turn away. I'd give him a minute to shake it off and act like nothing happened. I felt bad for him. We both missed Terry.

The second Halloween after we came back, Mr. McShay got sick; but the figures still went up. Jackie was mildly disappointed.

The following year, Mr. McShay was in a nursing home. I didn't go to see him as much as I should have. I was amazed when with the first cool, October breezes, the ghostly figures appeared on his lawn.

Jackie was not amused. Worse, it annoyed her that our kids were fascinated by them.

I was quietly ecstatic. Especially for the kids.

I was also curious. Was Mr. McShay hiring the figure construction and placement out? He had a younger brother I'd met and visited with a few times, but I couldn't remember his name. Was the brother taking care of it?

I went to see Mr. McShay before Thanksgiving that year, just before he died. I asked him who was putting up the Halloween figures in his yard and he smiled, but said he didn't know. We visited briefly, talking about baseball and the weather, and then he asked me if I'd seen Terry. I assumed he was confused. I told him I hadn't and he surprised me. He assured me I would. He told me I'd see "Shank" as well.

I barely remembered the name. *Shank*. One of Mr. McShay's old Vietnam buddies. Died in the war. Mr. McShay never talked about it much. Terry told me Shank had saved his dad's life.

"They'll try to enlist you," Mr. McShay said. "Be ready."

I nodded and smiled. I assumed he was losing his mind.

Two weeks later he was dead.

I saw his brother Seamus at the funeral. Pronounced *Shaymuss*. He laughed when I asked him about the Halloween figures. He didn't know anything about it. He said he remembered the old Halloweens at his brother's and said it was sad. He was putting the place up for sale, but felt like he was destroying a local landmark.

The morning after my wife called to report the appearance of Halloween figures in the McShay yard, she phoned early again. On her way out to work, she noticed another figure. She wondered if I'd found out anything.

"Not yet," I said. "But I'll get on it today."

When I got home, I stopped by the McShay place to get the realtor's name from the "For Sale" sign. But there was no sign. It was gone.

I had planned to ask the realtor about the Halloween figures. I assumed the house must have sold.

The figures swayed in the breeze.

I got out of the car, went to the front door and knocked.

No answer.

I knocked again, then froze. Just over my right shoulder one of the figures moved. I spun around and glared. It was dressed in black coveralls and wearing a hockey mask. An homage to Michael Myers from John Carpenter's *Halloween*. I could've sworn it moved.

Not swayed. *Moved.*

A chill ran through me. A core-shaking chill like I hadn't experienced since I was a kid.

Grinning, I turned around. Silly of me. I would have sworn to it, but maybe I'd just misjudged its position when I walked up. That was the only plausible explanation.

No one answered the McShay front door, so I walked back to the car. I gave the "moving" figure a respectable berth. But I grinned again. It was just the Halloween in me. Some of the old McShay magic.

For the rest of the week I quizzed the neighbors about the Halloween figures inexplicably popping up. Most considered Mr. McShay's Halloween interests unseemly and strange. When I played Devil's advocate and remarked some folks went overboard with the Christmas decorations, my neighbors looked at me like I was unseemly and strange. Public sentiment had clearly shifted and it seemed I was part of a dying breed. I decided to drop it.

"Who's doing it, then?" Jackie asked.

"I don't know," I said. "It's not his brother."

"Well, who else could it be?"

"I'm not sure."

My wife's fixation frustrated me. I came to realize that she had anticipated that Mr. McShay's death would mean the end of Halloween in the neighborhood. Jackie had been playing the long game. She knew her views on the subject would benefit from attrition. The appearance of the figures was forestalling her victory.

That Saturday night, I was up late. I couldn't sleep. Jackie was already in bed.

I sat up and watched old scary movies on TV until two o'clock in the morning. I even let the kids stay up (our little secret). It was fun to do every once and a while. And for Halloween to have any hope of survival, it was necessary, even.

After I put the kids to bed and went to make sure the front door was locked, I experienced another core-shaking chill. There was a lone, dark figure swaying in our front yard.

The sight took the breath out of me. I closed my eyes. It was dark out there. What had I really seen?

I looked again. The thing was still there. *And it was facing the house.*

Those effigies usually faced the street, the direction that Trick-or-Treaters approached from. Why was this one facing our house?

It was too much.

Was it the black figure wearing a hockey mask?!

I couldn't tell. Too dark. I wondered if it could see me.

I backed away from the front door slowly, never taking my eyes off the figure. After a couple of steps back, I could hardly see out of the front glass, but I noticed my reflection. I half-expected my dishwater blonde hair to be solid white. But it wasn't. I smiled, mustering bravado. It really was the Halloween in me. My imagination was just running wild. This was getting out of hand; it wasn't like me to get this rattled.

I went back to the door and peered out the glass. There was nothing there. The lone, dark figure was gone. Shaking my head, I opened the door.

There was nothing in my front yard. But now there was an extra figure at the McShay place.

"Not cool," I said, to no one in particular.

The next day I walked down to the McShay house and knocked on the door again and, again, got no answer. None of the figures moved, but there was another in addition to the one I'd noticed last night. I hoped there was a logical explanation. Either way I was unnerved.

Over the next couple of weeks, I was busy with work or the kids' practices; I didn't have time to sort out a logical explanation so I avoided thinking about it. My wife helped the children plan their non-Halloween costumes for the local Fall Festival. Whether I chose to think about it or not, more figures appeared at the McShay place and every new drive through the neighborhood gave folks an unwanted thrill.

I didn't know who was doing it, but I was secretly pleased. Jackie was just plain angry. I knew the neighborhood wasn't going to be the same without Halloween at the McShay place. *Where was the harm in one last "Hurrah?"*

Halloween fell on a school night, making the Fall Festival all the more practical.

The kids enjoyed the festival's inflatable playhouses, caramel apples and trickless treats. The bobbing for apples station of the mini-midway was the least visited—the parents didn't want the kids to get their costumes wet.

Not a scare in the place and it was depressing. But I concealed my displeasure.

We returned home around 10:00 p.m. and the Trick-or-Treating had frittered out. Just a few stragglers here and there.

Against my wife's wishes, I had left a big cardboard box full of candy on the front porch. It seemed only right. The box was empty and I was glad. I tore the box in small pieces and threw it in the recycling bin.

I went inside and helped tuck the kids in and told my wife I'd come to bed later. She nodded off quickly, and I decided to go back outside.

The weather had been perfect, low 60s, high 50s, no rain, light wind. It had felt like Halloween and I missed watching the costumes go by, the gags, the excited kids.

The ghostly mannequins were still out at the McShay place. No dry ice or strobe lights, but they were still there, swaying in the breeze. All Hallow's Eve was their dominion.

I walked toward them.

It would be melodramatic to say I was drawn there. I just had a yearning, a nostalgic tug.

As I walked, I felt like a kid again, fourteen, ten—eight. I smiled and laughed. Halloween had always been our night.

I approached the McShay place feeling like a big man, scared, but thrilled. Mystified, but also knowing—knowing as much as the parents, as much as other grown-ups. That was the thing on Halloween. It wasn't just the cheeky Trick or Treat threat. Kids were empowered and grown-ups were taken down a notch. They didn't know what was around the next corner any more than we did. They definitely didn't know what was happening at the McShay place. We were almost equals for a day. And in the possibilities created by uncertainty, there was magic and mystery again.

The McShay figures swayed. There were thirteen, a baker's dozen. A witch, a sunken-ship survivor (complete with a discolored, orange life preserver); a caped figure, maybe a vampire; a headless doctor, his stethoscope ear pieces still clasped to his stump of a neck; the figure dressed in black coveralls with a hockey mask; and the rest were soldiers. Mr. McShay always had soldiers. A sailor with a sailor's hat on his skull, a fighter pilot, a diver. The diver was new. I'd never seen a diver there. A diver in a frayed scuba suit and cracked oxygen mask. *Very cool.* There was also a tall Marine in desert camos, a regular Army soldier, etc.

Our improvised graveyard playground had tested our courage and we proved ourselves, again and again. Now, it was being offered to a new generation. I gazed in awe, transported through time—*then one of the figures grabbed my arm.*

Instinctively, I jerked my arm back; but the figure didn't let go. It was the Marine in desert camos. His face—a cracked skull—was expressionless. I struggled to free my arm, but the skeletal hand wouldn't release it.

I watched, stupefied as the figure with the hockey mask in black coveralls, stepped forward. This undeniable display of volition gave me the impetus to free my arm from the Marine's grasp.

"What the—"

"Bryan," the hockey mask said. "It's me."

I knew the voice. It—

"It's me. *Terry.*"

My head swam. I leaned too far one way and almost collapsed. The hockey mask grabbed my shoulder and steadied me.

"Stay with me, Bryan," the hockey mask said. "I'm real. *This is real.*"

"*Terry* . . . how?"

"Dad, Bryan. It was my dad."

"You died."

"Yes. But this—*Halloween*—it allowed me to come back. To visit."

Back. Visit. "With your dad?"

"Yes."

"Why are you wearing a mask?"

"It would be too much for the kids. And you wouldn't recognize me. There wasn't much left after the IED."

"Oh," I said, still bleary but recalling the way my friend had died. "Who's the Marine?"

"Dad's friend. Shank. Shank's been coming back since we were kids."

I could only offer a weak "Jesus" before I leaned again, irretrievably, and fainted.

When I came to, I was still lying in the McShay yard and two Trick-or-Treaters were standing over me. Captain America and a Ninja Turtle.

"Are you okay, Mister?" the Ninja Turtle asked.

"We thought you were dead," Captain America said.

"No," I answered. "Just frozen in ice."

They didn't get my joke.

"I'm all right," I continued, sitting up.

"Whatcha' doin' on the ground?"

"I just got tired. Listen, I don't think there's any candy left here tonight."

"Do you know the people who live here?" asked the Ninja Turtle.

"I used to."

"Who put up all the monsters?" Captain America queried.

"My uncle says a demon from hell lives here," said the Ninja Turtle.

"Your uncle is full of crap," I said.

"That's not nice," Captain America commented.

"Who said I was nice?" I sold it with a glare, suddenly wishing the kids would leave.

"I'm gonna tell my Dad," warned the Ninja Turtle.

"Listen," I said. "I'm a dad. And the man who lived here was a dad . . . not a demon."

"How do you know?"

"Because I grew up here. And he was my best friend's dad."

The wind was gone from my sails. These two boys were probably best friends just like Terry and I had been . . . or were.

Thankfully, Captain America and the Ninja Turtle moved on and I stood up. The Marine dressed in desert camos and Michael Myers were motionless again, but not for long.

"That was a little overboard, dontcha' think?" Shank said. His voice was deep and low.

"I think I'm losing my mind," I said.

"No," Terry replied. "It's just a lot to take in."

"McShay always said you was a good egg," Shank added.

"What's happening?" I responded. "How is this happening? How is this possible?"

"Can we talk in the back yard?" Terry asked.

If I was just talking to phantoms in my head, it made sense to do it where no one would see. "Sure."

We went to the back yard and stood in the shadows. The rest of the figures remained motionless.

The back yard was just like I remembered it, only smaller. We'd treed a squirrel or two in the old oak in the far corner and slept outside on old Army cots several times.

"I'm sorry, Bry," Terry said. "I know this is a shock."

"Is it really you, Terry?"

"Yes."

I struggled with it and thought for a moment.

"What baseball card did we fight over right here on this very spot when we were ten?" I asked, testing Terry.

"Nolan Ryan's 1979 Mets card. Topps, I think."

"Damn," I said. "*It is you.* How?!"

"Dad."

"Okay. But how?"

"I was first," Shank said. "I'll explain it the best I can."

Shank looked around and then lowered his head.

"I was in a place I can't describe," he said. "I saved McShay, Terry's dad, yeah . . . but I did some things, too. Bad things. War does that. And one day, I just lost it. I lost my shit and didn't stop losing it 'til a grenade launcher fragged me. *Benito Finito.* But the day I died was not a relief. No light, no tunnel. I was just on a different plane. Fighting the Vietcong was nothing compared to being at war with myself, battling my own demons. I had been my worst self. I was my own dull, sad, crazy monster, and I was stuck. But when I moved along that plane, I thought a lot about McShay. Thinking about Terry's dad kept me going. We'd had some laughs. We were friends. He was a good guy and I wondered what happened to him. It was an eternity before anything changed, but it did change. I kept moving along the plane and one day I just saw McShay. He was building something. Right there in the front yard. I couldn't explain it, but I was happy to see him.

"I watched him. I saw Terry when he was young. *I saw you.* And I just stayed. I quit fighting with myself. I quit wandering. I just hung around.

"Right before Halloween came, I came out. I came out to McShay just like we came out to you tonight. He was shocked, but he bawled his eyes out. He hugged me and held me in a way that made me feel like I was actually here. And I sort of was—just like we are now.

"And that's how it went. Year after year. Only Halloweens, mind you. I came back and hung around for Halloweens."

"The dry ice was Shank's idea," Terry said.

"Really?"

"Yep," Shank said. "That was after I'd been back a few times. It was fun. So, I got this reprieve every Halloween. A break from what might as well be called Hell. Just a chance to visit."

"And then I came along," Terry said.

"Yeah," Shank nodded. "Hated that. Your poor dad. No man should have to bury his son. I was worried."

"It was tough," Terry agreed.

"Yeah," Shank said. "After you—after you were gone, he asked me if you were out there. He asked me if I could find you. I said I'd try. And I enlisted some friends. Your dad just wanted to see you again, Terry."

"That's when the extra Army men began showing up?" I speculated.

"Yes, sir."

"That's why they looked so real."

"Yep. Because they were. We were. And we eventually found Terry."

"What happened, Terry?"

"IED, like I said. Never saw it coming. A click and a boom. Died instantly . . . *dumbfuck that I was.* I should have gone off to college with you."

"McShay never forgave himself," Shank said.

"It wasn't his fault," Terry said. "I kept telling him that."

"I talked to him awhile back," I said.

"Yeah?"

"Yeah. He actually tried to spill the beans about this, but I had no idea what he was talking about. Figured he was off his rocker. He even said y'all would recruit me."

"He was radio silence on the subject for decades," Shank said. "Can't blame him for slipping a little or wanting to confide. He was worried."

"Worried about what?"

"Worried about what would happen to us."

"Oh. Yeah. What will happen?"

"He's gone, Bry," Terry said. "He's gone. Somebody will buy this house and we'll be gone. We won't have a place to go. We'll lose this."

"Oh. *Oh*. Right. I wasn't thinking."

I stared at the back of the McShay place and then looked up the road to my house.

"Does it have to be Terry's house?" I asked.

"Not necessarily," Shank replied.

"Can it be my place?"

"It's a lot to ask," Terry said.

"My eyes welled up. "No, it's not," I said. "It's really not."

"War's over when we're here," Shank said. "Halloween's our R&R now, amigo."

Terry and Shank walked me back to the front yard and we hugged. Then, they assumed their positions.

"See ya, Bry," the hockey mask said.

"See you," I replied. "Next Halloween, I hope."

"We'll be there," Shank muttered. "We've never lost anybody on this detail."

The next morning, all the figures in the McShay yard were gone. The "For Sale" sign for the house was back up by Thanksgiving and the place sold before Christmas.

The new owners put up gobs of Christmas lights and a cardboard sleigh.

In early October of the following year, I bought a 1/2" EMT bender at a pawn shop, some EMT and some boxes and fittings. I put up two figures the first weekend of October and a couple more the week after. I dressed one in old jeans and a frayed, long-sleeve hoodie; I outfitted the other with my college graduation cap and gown. I may have been the only one, but I felt like I'd outdone myself.

When Jackie got home I braced for the worst.

"What is this?" she demanded.

"Just getting into the Halloween spirit."

"Well . . . get out of it."

We didn't talk anymore that evening. And the next day we ignored the subject.

That night I stood at the front door and stared at my creations, wondering when they might be joined by a figure I had not created. I slept very little that weekend.

I checked for "strangers" every morning as I left for work. I was pleased to find the figures I'd put up were disconcerting even in daylight; but there were no nocturnal additions. I began to fear that I'd have to put up all the figures myself. Had my reunion with Terry and Shank really happened?

On the evening of October 22, I cursed myself for a fool. Looking out my front window, it seemed it had all been a figment of my imagination.

It was only then I noticed an extra figure outside.

It startled me, but I wasn't frightened. In fact, I was relieved as I went out into the yard.

"This is sweet," a Marine in jungle camos said. Shank was back.

"Where's Terr—"

"Right here," Terry said. He was a janitor with a ratty mop.

"You made it."

"Was there ever any doubt?" Terry replied.

I hugged him. "I'm so glad," I said. "I'm just . . . so glad."

"Wouldn't miss it."

The last week before Halloween was a blur. More figures appeared in the yard. I picked up a fog machine and a strobe light. Jackie didn't like it, but didn't say much. Her silence was strange, but I didn't want to antagonize the situation any more than I already had. I'd even been going to church steadily for a couple of months to stay in her good graces.

Jackie made Fall Festival plans and I mounted the strobe light. I also made a special trip or three to a party store. I liked passing out candy on Halloween, but I knew you could buy plastic eyeballs, spiders and cheap plastic vampire teeth in bulk and thought it would be cool to hand these out along with the candy.

My kids were fascinated with the Halloween figures, and, as it turned out, enjoying a growing celebrity at their school. Other kids were asking what it was all about and making plans to drop by.

A few days before Halloween, I decided it would be fun to join the "creatures" in the front yard, so I bought myself a costume.

Jackie was perturbed but patient. I wanted more than anything to introduce her to Terry. It was the best way to explain. I just didn't know how she would take it. It was easy to imagine the encounter going south. Fast.

In the wee hours of the morning after midnight before All Hallows' Eve, I heard a tap on our master bedroom window. It was Terry. I met him out front. He was the only figure standing.

"Nice neighbors you got," said Shank from the ground.

Two men had come through the yard with bats, smashing the figures.

"Sorry," I said. "I don't know who would do such a thing."

"If I wasn't already dead," Terry said, "that probably would have killed me."

"I thought about shoving those bats up their asses, but we didn't wanna get you in any trouble."

"I appreciate that," I said, "but it seems like trouble is unavoidable. Anything like this ever happen to your Dad, Terry?"

"No. Never."

"A lot more humbugs these days I guess."

On Halloween night, Jackie was pleasant and agreed to let the kids hang out in the yard before the Fall Festival. It wouldn't really be dark by then, but I didn't complain. I knew the kids would be able to see the yard again after the Festival.

Everything was going well. The figures swayed, the fog machine belched creepiness and the strobe light trapped it all in an old-timey flicker-show frame. The kids that came through were thrilled and, though I couldn't see Terry's or Shank's faces, I sensed their grins. They were having fun and so was I. And that's what it was all about.

Looking back now, I know I should have seen the vandalism the night before as a warning. Maybe I should have taken it more seriously. When Mr. Jake showed up, I knew we were in trouble.

Mr. Jake had been a drunk when Terry and I were young. I'd

seen him at church a few times recently and assumed he'd sobered up. I didn't recognize him when he first started pacing in the street in front of the house, but soon he was saying things loud enough that I caught pieces of them, and then he was drunkenly shouting.

"This is a House of Satan. *This . . . is . . . a . . . house . . . of . . . Satan!*

When I finally heard him and realized who he was, the Trick-or-Treaters near the house were already fleeing. I took my mask off and approached him in the street. He started to scream about the house again and I said hello.

"It's me, Mr. Jake," I continued. "It's Bryan Nichols. Do you remember me?"

"No," Mr. Jake said. "Yes—what are you doing here?"

"I live here."

"In the House of Satan?"

"No, Mr. Jake. This is my house. It's Halloween. We're just having some fun. I just thought I might pick up where Mr. McShay left off."

"We thought that would be an end to it," he said. "This is a Christian town now. Why are you doing this?"

"Mr. Jake, you know me. I grew up here. This is what we did when I was growing up here."

"Well, it's a Christian town, now," Mr. Jake repeated, jerking his head. "*Can't you see?* We're trying to keep it that way."

"Mr. Jake," I replied. "Are you okay? You seem confused."

"I'm not the one's confused. You're making a spectacle."

Mr. Jake's seriousness made me uncomfortable. *Were we really debating this?*

"It's Halloween," I said.

"Halloween isn't good or wholesome."

"Says who?"

"Says me. Says lots of folks."

"Well," I said, my frustration growing, "Lots of folks have their own yards. I have mine. Don't you think it would be better if we tended to our own yards and minded our own business?"

"This is town business," Mr. Jake quipped. "Spreading deviltry is town business."

I was tempted to laugh, but I didn't want to upset him further. His sincerity stumped me, but I was truly annoyed.

"Well," I said. "If it's town business, pass an ordinance."

"We will. But you need to listen."

"No, Mr. Jake," I responded pointedly. "You need to listen to yourself."

Mr. Jake looked at me hard and I reciprocated accordingly. "Happy Halloween," I said.

Mr. Jake stared at me a moment longer and then turned toward his truck. I put my mask back on.

The people who had gathered in the street to watch dispersed. Mr. Jake had ruined the entire vibe.

And he wasn't finished.

As I reentered my yard, I couldn't see the headlights approaching. The strobe light was still flashing.

Mr. Jake drove his truck into my yard and mowed down several of the figures before I realized what was happening.

I heard passersby scream. I felt several impossible cracks and landed on my back.

Then, I saw Shank straighten, reach into the cab of Mr. Jake's passing truck and grab him by the neck. I couldn't make out exactly what happened next, but the truck veered sharply, slowed down and rolled into a neighbor's house.

As the passersby—not realizing I was actually among the figures that Mr. Jake had run down—tried to attend to Mr. Jake at the household next door, Terry and Shank came to my side.

"What happened?" I said. I could feel something poking through my rib cage.

"I went bobbing for apples," Shank said. "*Adam's apples.* I don't think Jake is going to make it."

"Am I?"

"Hang on," Terry said, lifting my head. "Just hang on."

"Medic!" Shank screamed. *"Medic!"*

"Jackie is going to be so pissed," I said, spitting up blood.

"Easy, buddy," Shank said.

Shank looked at Terry as he took my hand. "It's gonna be okay," Terry said. "It's gonna be okay."

Terry was wrong. That's just what you say when you know things aren't going to be okay and there's not a damn thing you can do about it. He had just been trying to make me feel better, allow me to go easier.

Now, I'm on the other side as All Hallows' Eve approaches. And the Halloween in me—it's all I have left.

Terry and Shank were able to get me back here, but we have no—for lack of a better word—venue to play, no refuge to inhabit.

Still, Halloween springs eternal.

My presence isn't a haunting. It's a longing.

I lost consciousness before my family arrived home from the Fall Festival, never got to say goodbye. I know my kids were fascinated by all the Halloween figures before Mr. Jake's rampage, but I realize what happened soured them on All Hallows' Eve.

Even so, I hold out hope. Jackie won't always be able to marshal them to the Fall Festival, and they may want to have their own Halloween someday.

I have to stick around just in case.

Thirsty Ground

By Summer Baker

Folks in the Great Plains see them every summer—long cracks in the dry caprock dirt. They appear overnight, yawning mouths opening down, down, down to the aquifer below.

Most people pretend these fissures aren't there, skirting around them, not looking. But the brave get close enough to toss in a rock or a penny. No echo of the object landing ever comes back up. Just air blowing through the crevice, like the sound of breathing.

The emptying aquifer thirsts; the crumbling ground above it hungers. We're watched through the wide brown eyes of dusty sunflowers and heard by ears of corn, grown from water sucked up from the parched earth.

Alicia stepped off a rumbling yellow school bus at a crossroads where the county pavement changed to caliche. Already, sweat trickled down through her hair and soaked her t-shirt where her backpack straps stuck to her shoulders. Even though the sun was going down, the air danced across the fields flanking the road; one side new corn, the other old sunflowers. Fine dust swirled up around Alicia's ankles as she started the half-mile trudge home.

Ahead, her trailer house shimmered in the heat, bleached of color like a hazy memory. Alicia longed for the window air conditioner cooling her bedroom and decided that, when she got home, she'd stand in front of it until Christmas.

It had barely rained a drop since April and the temperatures were soaring into the triple digits almost every day. Water conservationists were raising a ruckus on the news again as the local lake level dropped lower and lower.

Alicia twisted her backpack around, digging inside. Her fingers closed on crackling plastic and she pulled out a bottle filled with water from her family's well, sweet and clear. As she unscrewed the cap and raised it to her mouth, a gust of wind whispered past, bringing with it the semi-sweet scent of buffalo grass.

A faint shriek echoed through the sweltering air and Alicia's hand jerked, slopping water across her face and onto the earth. Liquid met dirt and the smell of rain rose up like a lie.

Looking all around her, Alicia saw nothing but plants and sky. Screwing the water bottle cap back on, she shouted "Hey! Who's out there?"

There was no response.

Then, something papery brushed against her leg.

Instinctively, Alicia swatted at it, thinking it was a wasp. But when she looked down, a crude cord comprised of braided yellow prairie grass ensnared her lower calf. The yellow prairie grass cord stretched off into the weedy ditch, vanishing between withered stems.

Alicia's eyes widened. She reached for the snare, but the yellow prairie grass cord drew tighter and yanked her feet out from under her. She was slammed to the ground back first, the air vacating her lungs.

She couldn't draw breath to scream as the rope bit into her flesh, dragging her along the ground, too fast for her to get up. Dirt buried itself under her fingernails and her fingertips tore open as her hands scrabbled along the road grasping for purchase.

When Alicia's feet hit the weeds in the ditch, the plants released an awful scent, sharp and bitter and broken. They slowed her momentum some, slicing at her skin, laying her bare legs and arms open, her blood watering thirsty leaves.

Ahead, at the bottom of the shallow ditch, a crack formed in the earth, splitting wider and wider. It opened and closed, a gaping, hungry mouth. Along its edges, long pale roots broke through the crust, like tendrils of saliva.

Alicia snatched at passing plants, anything to slow her progress toward the gaping abyss.

Several stalks broke free before she caught a double fistful of slick prairie grass and dug her heels into a cluster of ragweed, coming to a halt. Blood poured from her damaged ankle, but the snare tightened further, threatening to slice her limb in two.

The ground beneath her rumbled and shook. A voice, rough as gravel and deep as a canyon, said, "Give me my water."

Alicia whimpered. She needed to retrieve the knife in her pocket. But it was all she could do to hang on. Pain arced up her leg and down her cramped fingers.

"You've stolen it," the crack thundered. "Give it back!"

The pain in Alicia's ankle was excruciating and she knew she couldn't hold on much longer. She had to risk it.

Letting go with one hand, she slipped her knife from her pocket. But, just as she pressed her thumb along the warm steel to flip the blade open, the braided prairie grass snare tightened again. Alicia lost her grip on the grass and the knife. The weapon thumped into the loose dirt, half-opened. Receding out of reach. Useless.

"No!" Alicia screamed.

"Yes," the ground intoned. "So thirsty."

The crevice filled Alicia's vision. It was black as an oil pit and wide enough to swallow her whole.

Less than a yard away and nearing the edge, she spied the water bottle caught between her leg and the cord, carried along with her.

Seizing it, Alicia hurled it into the yawning crevice. "Take your damn water!"

The bottle spun upward.

Tone worshipful, the crevice said, "My water."

Releasing Alicia, the braided yellow prairie grass cord whipped through the air and wrapped around the bottle, squeezing. The cap popped off under the pressure.

Water spurted out, suspending droplets in the air. They glittered like diamonds in the sunlight.

The bottle disappeared into the crevice depths. Behind it, the crack shut with a hollow boom, startling a nearby flock of birds into flight.

Alicia didn't stop running until she made it home.

The local news the next day covered the disappearance of ninety-three people from the surrounding rural areas. All gone in one night.

"It's a mystery," a news anchor reported. "One that's got authorities stumped."

The wide brown eyes of the sunflowers watched and the maturing corn listened.

"But a bit of good news," the anchor continued. "It looks like we're finally going to get some rain. Maybe it'll seal up all those cracks we've been seeing around lately."

The Road Trip

By Dennis Pitts

McDowell had a free day before he was scheduled to be in Lubbock for his morning seminar. He was well prepared and had nothing pressing that needed attention. He could have lazed around the office until time to leave for Love Field. Flying in itself would have taken all afternoon. It was approximately a one-hour flight, but driving to the airport, parking, checking bags, going through security, picking up his bags, renting a car . . . well, the whole ordeal both before and after the flight was time consuming. And frankly, he was in the mood for a road trip.

According to the map app on his phone, it was just a little over five hours driving from Dallas up Hwy 114 through Seymour to Lubbock. But McDowell was in the mood for something more back-roads than that. He could take 80 to Mineral Wells, go north to Graham, and then take the really small roads, zigzagging through remote countryside on the way to Lubbock. Time consuming, yes, but it would be enjoyable to see small-town Texas, particularly in the spring.

He enjoyed the wildflowers that proliferated in the drainage ditches, creeks and open fields along the way. At some point, however, he realized that the small farming communities all looked the same: a Dairy Queen, a convenience store or two (that probably smelled of fried chicken), a small bank, a post office, a Baptist and a Methodist church (sometimes a Catholic church too, but not often) and a farm equipment company in the somewhat larger towns. Vacant buildings along the main highway were a testament to the dwindling economy of the area and they all started to look alike.

West of Haskell he began to wonder whether he was still on track or if he'd inadvertently taken a wrong turn somewhere. Pulling off the road into the weed-grown gravel drive that led to a tumbled-down farmhouse of gray wood roughly one hundred yards or so from the pavement, he checked his map app.

There was no service.

He continued down the two-lane highway a couple of miles until it made a sharp curve and appeared to go straight north. It would probably lead him up to 114, but there was no telling how long that would take. About fifty yards down the highway, however, was a smaller, unmarked road that seemed to go west, the direction he needed to go. He decided to give it a shot.

The road was barely two lanes wide and had very little shoulder on either side. Within two miles the road began twisting and turning, following a large creek that probably flowed into the nearby Brazos River. The road also began to climb, and the landscape became broken and rocky. He realized he was climbing up onto the Llano Estacado, the Staked Plains, the escarpment that marked the southeastern edge of the central plains.

McDowell knew that Lubbock was on the high land, so he was obviously going in the right direction. But he was still concerned that he was lost. He needed gas soon and he was hungry, so he decided to stop at the next gas station or convenience store he saw to get directions, gas and a snack. He had stopped around mid-morning for a Dr. Pepper and some crackers, but it hadn't held him for long. Surely, he thought, there's a little town somewhere along this road.

In one of the curves he caught a flash of something that looked like a sign in the bushes along the shoulder. Maybe it could tell him where he was. He stopped and looked in his mirror to see whether anyone was behind him. Seeing a clear road for a quarter mile or so behind him, McDowell slowly backed up until he could see the object that caught his eye. It was a sign as he had suspected. It looked as if it had been tossed off the road and had been in the brush for some time. It seemed to be attached to a makeshift sawhorse, and had been neatly painted at one time. The wood sign was warped and the paint was peeling, but he could read it. There was a skull and crossbones above a single word in all caps: "DANGER."

It was interesting, but not helpful. It had probably been used to advise drivers of some roadwork around one of these curves. Putting the car in gear, McDowell continued his drive.

Finally, the asphalt leveled and straightened somewhat, and down the road a few hundred yards he could see the roofs of a couple of buildings. They looked like abandoned farmhouses, but as he approached he realized they were the remnants of a small town.

On other road trips, he had learned the hard way that small towns often made their money with speed traps, so he slowed to a crawl. This place, though, looked as if it couldn't even support a single cop, much less a police station. On the north side of the road were about a dozen houses. All of the houses sat in yards with high weeds, and in the yards sat old appliances and an unusual number of junker cars. Spindly mesquite trees and even higher weeds grew in the vacant lots.

On the south side of the road were a handful of buildings with gravel areas in front. All looked to be in poor condition, but not abandoned. One, in fact, had a single gas pump in front, a pump that looked new enough to give McDowell hope of being able to get enough gas; but he suspected it would be very expensive. Smaller outbuildings sat behind the structures that fronted the highway. Roughly in the middle of the buildings, next to the place with the gas pump, sat a dingy, box-like structure with two large dirty windows in front and with a simple faded sign above the door that read "Eats."

McDowell was sure it was going to be lousy food, but under

the present conditions bad food and expensive gas was better than running out of gas and starving. And he figured that he could get directions as well.

Pulling slowly off of the pavement into the gravel area in front of the restaurant, McDowell stopped and turned off his engine. When the dust he had kicked up settled a little, he opened his car door and got out, suddenly aware of how tired his butt was from sitting for so long.

The first thing he noticed when he climbed out of the car was the smell. Not nearly as bad as the feedlot smells which are common in the west side of Amarillo, but earthy. Sort of a fart-in-the-bathtub smell. The air was warm and still, with some of the dust still hanging around his car. He'd seen birds all along the highway for most of his trip, but there didn't seem to be a bird in the sky here. Well, that wasn't completely true. He spotted three large crows in one of the trees across the road. All of them seemed to glare at him with black, beady eyes.

As McDowell turned to go into the small restaurant he saw a fat, bald man in a wife-beater undershirt step out of the building where the gas pump was. McDowell waved casually but got no response other than a stare.

At the top of the two wooden steps leading to the door of the building he noticed that there was a screen door, but the solid front door itself was standing open. This is going to be a particularly warm, smelly meal, McDowell thought to himself. The screen door had two balls of cotton clipped to the wire mesh, something his grandmother used to do to ward off flies, although he couldn't remember what she put on the cotton that was supposed to repel bugs.

The screen door clacked shut behind him as he stopped inside the building to allow his eyes to adjust to the gloomy interior. Even the windows didn't provide much light because of a film of grease and dust on them. The place was even smaller inside than it appeared from the car. There were two tables, one on each side of the door, and a counter that ran parallel to the front wall. Six old-fashioned swivel stools provided seating for the counter. A lanky, gray-haired man wearing faded overalls sat at one end of the counter with a coffee cup in front of him. Behind the counter was a short, stocky man with uncombed blonde hair. He wore a dirty apron over what appeared to be an equally dirty tee shirt.

McDowell looked at both tables, preferring to not sit any nearer to the two men than necessary, but both tables contained dirty dishes. With a mental sigh, he sat on one of the stools, not completely at the end of the counter but as far as he thought he could get from the other men and still seem polite. With only six stools that wasn't far. The Formica on the countertop was dull, scratched and spotted with cigarette burns.

The blonde behind the counter looked at him and said, "What can I do for you?"

No smile, no Hello. Better get this over with and get out of here, McDowell thought.

"Looking for a quick lunch and some gas, and you guys seem to be the only place around. Got a menu?"

The blonde hooked a thumb to a chalkboard on the wall between the kitchen pass-through window and the door into the kitchen. "It's all right there. Care for something to drink while you're making up your mind?"

"Yeah, give me a Coke please." You can't screw that up, he thought.

The chalkboard menu had a few breakfast items on it, bacon and eggs, pancakes and cereal. Everything else seemed to be just sandwiches of some sort. McDowell settled on a burger—again, how could they screw that up?

As he waited on his burger, McDowell sipped his Coke—a barely cool can taken from somewhere beneath the counter—and he could hear the blonde and someone else talking in the kitchen but couldn't really understand the words. Looking around he noticed other things. The breakfast cereal was in boxes that were like what he had at home; no small individual-serving boxes like he would've anticipated. Fly paper—when was the last time he'd seen that?—hung from the high ceiling at either side of the room and above the kitchen door. A glass pastry case containing nothing but crumbs sat on a shelf behind the counter.

The gray-haired man in overalls continued to stare into his coffee cup but seemed to be watching McDowell from the corner of his eye. McDowell turned toward him, and the man turned to face him, a polite smile on his face that didn't reach his eyes.

"Uh," said McDowell, "is there a restroom?"

"Behind you," the man responded, his voice dry and raspy.

Turning around, McDowell felt foolish to find a door along the sidewall just behind his stool, with a faded stick-on sign saying "Restroom." He took another sip of the quickly warming Coke to hide his embarrassment, then slid off the stool and went into the toilet. It was everything that he assumed it would be. The fixtures were old and discolored, the sink stained a rusty red. The vinyl flooring was dark from water leaks. There was a lingering odor of urine. McDowell raised the toilet lid with his toe and quickly did his business. He reached for a paper towel to flush with so that he didn't have to touch anything and found there were no paper towels. Instead there was an old machine that contained some sort of roller system on which a continuous cloth towel was pulled out of the box to give the user a clean section of the towel to use. Apparently, the idea was for the dirty portion of the towel to be re-rolled in the machine when a clean section of the towel was pulled out. However, here the towel was pulled out and hanging down to the floor. It looked as if it had never been clean.

McDowell managed to flush the toilet using the toe of his shoe, praying that he didn't lose his balance and have to catch himself on one of the fixtures. With no paper towels to use over the faucet handles, McDowell didn't wash his hands. When he turned to leave the room, he stared at the door a moment, then took his handkerchief from his back pocket and used it to turn the knob.

Back on his stool he noticed the guy in overalls staring at him. "Can I get to Lubbock on this road?" McDowell asked.

The man poured himself some more coffee from a carafe on the counter and replied, "Yeah, you come out a few miles south of Lubbock."

"I haven't noticed any cars on the road. Made me wonder if I'd taken a wrong turn somewhere."

The man took a sip from his cup. "Not many people come this way, particularly not locals. Not that there are many locals other than those of us here."

McDowell took another sip of his now-warm Coke and, hoping to avoid more conversation, looked around again. He gazed at a picture above the kitchen door that he'd noticed earlier. It was a large, panoramic picture that appeared to have been taken behind the now run-down business buildings. He could see the road beyond the buildings that were in the background of the picture. In the foreground were several wooden picnic tables that looked to be loaded with bowls and plates containing what was probably food lined up end-to-end. Behind the tables were people, a dozen or so men, a half-dozen women and several kids of various ages. The picture was dated by eight cars parked behind the people, fronts facing the camera, between the people and the buildings. All of the cars were late 40s or early 50s sedans although McDowell was just guessing. It seemed as if the people were proud of the cars; why else have them in the picture? He guessed that the eight cars had something to do with the celebration, but he couldn't imagine what the connection would be.

At that point, a young boy came from the kitchen carrying a plate with McDowell's burger. The kid, who looked to be about twelve years old and was thin and pale, put the plate on the counter. He reached under the counter and brought up ketchup and mustard bottles, each with a crusty-looking lid. The boy looked at McDowell as if expecting something, then turned back to the kitchen.

The burger looked oddly unappetizing—a patty of grayish meat on a dry bun, a few pickle slices on the side along with a limp piece of lettuce. The room's smell of greasy cooking, along with the outside dust and sour background odor, overpowered what little aroma that might have come from the meat.

The kid and the blonde in the apron came to the kitchen door, and the man in overalls looked over his coffee mug at McDowell. All of them looked as if they were waiting for his reaction. McDowell hadn't been expecting a particularly good meal, but certainly not a burger that put him off just by its appearance. And the fact that the three watching him seemed to expect something of him made him wonder how he was supposed to react to his meal. But his stomach rumbled, and he decided to gobble it down and hit the road.

One bite was all that he could stand, however, even with the mustard and ketchup he'd applied and the pickle that he added. He thought about asking for a slice of cheese and some chips to hide the gamey flavor of the meat, but realized that nothing would help it. He finished the rest of the Coke, and took out his billfold.

"How much do I owe you?" he asked the blonde.

"What's the matter, you don't like my cooking?"

"No, my stomach's been acting up, and I . . . uh . . ." He couldn't think of anything else to say.

The man in overalls swiveled his stool toward McDowell and smiled another humorless smile. "We have a special recipe for some things around here and not everyone likes our meat. That's unfortunate since we dress the meat ourselves. Very fresh and healthy."

McDowell fished a twenty out of his billfold and dropped it on the counter. "No offense intended. I've just never cared for wild game. I'll just go next door and get some gas and be on my way."

He stood and turned toward the door, then noticed several men gathered around his car. A couple of them were talking heatedly but in low voices.

"What's going on out there?" he asked the man in overalls.

"Oh, just some of the local boys admiring your car," he replied. "Trying to decide who gets it."

It took a moment for the words to sink in.

"What the hell do you mean 'who gets it'? Nobody gets it. I'm driving it away from this place." McDowell tried to control his rising voice.

He realized that the men outside had stopped talking and were all looking at him through the screen door. McDowell saw the man with overalls get off his stool and take a step toward him, his eyes flat, a smirk on his narrow face.

"No," the man said quietly as he took another step toward McDowell. "I don't think that's going to happen. Come on outside and we'll take care of your car and then move on to other matters."

McDowell was incredulous but felt clear-headed. He knew he needed to get outside where there was some room to move around. If he couldn't get into his car, which looked to be the case given the suddenly aggressive stance of the men outside, he'd run. He jogged at times and probably could outrun any of these guys. As he backed through the screen door he pulled his phone from his pocket. Damn! Still no signal.

"Yeah, that's another reason there aren't a lot of people around here," the man in the overalls said. No phone reception. Inconvenient at times, but some of us like being off the grid." He followed McDowell through the door and down the steps.

The small crowd moved away from the car slowly, stepping toward McDowell. He began to panic and backed away from the men. When he reached the corner of the building he saw the fat man next door coming across the gravel, carrying what appeared to be an axe handle. McDowell whirled and dashed up the side of the restaurant. His hope was to get through the out buildings in back and into the open ground beyond them. It appeared brushy and rough, but he was wearing a pair of his old running shoes and jeans and felt that he could make it through the rough ground faster than the guys behind him, especially the fat guy with the club.

As he got to the back corner of the building, however, his head exploded in a white flash. There was no pain initially, just shock and loss of his stability. McDowell fell against the dusty side of the building, trying not to go down completely. He knew that he was doomed if he ever lost his footing. With one hand to his forehead, he tried to push off the wall with the other hand. But as he regained his feet there was another blow, this time a fist to his stomach. He staggered, still trying to stay upright, but unable to breathe.

Rough hands grabbed him under his arms. The hands bent his body at the waist, and someone grabbed his polo shirt, roughly yanking it over his head. His mind was spinning, and he couldn't figure what was being done to him, certainly not why. When the shirt came off his arms, the rough hands stood him mostly upright. At that point, his arms were pulled behind him and his wrists bound together tightly. Standing in front of him was the blonde, holding a skillet of all things with a smear of blood on the flat bottom. One of McDowell's last coherent thoughts was that this was more than just a beating and a car theft.

He was dragged, his toes making lines through the dirt and gravel, to a large shed. The pain in his head was almost overpowering by this time, and he was aware of wetness on his forehead and blood running into his right eye. He was dropped roughly, the side of his face smashing against a sticky wooden floor. He tried desperately to regain control of his thoughts, but was suddenly rolled over onto his back. His shoes were yanked off, his belt unbuckled, and his jeans tugged down his legs. His socks and underwear quickly followed. Something about being naked increased his panic. His breath, already painfully shallow from the blow to his stomach, became more and more rapid.

He could see very little, and his vision, pulsing with his heartbeat, was limited to one eye. Even that eye could only see a cloudy image of ceiling framing above him. He could hear voices, but couldn't tell what was being said. What he heard was just muffled mumbles.

Before he could do anything, he felt people moving his feet and legs and suddenly felt something tight around his ankles. "Okay," he finally heard someone say. "Pull."

His feet were yanked up off of the floor, and his body bent at the waist as his legs went up. Hands now on his shoulders hoisted his upper body into the air as his legs continued to rise. One bare shoulder scraped the edge of some sort of large tub.

In a moment McDowell hung suspended by his ankles, his limited vision disoriented from seeing things inverted. He was physically and emotionally exhausted, unable to do anything to resist whatever was happening. He felt as if his legs were being pulled off. Trying to make sense of what little he could see, he realized that a group of men were standing around him. Directly in front him seemed to be the man with the apron, his arms crossed over his chest, one hand holding what might have been a long, thin knife. Beside him was someone smaller. Probably the kid from the restaurant.

There was conversation that he couldn't follow. He closed his eyes, the pain in his ankles, his hips, his wrists and his head (although he couldn't have catalogued his pains that clearly) was unbearable.

When he felt someone touching his face he opened his good eye. It was the kid who brought him the gamey burger.

Expressionless, the boy leaned in and licked the blood off McDowell's forehead.

Cemetery Games

By Keith West

I presume my attorney explained the conditions of this interview.

I talk; you listen, take notes, record me, whatever. Just no questions.

And no, I won't talk about the murder.

I said all I intend to ever say on that topic when I was convicted. When I made a statement to the court and the kid's parents, that was it. I'm through talking about it.

It's my death row confession, and I'll say what I like. You got a problem with that, you know where the door is. This is your only chance to get an interview. I've got less than forty-eight hours left, and the governor won't give me a reprieve. Not if he wants to be reelected next month after campaigning as a supporter of our three-strikes-and-you're-out justice system. And this is it. I've struck out, and now I'm being sent to the dugout. *Permanently.*

What I'm going to do is answer all the questions the pop psychologists and self-appointed experts on the tube think they know the answers to. I'm sick of hearing all the crap they're spouting. Not one of the fools has any idea what he's talking about. I don't expect anybody to believe me, least of all you. Your reputation for skepticism is why I requested you. I know you'll report what I say without embellishing it with psychobabble.

Anyway, enough with the ground rules. Let's get on with it.

Capture the flag was our favorite game the summer my childhood ended.

You know how to play, right?

Two teams, each with a flag hidden somewhere in their own territory. The object is to sneak into the other team's territory and steal their flag without getting captured, and do it before they can do the same to you.

We played in the cemetery down at the end of the street, nearly every night once school got out in May. It wasn't used much anymore, not since the new cemetery opened on the other side of town, which made it the perfect place to play. We practically lived there every summer, at least until April Townsend showed up.

The trees provided some relief from the heat with their shade. Mom wouldn't turn on the air conditioner until the temperature was in the nineties, and the city had closed the pool years back and never reopened it. In small west Texas towns, there often aren't a lot of shady spots except the cemetery.

In the daytime, it was great for playing hide and seek or army or just riding bikes down the gravel paths. Old Man Smitty was the caretaker. He didn't really care what we did as long as we didn't vandalize the place or bother people paying their respects to their loved ones. Most of the time he stayed in his office, drunk usually.

But night was when the place really came alive, if you'll pardon the grisly turn of phrase. The trees gave lots of shadows, which are what you need if you're going to play capture the flag right. You need lots of hiding places.

I was twelve that summer, and my brother Greg was fifteen. I'd pretty much outgrown the games the younger kids played. Capture the flag, though, that was a game for the older kids. It had been going on for several summers, with younger kids taking the places of the older kids as they got cars and jobs and moved on. My brother and his friends let me hang out with them. None of them had steady jobs yet because most weren't old enough, so they had a lot of time on their hands. I think some of them even liked me, although I'm sure much of the time they just tolerated me.

Anyway, they let me play. Usually there were about a dozen of us, although on some nights there'd be twice that. We ranged in age from twelve to sixteen. I was usually the youngest, but sometimes Randy Martin's mother would let him play with us. Randy was four months younger than I was.

It was mostly guys, too. Not many of the girls wanted to play, at least not in the cemetery. Some of the high school age kids would use it as a make out spot, but not often. There were better places for that. People, the girls especially, didn't like making out in that environment. It gave them the creeps.

Not us, though. I guess we'd gotten used to it because it never bothered us once. At least not until the summer in question.

Don't get me wrong. We had a few girls join us from time to time. The two most frequent were Lois Hightower and Julie Shaw, who were regular players and reputed to be dykes. They weren't. They were just plain, homely even, and from the wrong side of town, and therefore victims of rumors.

Then April Townsend showed up. We didn't know where she came from. She just walked around a mausoleum one night as we were picking teams.

"I want to play."

We all turned and looked. Some of us jumped. At least I did.

She was leaning on the corner of the mausoleum. Her hair was long, and it was feathered, which wasn't the style then, hanging past her shoulders, a sort of dirty blond shade that used to be called dishwater blond. Her jeans were bell bottoms, with a flare on them that had been out of style for a number of years, and her shirt had a psychedelic pattern to it. She wasn't wearing much makeup either.

The clothes weren't a big deal, being out of style and all. Anyone in my part of town who had an older brother or sister usually wore hand-me-downs, passed down through two or three siblings, or sometimes cousins. It wasn't because we wanted to; our parents just couldn't afford to keep up with the changing styles in clothes. You see them in every school. Kids who aren't part of the popular crowd, not because they are socially awkward or even ugly. They simply don't have the economic means to fit in. They're there if you look. They often are invisible, and sometimes that's by choice. It's easier to not be noticed than to be reminded of how you aren't accepted and never will be.

Like I said, the clothes weren't a big deal, but the hair and lack of makeup were. Even the girls in my neighborhood were willing to go without eating to make sure they had the latest makeup or hair style. I found out a few years later that some of them often did.

Don't get the impression that she wasn't attractive, because she was. Her features were finely chiseled, and she had a good figure. She looked to be about sixteen and, when she pushed off from the mausoleum and walked over to us, she moved with a grace that none of the girls I knew had yet mastered.

"Well?," she said after we all just stood there gawking at her and not saying anything. "Can I play or not?"

"Uh, sure," Greg said. He took a step toward her. I could tell from the look on his face that he was smitten, and hard. "We're playing capture the flag. Know how to play?"

"Of course, doesn't everybody? Two teams, two territories, try to find the flag hidden in the other team's territory and get back with it without getting caught."

Greg just smiled at that. "What's your name?"

"April."

"What's your last name, April?"

"It's Townsend," she said. She took a step closer to Greg, like she was meeting some sort of challenge. In a way, she was. New kids always seem to have to prove themselves before they're accepted, and our group was no different. If you didn't have a streak of toughness, you were dog food.

"You got a name?" April continued, looking at my brother.

"Greg Phillips." He started to make introductions. "That's Joe

Turner; the tall guy over there is Aaron Semple. The red-haired girl is Julie Shaw, and the girl next to her is Lois Hightower." April was greeted by a chorus of "hi's", "hello's" and the inevitable Texas "howdy's" as he continued. Of course, I was introduced last. "And finally, the runt over there is my kid brother, Mike."

"Hi, Mike," April said. I was the only one she spoke to when introduced. She'd merely nodded at the others. I got the impression she was putting up with the introductions as though they were something she had to endure, almost as if she already knew who we were.

We proceeded to pick teams. Greg and Aaron were captains. We rotated captains when we played, but as those two were the oldest they tended to be the default captains. The only person who didn't get to be a captain and pick teams very often was me, because I was the youngest of the regular players.

We also rotated the boundaries. The cemetery was rectangular in shape and had a main drive paralleling the short sides that more or less bisected it. In the middle of the intersection of the main drive with the main crossroad was a gazebo. What purpose a gazebo served in a cemetery, I don't know, but it was there. A number of side roads branched off these two. We usually made either the main road or the crossroad the dividing lines between the territories. This resulted in territories that were long but not deep, or deep territories that were not too wide.

Greg got first choice, so naturally he chose April. No big surprise. I was the last one picked. Usually was, but I was used to it, and it didn't bother me.

Since Greg picked first, Aaron chose the boundaries and which side he wanted. "The long road is the dividing line," he said.

There were several groans at this. It made the boundary hard to watch because of its length and the shade from the trees that overhung it in places. The veterans' section at the west end of the cemetery didn't have any trees, so that helped.

"The black and spic cemetery on the other side of the fence

down there is off limits," Aaron added. Since it usually was, I figured he was saying that for April's benefit.

We went to our respective sides. I was on Aaron's team. We hid the white flag by draping it over a fresh floral arrangement with a lot white flowers in it. Our jail was in the corner of the veteran's section between four white crosses. After five minutes everyone dispersed to either try to sneak into the other team's territory and look for their flag or watch for people from the other team trying to sneak into ours.

Everyone except me that is. I got stuck with the job of being the jailer, even though I was faster than half the people on my team. April was the first person caught. It was my job to watch her and make sure she didn't sneak back across the boundary without being tagged by someone from her team first. It was also my job to watch for members of the other team trying to free their teammates.

"So you're Greg's brother, huh?" she asked after Julie, who'd captured her, left.

"Yeah."

"What's he like?"

"He's a big brother."

"That doesn't tell me anything."

"That means he's all right some of the time and a jerk most of the time. Why are you asking? You wanna go out with him?"

"I didn't say that. I'm just curious, that's all."

I was wondering why she was so interested in Greg when it occurred to me she could be asking me stuff to distract me. She had acted like she knew how to play when she showed up, and maybe she really did. I turned around. I didn't see anybody, but that didn't mean anything. Someone could be hiding behind a shrub or a tombstone on the edge of the veteran's section, waiting for me to turn my back or drop my guard. I ignored April and walked a few rows over.

"Hey," she called after me. "I didn't mean to make you mad."

I didn't say anything.

"I'm sorry if something I said upset you."

"It's not that," I called back over my shoulder. "I don't want you distracting me. Aaron'll kill me if I let someone from the other team sneak up and tag you."

"Oh."

She didn't say anything after that.

I stood and watched the trees, scanning the shadows for any sign of movement. A slight breeze had sprung up, hardly more than a breath, but it felt good on my back and dried the sweat on my arms.

Sure enough, a few minutes later Greg came sneaking along the back fence line. He headed straight toward April, and I ran to cut him off. April shouted encouragement at him. He dodged around a cross as I got close to him and kept coming. Greg was one of the few people playing that night I couldn't outrun.

But I got lucky. He tripped and almost fell. I was able to get between him and April and was moving to tag him when he turned tail and ran, stumbling the first few steps as he tried to get his balance back. I let him go. We usually played two or three games a night. If we played another game, I would probably not have to be jailer again, and I wanted to save my energy.

I watched my brother scamper across the road marking the boundary and into the safety of his territory.

"Coward!" April called after him. He just jogged to the left and into the shade of the trees. I knew he would make another try to rescue her.

As it turned out, he didn't get the chance. Someone on our team, I never found out who, managed to find the other team's flag and carry it back across the line without getting caught.

We chose teams again, this time with Lois and Julie as captains. Julie wanted to make the boundary the main drive, which gave us deep territories with a short perimeter to guard. April, Greg and I were on Lois's team.

Greg suggested the three of us make a concerted rush into the other territory. Since I had spent most of the last game standing around waiting, that was fine with me.

April and Greg went on one side of the gazebo, while I took the other. The idea was for me to create a distraction, hopefully without getting caught. Greg said I should be the first across because I was one of the fastest players. I started to respond that he should be the first across because he was faster than I was, but I could see that wouldn't work. He clearly wanted to spend time with April. This suggestion was just his way of ditching me. Greg and April would wait to see how many of the other team I flushed before they crossed the boundary.

It worked, for them. Julie and Joe Turner took off after me. I don't know how many other people were guarding the boundary. I didn't turn around to look. I could outrun both Joe and Julie, but just barely. I'd crossed about three rows of graves when Sammy Garrett popped up from behind a double headstone. There was no way to avoid him. If I slowed down to turn, either Julie or Joe would catch me. I let Sammy tag me and lead me away to the jail, which was in the intersection of the main crossroad and a smaller road paralleling the fence. I spent the rest of the game there.

By the time the other team found where we'd hidden our flag and took it back to their territory, it was almost midnight. Most of us had to head home.

Greg was saying goodbye to April when I walked up to the gazebo.

"You're really good," he said.

"Thanks." She smiled at him.

"Are you staying with family for the summer?" he asked her, and that was when I knew she had him hooked.

"Yeah, you could say that. All right with you if I come back and play again?"

"Sure."

"Good, then I'll see you tomorrow night." She turned and

walked off. Before Greg could say anything, she was gone.

"Come on, Romeo," I said. "Mom'll kill us if we aren't home soon."

"Shut up," was the only response I got.

April was back the next night, and the night after that. She and Greg had ended up on different teams both nights, and he hardly got a chance to say more than a few words to her. Then, Friday when Mom got off work, she took us out of town to our grandparents' house for the weekend. They weren't doing too well, and Mom wanted to check on them. She was afraid she'd have to put them in a home. It was raining when we pulled into the drive Sunday evening. The rain didn't cool things so much as just make the humidity feel muggier.

We stayed in that night. Old Man Smitty didn't have many rules and pretty much left us alone, like I said, but one thing he insisted on was we didn't play when it was wet. Too much risk of someone slipping on wet leaves or grass and hitting their head on a tombstone. He didn't want to have to deal with that much liability.

We sat around watching television while the fans moved the hot, sticky air back and forth in the room.

We didn't go out Monday night, either. The rain had stopped when we got up that morning, but by noon it was pouring again.

Greg was impossible to be around. He was twitchy and cross and a total ass. I could tell he wanted to see April, although he wouldn't say so and displayed a complete lack of interest when I tried to tease him about her. Even so, something in his response made me drop it. He'd been getting mean the last couple of months, and I didn't want to push my luck. Instead I watched cartoons, played video games, leafed through comic books I'd read a dozen times and tried to stay out of his way.

Tuesday was bright and clear, and it started to look like summer was settling in for good. The temperature hit the high nineties by early afternoon, and Mom called from work to tell us we could turn on the air conditioner so long as we didn't change where she had the thermostat set. We decided to stay in and enjoy the AC while we could.

Just before dark we headed down to the cemetery. Mom had come home, fried chicken, then decided the heat wasn't so bad we couldn't open up the house to save on the electric bill.

I couldn't really blame her, although I hated it at the time. There weren't many jobs, much less jobs that paid well, in small west Texas towns, at least not for women with a high school education whose husbands had died six months after running out on them. My Mom did what she could, and she did her best; but when you're a kid, you can't always see that, especially if a lot of the other kids at school are always rubbing your nose in what they have that you don't. Being poor sucks when you're a kid.

It was the last summer I would live like that, and I would give anything to be back there in that house, no matter how hot it was.

Anyway, we took off for the cemetery. While it wasn't cool there, either, it was at least less hot. Greg was antsy the whole way. His hands were shaking with anticipation. When he saw me looking at them, he shoved them in his shorts pockets and walked on in front of me. I pretended the sun had been in my eyes and I hadn't seen anything. Greg hurried on ahead, while I hung back dragging my feet.

By the time I got there, they were ready to start picking teams. Greg and April were captains. I could tell he wasn't happy about it, but he wasn't pissed off, either. He and April seemed to have a rivalry going.

"My team is gonna kick your butts," Greg said as I walked up.

"Big talk, little man, big talk." April's tone was light and flirty, but I thought I heard an edge to it. One thing Greg didn't like was being called little. I was never sure why. It was something he refused to talk about, and I had learned the hard way not to hassle him about it. He tried not to scowl but wasn't entirely successful. "So, who gets to choose?"

"Ladies first," said Greg with a mock bow.

"Fine, I pick Joe."

"Okay, I want Julie."

April looked directly at me. None of the other kids had noticed I was there. "I'll take Mike," she said.

I was caught a little off guard. Like I told you earlier, I was usually picked last.

"What do you want him for?"

April turned and grinned at Greg. "So we can beat your butt. C'mon, Mike, you're on my team."

I didn't say anything, simply walked over and stood behind April.

"Losers," said Greg, but he smiled when he said it.

He named his next choice, and the process continued until the teams had been selected. Greg decided he wanted the main drive to be the boundary.

Greg kept taunting April. I guess it was his way of flirting. Finally, she challenged him to put his money where his mouth was. "Okay, little man, you're starting to get on my nerves. Put up or shut up."

"Fine, I will. Let's make a wager."

"What kind of wager?"

"We win, you go out with me." I guess Greg said this because he was too nervous to just ask April out.

April stared at him, then said, "Alright, and if we win?"

"Name it." Greg grinned. He didn't think he would lose.

"I will. Later."

"What do you mean, later?"

"I mean, if my team wins, I'll name my price later. You're not chicken, are you?'

A pause.

"No," Greg said. "It's a bet."

"All right, then," said April. "It's a bet." They shook on it, and that was that.

We grabbed our flag and headed off to find a really good place to hide it. As we passed a mausoleum, April said, "Let's put it in here."

She pointed over to where a door was slightly ajar. There was just enough light from the moon to see the darkness between the door and the doorjamb.

"Uh, we'd better not," said Aaron. "It's against the rules. The flag has to be out in the open. It can't be under or inside of anything."

"Besides," I said, "if old man Smitty catches us going into one of those things, he'll run us out of here. He's told us it would cost him his job if we got caught playing in one of the mausoleums."

"Who's this old man Smitty, anyway?" April asked.

"He's the caretaker. We're not really supposed to be in here after dark, but he lets us play as long as we don't do any damage. He says it keeps us out of trouble." Aaron's chest swelled a little as explained this to April. Greg wasn't the only guy who wanted to impress her.

"Spoilsports," said April. At first, I thought she was going to argue, but she didn't. Instead she got a thoughtful look on her face and kept walking.

"Hey, April," said Lois, "isn't that your last name on that mausoleum?"

She was pointing to the one April wanted to hide the flag in. Across the top was the name "TOWNSEND."

"Yeah, so?"

"So, are they any relation to you?'

"Yeah," she said, turning away so none of us could see her face. "You could say that." She headed off without another word. Lois let the subject drop.

We ended up laying the flag on a slab of white marble in the full moonlight. It was almost invisible unless you were standing on top of it. April appointed herself and me to patrol our territory and capture anyone coming over. Everyone else was assigned the task of penetrating Greg's territory and finding the flag.

April and I alternated being the jailer. When one of us caught someone from the other team, we switched. The person who was jailer went on patrol, and the other person got a rest. This turned out to be an efficient strategy. We ended up with most of Greg's team in our jail, and they still had no idea where our flag was.

When it was just Greg and Mark Campbell left, Greg tried a rescue. If he could tag the people in the jail without being caught, they were free. Mark was one of the slowest players, so Greg left him on their side of the boundary. That way, if Greg was captured the game wouldn't automatically be over, although for all practical purposes, it would be. Mark wasn't fast enough to rescue anyone.

I was jailer when Greg made his attempt. I saw him coming and positioned myself to try to intercept him. I didn't figure I would have a lot of luck. He seemed pretty pissed off. Greg was never a graceful loser, and having most of his team in jail wouldn't be doing anything for his mood.

That was when April came out of nowhere. I knew at the time, or at least thought I did, that she couldn't have just appeared out of nowhere, but that's what it looked like. One second she wasn't there, and the next she was bearing down on Greg. And fast. I had never seen anyone run that fast before. She practically sailed over the grass and footstones. April caught up to Greg before he was halfway to me and lightly tapped him on the shoulder. He never even knew she was there until she touched him. The look on his face was classic. He turned and stumbled and then brought himself to a halt.

"Gotcha, Greg. You're mine now, little man. *Go to jail, go directly to jail, do not pass Go, do not collect two hundred dollars, and do not win the game.*"

Greg growled and put himself in jail. He wasn't a graceful loser, but he could admit when he was beat.

Aaron stayed as the jailer. I went with April and the rest of the team to search for the other team's flag. It didn't take us long to find it. Anytime Mark got near us, we simply outran him.

April carried the flag back and waved it in Greg's face.

"I win. You owe me."

"Just what do I owe you?" he asked.

"I'll let you know later. When the time is right." She gave him a smile and a wink and turned to go.

"That's all for me tonight, folks," April said. "I'll see y'all later. Especially you, Greg." She walked off among the tombstones.

Once again none of us moved until she was gone. It was as though she'd cast a spell on us. Greg took a little ribbing, but not much. I think most of the guys were jealous of the attention he was getting. April was the finest girl to ever hang out with our crowd, and everyone knew it. Nobody wanted to jeopardize her friendship by making light of her interest in Greg. Most of the group were also old enough to have outgrown that kind of thing. I kept my mouth shut because I didn't want to get the crap beaten out of me.

We tried to play another game, but everyone was too tired. At least that's what we told each other when we called it off without a winner.

April always joined us for the capture the flag games, but she never stayed around after they were over. No one ever saw where she went when she left, either.

Greg began spending more of his time at the cemetery. I don't mean at night; I mean during the day, even the hottest part of the day. April was often there with him. Other kids were there, too, but I doubt Greg even noticed them. They came and went and were completely interchangeable, at least to him. There was no one else there except April as far as he was concerned.

Not that things were progressing very fast. They talked, flirted a lot, hung out in the shade. That was about it. I never saw them hold hands, and I had the impression that April wasn't the hand-holding type. Aaron and Joe were kidding Greg one day about having kissed her. More of a good-natured interrogation, really.

Hey, Greg, is she a great kisser? Does she use her tongue?

That kind of stuff.

Greg got really mad, not so much at them, I think, but at the fact that in the physical arena he wasn't getting anywhere. I knew him well enough to realize she was more to him than someone to make out with, but that was definitely part of her attraction. He was a fifteen-year-old male, after all.

After a few days of this, I stopped going to the cemetery during the day. The temperatures were high, even for late June in Texas. I preferred to stay inside, especially since Mom was letting us run the air conditioner.

One day, Mom came home from work at lunch. She usually packed her lunch and stayed there. I'd gone down to the Minit Mart on the corner for comics. She was sitting at the table when I got home, brochures from nursing homes spread out in front of her. There weren't any assisted living centers in that part of Texas back then. I knew she was facing the decision about putting Grandma and Granddad in a home. And worrying about how to pay for it.

"Hi, Mom."

"Hi, Mike. Where've you been?"

"Getting some comics." I wiped sweat out of my eyes with a paper towel. My shirt was sticking to my back. I set the comics down on the counter and fanned myself with the hem of my shirt. It didn't keep my shirt from resticking, but the breeze felt good.

She looked up from the brochures. "I see. Where's your brother?"

"I'm not sure."

"Mike," she said, in that tone that told me she knew I wasn't being entirely truthful but was willing to give me another chance to come clean.

"I think he's down at the cemetery." I hoped my saying "I think" would get me off the hook if Greg got in trouble and accused me of squealing on him.

"He's been spending a lot of time down there lately." While not worded as a question, Mom clearly intended this apparent statement of fact to be one.

"Yeah, well, there's this girl."

"Oh." Mom's eyebrows went up. "And what girl would that be?"

"Her name's April. She showed up one night and started playing capture the flag with us."

"I see." This was mom-speak for *I don't see but I expect you to tell me* or maybe *I'm beginning to see but want to know all the details.*

So, I told her. I didn't mention April's last name. I don't know why I didn't. It wasn't like I was trying to hide anything. It just never occurred to me to mention it. Probably it was the mindset kids develop of don't tell your parents any details they don't ask for.

Anyway, Mom didn't ask her last name. If she had, maybe it would have made a difference and things would have turned out better. Or maybe it wouldn't have made any difference at all and things would have turned out the same. I'll never know.

I wouldn't have thought there was that much to tell, but apparently there was, because while I was talking, Mom got up and made us both sandwiches. Hers was gone by the time I finished. Mine only had two bites taken out of it.

"You miss your brother, don't you?" she asked, when I'd finally run out of words.

"Yeah, in a way I guess I do. I mean, he can be a real jerk sometimes, but he still looks out for me and hangs out with me. Or lets me hang out with him and his friends. At least he did until April came along."

Mom smiled, just the corner of her mouth crooking up, but it was the first genuine smile I had seen on her face in a while. It would also be the last.

"And you're a little bit jealous."

"Well, yeah, kinda."

"Sweetie, he's older than you. Your brother is at the age where he needs to hang out with girls more than he needs to hang out with his younger brother. It doesn't mean he doesn't love you anymore."

I hated it when she talked like that. No twelve-year-old kid wants to admit that he loves his older brother. Especially when it's true. "Mom, really. It's not like that at all."

"Okay, so tell me. What is it like?"

"It's, well, it's like . . ."

"Yes?"

"It's just that his brain has stopped working."

"What do you mean?"

"Oh, you wouldn't understand." Backed into a corner like that, I did what any twelve-year-old would do. I got up and left the room.

Old Man Smitty came by the next night. It was after the first game. We were standing around trying to cool off before we picked new teams and played again.

None of us knew how old he was, but he had to have been somewhere in his mid-fifties. By teenage standards, that made him older than dirt. He'd been the caretaker for as long as any of us could remember.

The air was still, dead still. The only breeze was the one you made as you ran. Even the crickets were too hot to chirp. The night was so quiet the stillness was almost audible.

When old man Smitty walked up, none of us heard him until he was standing between Aaron and Lois. It startled some of the group. Not me, though. I'd seen him coming. He could look pretty creepy, so I couldn't blame any of the kids who jumped.

Smitty was tall, thin as a post oak and the top of his bald head seemed to have an eerie glow where it reflected the moonlight. He wore a long-sleeved shirt during the day to protect his arms from the sun, and he still had it on in spite of the heat. Tucked under one arm was a tarp that had become partially unfolded and was dragging the ground.

He smelled of alcohol. He didn't say anything until he was in the middle of us. Smitty's voice was raspy from the cheap hooch he drank. "You kids stay away from that grave I dug this afternoon, y'all hear?"

Part of his job as caretaker was to be the gravedigger. It wasn't something he did often, but occasionally someone would be buried in the cemetery, usually a widow whose husband had bought the plot decades ago. We'd seen the grave and kept our distance from it. Nobody wanted to risk breaking something by falling into it. That would have ended our games for good.

There was a chorus of mumbled *Yes sirs.* Then Smitty continued: "I don't want to have to haul one of y'all outta there. And I sure don't want to have to redig part of it tomorrow, so stay off the dirt pile." Smitty was all heart.

He looked off at the western sky, staring so intently I wondered if he was having the DTs. In spite of that, I turned and looked. On the horizon was a flicker of light, followed by another.

"You kids need to git on home. Radio says there's a storm coming. A big 'un. If I don't git that dirt covered," he raised his tarp, causing it to unfold some more, "it'll wash back into the grave, and I'll be digging mud outta that hole right up to the funeral tomorrow."

As Smitty struggled to hold the tarp, his gaze dropped from the sky toward his hands. That's when the change came over him. Something caught his eye, and he dropped the tarp. His hands began shaking.

"That girl!"

His voice was a raspy whisper, but it contained all the intensity of a shout. He pointed where he was staring.

We all turned and looked. The area he was pointing toward was empty, but I could have sworn April had been standing in the same spot a moment earlier.

"There's no one there, Smitty," said Joe.

"What girl? Do you mean April?" asked Greg.

Smitty reached out and grabbed Greg's arm. "What do you know about April? There was no April here. Do you understand? *There was no April!*" He was shouting now, and his enunciation improved with volume.

"Ow," Greg shouted in kind. "That hurts. Let go of my arm."

Smitty dropped Greg's arm and shoved him out of the way. He went stalking toward where April had been standing. "Stay away from that April, y'all hear? She's trouble." He continued to mutter more of that kind of thing until he was out of earshot.

We headed out of the cemetery, shocked and surprised. Smitty had never been violent before. Gruff, sure, and usually drunk, but not violent.

Greg kept rubbing his arm on the way home. "Don't tell Mom."

"Don't worry," I said. "I won't." This was just the sort of thing Mom would have gotten upset about and forbidden us to go back to the cemetery.

"Where did April go?" I asked.

"Who knows? Wherever she disappears to every night."

Mom was already asleep when we got home. I tried to play video games with the sound down. After failing to get past the second level on the fighter pilot game, the one where I was the household champion, I went to bed.

The storm hit a few minutes after I turned off the lights. It was a west Texas thunderstorm, full of wind and lightning and thunderclaps that sounded like a bomb was going off outside my window. But there was something different about this one. The howl of the wind contained a woman's wailing.

We got over three inches of rain during the night, an unusual occurrence, especially for that time of year. The next day felt more like east Texas than west Texas. The humidity, combined with the heat, made everything unbearable. I wasn't used to the stifling humidity, and it was an effort to breathe.

Old Man Smitty never got his tarp over the dirt. The funeral home people found him the next day. He was at the bottom of the grave, face down in a shallow pool of water, his tarp next to him. The police concluded Smitty slipped in the mud while trying to put the tarp over the dirt piled next to the grave. The fall knocked him unconscious, and the ground was so hard it couldn't absorb all the water before he drowned in it.

The whole town was shocked. Smitty didn't have any family, least none willing to come from out of town to the funeral. Since he was a city employee, the city benevolence fund paid for a gravesite, and the funeral home took care of the embalming and a cheap casket for free. The service was a small graveside affair. The only attendees were the mayor, a few city employees and most of the capture the flag crew. April wasn't one of them.

It made us nervous being there. We outnumbered the city workers who attended, something they were sure to notice. Nobody said anything to us, but there were plenty of looks. Wouldn't you wonder why a bunch of kids showed up to the funeral of an old drunk gravedigger when no one else would?

The minister from the First Baptist Church said a few words, offered a prayer and that was it. When no one was willing to throw a handful of dirt on the casket after it was lowered into the grave, Greg stepped forward and did it. That attracted a new round of looks and some whispers. Then the group broke up and everyone went home or back to work.

We'd all agreed to stop playing for a few days, at least until after the weekend. It would give things a chance to settle down. It didn't hurt that the Fourth of July was coming up that weekend, and most of us would be busy or leaving town to visit relatives. Considering the looks we'd gotten, and the whispers Greg had caused when he tossed the handful of dirt on the grave, taking some time off was a good idea.

Like I told you earlier, the cemetery was pretty much full. Most of the unused grave sites had been purchased years earlier as part of family plots. The one Smitty fell into was one of those. The cemetery was also old enough it held moderately well-to-do to wealthy white folks. Smitty was buried in the smaller cemetery just to the west of the main one, the one reserved for blacks, Mexicans, Indians and some white trash.

I realize that last remark offends your reporter's sense of political correctness, but that's the way it was. The reason I mention it is because we had to walk through most of the main cemetery on our way home, including past the Townsend mausoleum. A glint of sunlight on metal caught our eyes, and we walked over to investigate. As we approached, we saw a fresh padlock on the door. The metal clasp holding the door shut had been bolted into the granite, and the padlock hanging from it was the biggest I'd ever seen up to that point in my life.

"Where'd that come from?" I asked.

Greg pulled on his lip and stared at the lock without saying anything for so long I thought he hadn't heard me. "Smitty must have done it after he left us the other night."

"What, during the storm?"

"Before, I imagine."

"Why? I thought he had to cover the dirt with that tarp."

Greg shrugged. "I guess he thought he had to do this first."

"But why? What was so important about putting this lock on? The door had been busted open for days. None of us had gone inside." My voice was rising with my frustration. This was the first encounter with death I would deal with that summer, and I was struggling to come to grips with it. It made no sense to me for Smitty to have lost time putting a lock on a mausoleum door when he had to get a tarp over some dirt before a storm came.

"I dunno," Greg said. "It doesn't matter now. Let's go home."

Mom took me out of town on the weekend of the Fourth, which was on a Saturday. Greg convinced her to let him stay home. He said he wanted to hang out with his friends, but I knew he really didn't want to be away from April. He'd hardly seen her since the night Old Man Smitty died. I think Mom knew it, too. She agreed to let him stay provided he didn't have anyone over and was home by eleven each night. Greg grumbled a bit at the restrictions, but that was mostly just for show. He knew he was getting a good deal.

What Mom wouldn't agree to was letting me stay with him. She said I was too young. On this point, Greg was in full agreement with her.

So, after a great deal of ineffective arguing, I went along with Mom to see Grandma and Granddad. It wasn't a fun weekend; in fact, it was terrible.

We ended up putting Granddad in the nursing home. Grandma would continue to live at their house, but we all knew it was a matter of time before she joined him.

Mom and I kept getting on each other's nerves. She was upset at the whole situation and tended to take it out on me. I didn't understand everything that was going on, and as a result was scared. Scared Granddad was going to die and I would never see him again, scared someone would put me in one of those places when I got old, scared because I didn't understand all the grown-up dynamics that were taking place. When I wasn't scared, I was bored. There wasn't anything to do, my mother and grandparents were too busy to talk to me, and I was missing out on all the firework festivities back home. As a result, I did things to get attention I normally wouldn't do, such as interrupting conversations, refusing to comply with simple requests, playing the television too loud, that sort of thing.

That Friday would have been Mom's eighteenth anniversary, although I didn't know it then. Mom had never really gotten over being abandoned to raise two kids on her own, and I'm sure now the anniversary was eating at her that weekend, as well, although she didn't say anything about it.

We got back into town Sunday night. By then Mom and I were hardly speaking. Sometime during the night a dust storm blew in. The wind was making that weird sound again, as though some woman somewhere was having her heart ripped out. Previously it had sounded strange, but for some reason, now it was terrifying. This time I was asleep when it started, and it woke me up.

I must have been hearing it in my sleep and cried out because Mom was sitting on my bed within seconds of my waking up. She held me and shushed me and patted my hair while I tried to calm down. All the friction between us was forgotten. She didn't say anything, didn't even ask if I'd had a bad dream, just held me and rocked me until I settled down. Eventually I did and drifted back to sleep.

That was the last time my mother ever held me without reservation. The few times afterward, she always had a stiffness about her, a sense of distance that could never be bridged. A sense of blame. For the last time, I was her little boy again.

I tried to talk to Greg about what happened over the weekend, but it was a lost cause, both in regards to his weekend and mine. He didn't want to hear about mine, I think because he was upset about Granddad going into the nursing home and didn't want to admit it, and he wouldn't answer any questions about his. I knew he had stuck to Mom's rule of not having anyone over because I heard her asking the neighbors how things went. Still, he had a cat-that-got-the-canary air about him, making me think something was up. Since he completely refused to even acknowledge any questions about April, I figured it involved her.

We hung out at the house most of the day before heading to the cemetery around dark. As we were leaving, I saw Greg stick a small flashlight in his pocket. It was odd because not only had he never taken one with him before when we played, a flashlight wasn't exactly something you wanted to use. It could give away your hiding place.

When we got there, Greg and April didn't speak. They just gave each other glances and little half smiles. Something was definitely up. Aaron and Joe were the captains. I was picked last again, by Aaron. When he had picked Greg earlier, Joe had immediately chosen April as his next team member, almost before the sound of Greg's name had died on Aaron's lips. It made me wonder if Joe and Aaron were trying to keep Greg and April apart. My curiosity about the weekend only grew.

I decided to see if I could get some answers. When Greg headed out, I followed him. He wandered around for a minute, not really going anywhere in particular, just moving about. Once when he reversed directions, I thought he heard me, but he strolled right past the headstone I was hiding behind and didn't notice me.

After about ten minutes of this, he stopped, looked around, and started moving in a definite direction. I followed. He went straight to the Townsend mausoleum, which was on our side of the line. As he got there, April stepped out from behind a tree.

"Did you bring a flashlight?" she whispered.

"Yeah, I got it right here."

"Good." She walked over to the door of the mausoleum and pushed. It swung inward, and April went inside. Greg followed her.

I crept closer. The night was hot, but not still. A warm wind was blowing out of the southwest, rustling the trees. I had to get right next to the door of the mausoleum to hear what they were saying. There was no sign of the new lock.

Trying to make myself as small as possible, I knelt by the door and peeked around the corner. Sand on the threshold scraped my palms and knees, and a strange, dusty smell wafted out of the mausoleum. I wanted to sneeze. Instead I rubbed my nose, and the sensation lessened.

They had set the flashlight on a shelf next to a coffin. From the light, I could see the mausoleum had shelves on three walls. Each shelf contained places for three caskets, with one shelf a foot off the ground, one at waist height and one at shoulder height. All of them were full. The flashlight was on the bottom shelf of the back wall.

I could tell I'd already missed some of the conversation, because April was saying, "...ever made out with a ghost?"

"You don't look like a ghost to me. I think you're definitely flesh and blood."

Greg reached out and put his hand on her breast. I was both shocked and impressed. Although I'd dreamed of doing that with a number of girls, I never would have had the nerve to try it.

I shifted to get a better view. If he'd done that to Lois or Julie, they would have broken his arm. April didn't seem to mind. She let him get a good feel, then stepped back, just out of his reach.

"Yep," Greg said, "definitely flesh and blood."

"You think so, little man? How sure are you I'm not a ghost? Want to lose a wager about that, too?"

"There you go with that wager stuff again. That's all I heard all weekend. When are you going to tell me what I've supposedly bet?"

"What's your rush to find out?"

Greg's tone became harsh. "No rush. You've been going on about that for days, and I'm getting tired of your games."

I'd learned to fear that tone. It meant I was about to cross a line best left uncrossed. April didn't realize just how on thin ice she was, or else she didn't care.

"What's wrong with my games?" April teased. "Are you afraid you'll lose?"

Greg took a step toward her, and April stepped back in synch with him as he did.

"I don't lose."

"Funny, I thought you did. To me. At capture the flag. We even had a wager on it. Or don't you remember?"

"That was just one game. Over the long run I don't lose."

I began to get nervous. Sweat dripped into my eyes, and it

wasn't all due to the heat. Greg had a temper, and he was showing signs he was about to lose it.

"Don't be too sure of that." April stopped backing up and took a step toward Greg. She was now within his reach, but for some reason he didn't try to touch her.

"What would you say, little man, if I told you the wager was for your soul?"

"I'd say you're full of it."

"You don't sound too sure of yourself, little man. Are you afraid to wager your soul?"

"No."

"Poor little man, not sure if I'm worth his little soul." April was wiggling her shoulders. The movement did things to the rest of her body that were pretty impressive, even over where I was hiding. I could only imagine the effect they were having on my brother.

Greg's voice was huskier when he replied. "C'mere and I'll show you how big and sure I am." He reached out with both hands and, taking her by the shoulders, pulled her to him. They went into a deep kiss.

I was beginning to wonder when they were going to come up for air when I realized that was exactly what Greg was trying to do. April had her arms around his neck. She didn't seem to be holding him tightly. In fact, her arms looked relaxed. But Greg began to struggle and try to pull away. April held on and kept kissing him. Greg began making a strange noise and pushed at her more violently. It didn't have any effect. April's grip on him never loosened. Then his struggles weakened and he just went limp, his arms dropping and his knees sagging. April kissed him for a few more seconds, then let him drop to the ground.

I must have made a sound, although to this day I have no idea if I inhaled audibly, or shifted and April heard the sand scrape. Whatever it was, she looked up and made eye contact with me. Her face was different somehow, more gaunt and tormented than

I have ever seen a human face. And no, it wasn't an effect of the flashlight. Of that I'm sure.

"Hello, Mike. Please come in."

I don't know why I did. It was as though I had no other choice.

I wanted to run. I was a twelve-year-old kid, and what I had just seen was way beyond anything in my experience. The whole situation was terrifying.

"Is he dead?" I managed to croak.

"Yes, Mike." Her voice was distant. "He is."

"Why?"

"His father raped me after prom my sophomore year. I got pregnant. He told me to have an abortion. I was terrified my parents would find out, so I went along. I started bleeding the next day. I had to be taken to the emergency room. I was so hurt and ashamed. I committed suicide."

"But why Greg? He didn't rape you, did he?"

"No, but he's his father's son. The bloodline ran true. It would have only been a matter of time before he did."

"Are you going to kill me, too?" I felt urine run down my leg and drip from the hem of my shorts.

"No, Mike." And this time there was a sadness in her voice. "You and Greg don't have the same father."

Then she vanished, fading out like you see in the movies. Behind where she had been standing I could see the nameplate on the casket in the light from the flashlight. It said April Townsend. Below her name was a date, July 6. The year next to the date was twenty years earlier.

I reached over and tried to rouse Greg, but it didn't do any good. He was really dead. In a panic, I took off running. I guess I must have tripped and fell and hit my head. Some of the other kids found me unconscious outside the mausoleum a little while later.

When I regained consciousness, I was completely hysterical. Once they understood what I was saying about Greg, they opened the mausoleum. How the door had gotten shut, I don't know. I certainly didn't shut it. The police and an ambulance came. Greg was pronounced dead at the scene. They had to give me a shot to calm me down.

The coroner did an autopsy, and his report concluded that Greg was hiding in the mausoleum when the door somehow shut and he couldn't get it open again. The cause of death was listed as asphyxiation

The police questioned all the kids playing capture the flag that night, as well as any others who had played in the last couple of weeks. They looked for April but were never able to find her. The only April Townsend anyone knew about had committed suicide to the day twenty years before. Her family had moved shortly after her burial, a burial that occurred in the mausoleum where my brother died. No one remembered where the family had gone. There were no other Townsends anywhere in the county.

There was some speculation around town that I had shut Greg in the mausoleum, with reasons ranging from deliberate murder to a prank turned deadly. There was also some speculation one of us kids had pushed Old Man Smitty into that open grave. Nothing ever came of the talk. It was just small-town gossip, but it still cut deep.

The city council passed a resolution making it illegal to be in any cemeteries after dark. The gates were locked at night, and for the rest of the summer the police made regular patrols by all three cemeteries in town.

Needless to say, capture the flag lost its appeal. As far as I know, the games never resumed, in the cemetery or anywhere else. If they did, I was never invited to play.

I never talked to Mom about what April told me. She wouldn't have believed me in the first place, and in the second place, I didn't know how. I mean, I was only twelve. Mom had gotten married eighteen years earlier and had only been married once. Yet my fifteen-year-old brother and I had different fathers. How was I supposed to ask her about that?

Mom was devastated by Greg's death. Although she never said so, I've always felt she blamed me. After she got the news, she was distant. She never held me like she did the night we got back from putting Granddad in the nursing home. When she did embrace me, it was always stiff and formal, and she always broke contact as quickly as she could.

She also started drinking, something she had never done. You know the rest. It's been in all the papers and on all the tabloid news shows. How that fall she died when she failed to make a curve and ended up wrapped around one of the oldest trees in the county. The amount of alcohol in her bloodstream was more than three times the legal limit.

I ended up as a ward of the state, which is a fancy way of saying I became a kid nobody wanted. Foster care and I didn't exactly fit well, and I rebelled the only way I knew how. I don't need to review my criminal record for you. I imagine you did homework before coming here.

I just want to correct one thing that everyone, including the prosecutor, got wrong. I wasn't high the night I killed that girl. Just the opposite. I was going through withdrawal. That was why I was in the house in the first place. I was looking for something I could sell so I could score a hit. The place was supposed to be empty. I didn't want to hurt anybody. That's the truth. It was just when she came into the room, she was the spitting image of April Townsend.

I thought April had come back for me, that it was my turn to die like Greg, and I lost it. There was a fireplace poker.

I don't remember picking it up. I just remember coming to.

The poker was in my hand and she was there on the floor. There was blood on the walls and the carpet and me, and I panicked and took off.

I said I didn't want to talk about it. I guess I wanted to after all. That's what this whole thing has been about, hasn't it?

Anyway, that's what I've never told anyone about that night before now. I thought April had come back for me.

Did you ever go to Sunday School as a kid? No, I didn't think you did.

We used to go until Mom found herself raising two kids on her own, then we stopped. We didn't feel welcome there anymore. I still remember some of the lessons, even though you wouldn't think I did after how my life turned out. There was this Bible verse we talked about one time. About the sins of the fathers being visited on the children. I've been reading the Bible a lot since my sentencing, and I came across the verse the other day. Your mind tends to run in those veins when you're waiting to be executed.

No, I don't think I'm being punished for my father's sins. Anyway, it's not my father's sins, it's Greg's father's sins. And I'm not sure Greg was like his dad or would've done like his dad. I'm not sure I believe that. I don't believe that.

But I do believe I'm dealing with the consequences of Greg's dad. Have been for the last ten years of my life. That's what "visited upon" means.

One last thing.

My attorney has a packet of documents, family photos and such, mostly. He has instructions to give them to you after the execution if you request them. If you decide to print this interview, you're free to use any of it you want. In one of the photos two boys are standing on a pier holding up fish they've caught. They're not much as fish go, merely a couple of little crappies. The boys are about eight and eleven, and they couldn't be prouder of their catches. Behind the boys, kneeling down so that his hands are on their shoulders, is a man. The picture was taken shortly before the man left. Neither boy resembles him very much, so it's hard to tell which is his son. I plan to find him in the next life and ask him.

I have no intention of looking for April Townsend.

The Back Forty

By S. Kay Nash

When Billie Thompson called his office at 8:01 a.m. complaining of trespassers, Sheriff Jim Hollis had no choice but to get in his truck and head out to her place. He'd normally send a Deputy on a call like this one, since the farm was outside the city limits of Sulphur Springs. Mrs. Thompson, however, was a close friend of his mother's, and he'd known her all his life. He didn't want to risk Mrs. Thompson's temper. When she was his high-school English teacher, he'd seen her transform the rowdiest, testosterone-crazed teenagers (including himself) into mumbling cowards with just a few well-placed barbs. She never spoke blasphemy, but the woman could cuss like a trucker.

He lit a cigarette and blew the smoke out in a huff. He had better things to do today but if he didn't show up in person, he'd hear about it from his mother, and that was another situation he would prefer to avoid.

Jim enjoyed the drive out to the Thompson's farm despite himself. He rolled the windows down and appreciated the cooler Fall weather. When he saw the hand-painted sign advertising the produce stand on the county road, he followed the arrow to the side road which bordered the property line. Like most of the folks out this way, Billie had posted official-looking notices on her fences to warn hunters away. A wooden farm stand with a little clearing for parking marked the entrance to her driveway. At the corner of the fence, one sign declared: STRAY DOGS WILL BE SHOT.

After what happened to her husband six years ago, nobody

blamed her one bit.

Absent the body, present with the Lord.

Mike Thompson heard the words and knew he was dead.

A pack of dogs from the neighboring farm had attacked while he and Billie worked in their garden. He recalled gunshots, pain, the sound of snarling. Billie's face, stricken with fear as she tried to pull him inside the cab of the truck with her, was his final memory. He'd used the last of his strength to slam the door, keeping his wife safe inside as the dogs dragged him away.

After that; nothing, until he heard Billie's inconsolable weeping. He knew he was supposed to move on, but that radiance of peace and the promise of Heaven never came.

The only light he saw was Billie, shining in the darkness. He could see her clearly, but not the crowd that filled his house. These must have been his grown children, friends, neighbors, his church family; but they seemed insubstantial, their faces vague and unfocused, hovering like shadows around his wife.

Days after the funeral, he trailed behind her from room to room as she boxed up his clothes for charity. He stayed close, sharing his memories of their life together, hoping she would hear and know he watched over her. He repeated his wedding vow. *In the name of God, I, Michael, take you, Wilhelmina, to be my wife . . .*

She never answered him.

If the Lord didn't take him home, it meant he still had work to do. It made sense. He'd been a simple man, a good husband and a father, farming the land passed down to him through four generations of Thompsons. Perhaps he was meant to be his wife's guardian angel, sent by God to keep her safe until they could be reunited in Heaven.

Billie waved and called out a greeting from the porch as Hollis pulled up. She pointed up the dirt road that wound around the side of the house as she approached the passenger window of his truck, with a varmint rifle slung over her shoulder. He leaned over the passenger seat to open the door for her.

"Sorry for the rush, Jim," she said, talking as soon as the door opened. "But I want you to see this before they come back, and if they're around, I want the law with me."

"When did you find out you had squatters?" He put the truck in gear and eased down the rutted road, going slow past the farm-house.

"Yesterday, but I've been smelling campfire smoke for a while. Thought it was hunters, but I walked back there and found some kind of camp on the edge of the back forty." She eased the rifle to rest beside her leg, the barrel pointing at the floorboard.

The long dirt road ended in a bare patch of ground with a few rusting remains of antique farm equipment off to one side. Billie was out of the truck and walking toward the field before Jim could kill the engine. He caught up to her as she headed into the brush.

"Now, you follow right behind me and be careful. It's still warm enough for snakes."

The land ran wild with overgrowth, plants twisting across the ground in a tangle of leaf, stalk and late-season pumpkins. Three buzzards hovered over the trees near the river, lazy in the still morning air.

"What am I looking for?" Jim asked.

"Well, just follow me, and I'll show you. Those assholes made a fire pit out of river rocks, left trash everywhere and they went and dug a bunch of holes all over the place." She brushed aside yel-lowed corn stalks and bunches of wild sunflower as she walked.

Jim concentrated on keeping his footing as they got deeper into the tangle. For a woman pushing seventy years old, Billie was stronger than she looked.

As they moved around a brush pile, Jim caught the sickly-sweet scent of rotting meat.

He stopped on the path. "Mrs. Thompson, hold up a minute. What died out here?"

She spat out, "Dog." She pointed to a patch of wild sunflowers.

"Over there. I've about had it with city people dumping their dogs out here for no good reason. I've half a mind to shoot their owners, too."

Jim pushed through the wild sunflowers, following the stench. The first dog he found was nothing more than a few patches of hide and bones concealed by weeds. Just beyond it was the likely source of the smell, a dog that the buzzards had already picked clean and abandoned. The ground under the scattered remains squirmed with beetles as big as his thumb. He gagged and turned away.

"I have every right to shoot those dogs, you know," Mrs. Thompson said.

"I understand, ma'am," Jim fought his way back to the trail, eager to get away from the stomach-turning reek.

He reached into his shirt pocket for a cigarette.

"You're not planning on setting a fire in my garden, are you?" Her tone of voice and the look on her face sent him right back to high school.

He coughed nervously and left his smokes alone. "No, ma'am."

Everywhere Billie went, Mike followed. The land entrusted to his stewardship was hers now, and after fifty-one years of working beside him, she knew it as well as he did. She still managed the property herself, leasing out the hay fields and hiring local boys to do the work she couldn't.

For a long time, Billie stayed away from the garden at the back of their property. Every now and again, she'd stand on the dirt road, staring like she meant to walk down to see it. That garden had been their retirement project where they grew vegetables for their produce stand and the food pantry at church. It was also the place where Mike had given his life for hers.

Mike tried to urge her along with words, fragrant as vitex trees and honeysuckle blooms awash in the summer heat, but she turned away with tears in her eyes. He wandered through their garden, troubled by the state of the field. Choked with volunteer squash, corn stalks and opportunistic weeds, the field had lain fallow too long. This was something he knew how to fix. It was his land, after all, and he would shape it as he saw fit.

He reached into the ground and sensed life there, pulsing at his touch. Deep in the soil, he felt seeds longing for rain and sun. His hands pulled melons, corn, squash, tomatoes and sunflowers into the sunshine where Billie would find them.

If he couldn't speak to her, maybe he could show her some other way. He wrapped his words into the wind, letting the scent of young grass beneath her feet become his voice.

You're going to be all right, Darlin', he said. *Come and see. Come and see how much I love you.*

That night, he talked to her as she slept. He told her of the fallow field bursting with life, of deer grazing peacefully and the antics of squirrels and 'coons, possums and armadillos. His words carried the scent of rain-washed earth and the heat of the sun on broad green leaves.

Billie woke with the sun. In the cool of the morning, she slung a rifle over her shoulder and walked down the dirt road with resolute determination. Mike glowed with pride as he followed.

She had heard him, she'd listened and she would see what he'd done for her.

She walked out to the middle of the field and stood there, dumbstruck. Melon vines twisted around her ankles and stalks of corn stood two feet high, shoots of string beans already curling at their lowest leaves. The tears of wonder in her eyes gave him a deep satisfaction.

"Michael," she finally spoke in a thick, broken voice, "I wish you could see this."

I'm right here, Darlin,' he replied. I will always watch over you.

The downed fence was obvious once they got close. It looked to Jim like the squatters had gone through there several times, leaving a path through the brush and down to the creek. He followed their trail into the garden, weaving around piles of brush and dead wood that concealed the camp.

It was exactly as she described, with a rough fire pit and a torn, bloody sleeping bag on the ground. Walking a little farther, he found a makeshift latrine. He poked around the area and discovered that some of the weeds towering over the low brush were exactly that—weed. The scent of it was unmistakable. Cut stalks farther in told him the growers had already hauled out most of it. They'd be back for the rest, and soon.

"Well, hell," he cursed softly, hoping she wouldn't hear and give him an earful for blasphemy.

He walked back to Billie, holding up an accusing finger to point out the plants. "That's what they're here for. Dope plants. Marijuana. Bet they had to take the fence down to get their crop moved out." He poked a shred of the sleeping bag with the toe of his boot, "Looks like one of them got hurt. Maybe that's why they haven't been back."

He followed the path through the fence and down to the creek. It looked like the growers moved the plants on foot, probably down to a vehicle parked on the county road a mile downstream.

He pulled his phone from his belt and dialed his office.

"Deb, get me through to Bill Stetler at Tyler DEA," he paused to listen to his clerk, "Yeah, we found a grow operation out here at the Thompson's."

Mike didn't mind the visitors in the field, at first. They planted and tended their bit of garden well out of the way, and never stayed long. This was a place of plenty, and he knew the Lord's decree that fallow fields belonged to the poor and the sojourner. If they needed sustenance from his land, he didn't begrudge their gleaning from his bounty. But he kept an eye on them, just in case.

As the weeks wore on, more men appeared, and while he couldn't tell them apart, he saw their weapons clear as day. They carried rifles that were more like soldiers' weapons than a farmer's trusty gun. They stayed on the land and built fires when the nights got cooler. Their voices faded in and out like a radio not quite tuned in, but when they spoke about the old lady in the house up the way, he heard them loud and clear. When they talked about how they could get her out of the house and use the land for themselves, anger stirred in Mike's heart like a nest of wasps.

He'd sworn to protect her, but what could he do? The land was his to shape as he wished, but he had no sway over living men.

At the campsite, he watched as they stuffed trash bags full of the plants they'd grown. They took the bags down the river, wading through the shallow water. One man stayed behind, asleep beside the embers of the fire.

Fear chewed at Mike, building into rage. They wanted to hurt Billie. They wanted to steal his land. If he was Billie's guardian angel, it was time to step up and do his job. He knew he was supposed to forgive trespass, but the men had threatened his wife. He recalled Samuel from the Bible, and how he had called for vengeance against those who threatened the children of the Lord. Mike didn't have an army to fight against men with rifles, but he had the power of the land that God had surely granted him. He would have to make do with what he had.

The first time Billie shot a dog, she kicked the corpse, spewing filthy words that would have shocked her husband in life. She dragged the dead canine down to the place where Mike died, left it on the bare dirt, and wept. Others had followed, and Mike knew where every one of them lay, their bodies left to rot.

Now he understood. Her grief had given him the army he needed. He knew the power of rage, sharp teeth, and how a feeble old man could be brought down by a handful of crazed beasts. Surely a sleeping man would be no different. Taking a life pained Mike, but he saw no other choice. The threat to Billie was clear. He had to keep his promise to her.

He found the remains of the dogs and knitted their bones together with tendrils of wild primrose and melon, then willed them to rise.

The dogs reconstituted and came to heel just in front of Mike, silent but for the rustle of brush, each of them an incarnation of his anger, as easy to control as the plants of the earth had been.

Fleshless jaws with shattered teeth tore into the sleeping bag, then raked it open with rotted claws. The man woke up as the dogs seized his arm, dragging him free of the bag. He made a single cry, but the biggest dog shook him by the throat, and he didn't scream again.

Mike watched and mourned as the memory of his own death replayed before him. He'd sacrificed himself for his wife, like any good man would have done. But the criminal writhing before him was not a good man. This was righteous. This was the reason Mike had not been called home.

The man curled on the ground, unmoving. Mike waited until the sputtering of blood and air from his torn throat grew still.

It was over. Billie was safe, for now. Mike thought of leaving the body there as a warning but realized it would only bring the men with rifles closer to Billie's door.

At his command, the dogs dragged the body to a brush pile of storm-felled trees that marked the north end of the field. Mike covered the corpse with a living shroud of saplings and vines, growing beneath his hands like snakes slithering through the brush.

When it was done, he sent the dogs back to their rightful places in the field, then went home to Billie.

Don't be afraid, he told her. I will always watch over you.

Within two hours, Agent Stetler arrived to survey the area. By one o'clock in the afternoon, he and Jim had pulled together a team to survey the site and Bill called a company that the agency used for cleanup to remove the plants. They agreed that it would be best to get it taken care of that day, since a front was blowing in from the west, bringing rain and high winds.

Men and equipment descended on the Thompson farm. Jim did what he could to keep Billie calm. When they unloaded a borrowed windrower to clear a path across the field, her legendary temper exploded.

She stood in front of the machine with her arms folded, daring them to roll it over her. She'd been spouting scripture and profanities for half an hour.

"This land is touched by the hand of God!" she yelled, "You can walk in and walk out like everybody else, but you sons'a bitches will not go tearin' up my field!"

"Mrs. Thompson," Jim tried to reason with her, "please don't make me arrest you for obstruction. My mama would kill me, and I am not ready to die just yet." As soon as the words were out of his mouth, he knew he had his answer. He called his mother. Twenty minutes later, her car rolled into the driveway.

Margaret Hollis calmed Billie down and assured her that the men wouldn't damage more than they had to. After all, hadn't the Spencer boys gone through that field a time or two with a Bobcat after that storm took all the trees down? Billie relented, shot Bill Stetler and his men a vicious glare, then followed Margaret into the house under the pretense of making coffee.

Within an hour, the windrower cut a clear path to the site. The disposal trucks moved in, and the men got to work. Jim had done his best to steer them around the dog graveyard, but the scent of decomposing flesh trailed them to the campsite.

The disposal company out of Tyler was used to cleaning up toxic meth labs. The relative ease of tearing out a pot farm had them in a good mood. Fifty-five plants still stood, and Stetler estimated that as many as eighty had been there.

The surveyors bagged up the remains of the shredded sleeping bag, beer cans and fertilizer bags as evidence. One of the guys joked about getting DNA evidence out of the latrine, and everyone laughed until Jim told him it was a great idea and handed him an evidence bag.

Around four o'clock, Margaret called Jim's cell phone to tell everyone to come up for a break. They munched chips and sandwiches and drank cokes, then headed back to the job after offering generous praise to their hostess. Billie didn't seem much happier, but at least she wasn't shouting abuse at them anymore.

Back at the site, buzzards circled over the river in lazy spirals, drifting as they rode the gusty air. The wind shifted, carrying the reek of decay with it. Everyone cursed and covered their faces as the scent washed over them.

Stetler gave Jim a dirty look, "You sure that's a dog?"

"Yeah," he grimaced, "Saw 'em myself. My guess is there's prob'ly half a dozen piles of buzzard bait out there. One I saw this morning was nasty."

The team cut down the plants and stacked them into a silage truck. It would be transported to Dallas for proper disposal. The jokes about burning it at the landfill to get the whole county high were getting old, as were the wisecracks about burning some now, just to get rid of the dead dog smell.

Around sunset, the team finally rolled out. They offered Jim a lift back to the house, but he waved them off. He wanted to delay getting back to his mother and Mrs. Thompson for as long as he could.

Jim paced through the clearing where the plants used to be, kicking at a clod of disturbed earth. He figured he'd come back on Saturday to help re-string the barbed wire fence. It might make Mrs. Thompson feel a little better. He pulled a cigarette out of his shirt pocket and lit it, blowing a thin stream of smoke into the air. The breeze rustled the trees by the river, bringing another gust of fetid decay.

Jim blew out another lungful of smoke, then frowned. The smoke drifted south, toward the place where he'd seen the dead dogs. Was there another one nearby?

He walked through the cleared pot farm into the brush where storm-felled branches and undergrowth made for tricky footing.

As he got farther in, the smell got stronger, so cloying that even the tobacco couldn't touch it. The wind stilled, and he heard the buzzing of flies.

Following the sound, he carefully picked his way toward a pile of tree limbs swarming with fat green flies. There, under the fly-laden branches, he glimpsed the source of the stench. He covered his mouth with his arm, trying to filter the air, but it didn't help. He stepped up on the trunk of a fallen tree to get a better look.

A dead man's face grinned up at him, bloated, egg-spotted and dabbed with tiny masses of squirming maggots on the skin.

It was more than Jim could take. He turned and vomited, sending up a cloud of buzzing flies as he choked and coughed on the lung-searing air. He spat, flung the cigarette butt to the ground and gathered his nerves to turn back for another look.

It was now a murder investigation.

Something wasn't right. Shoots of thorny greenbrier curled around the body, tearing through the denim work clothes it wore. Whip-like saplings, waist-high, grew through the body. One split through the dead man's arm, and another pierced a leg. Nature said the body had been there for months, but the state of decay and the flies spoke of two days, maybe three.

Jim backed up a step, reaching for the cell phone at his belt. One of the saplings trembled in his peripheral vision. Jim jerked his head up and peered at the brush pile, wary of scavengers.

One sapling thrashed, then another. The corpse's arm twitched, fingers curling, spastic. Its legs moved, scraping the ground, sending up another cloud of flies. The greenbrier vines that wound around the body seemed to grow longer and thicker, twisting around its arms and legs, spreading as he watched them twist over the corpse in a matter of seconds. Jim backed away slowly, his phone forgotten, his instinct to run overridden by his need to understand what he saw.

The corpse rolled to one side. Flat, dead eyes stared up at him.

Jim screamed and jumped backward, tripped over a branch, and landed on his backside. He scuttled back on hands and heels, every breath a moan of terror. The sound of wood and leaf ripping through dead flesh made him retch again. He couldn't see the body from where he fell, but he couldn't look away.

The corpse rose from the ground. Maggots fell from its face, the red glow of the setting sun glinting on the squirming larvae like bloody tears. The thing lurched forward, clambering toward him.

Panic gripped him by the throat. *What the hell—?*

He rolled to his hands and knees, crawled until he could get his legs under him and stumbled up from the ground into an unsteady run. Pushing through the tangle of vegetation, he rushed into the clearing. His foot caught a hole left behind by the disposal unit. Pain flared through his leg, and he tumbled to the ground. He tried to stand, but the blinding pain in his ankle brought him down again.

Something moved on the other side of the clearing, creeping shapes that stalked low to the ground. They moved on four stiff legs, hobbling as if they didn't quite know how to walk. They made no sound louder than the wind in the brush. One raised its head and turned toward him, eyeless. Weathered bones, scraps of leathered hide and vines curled around skeletal jaws full of teeth.

The dogs. Oh God. The dogs.

Mike watched his wife stand in defiance against a crowd of featureless men with guns on their hips and heard her protest at their trespass. They'd come for her, just as they said they would. His anger grew as he watched them surround her and felt her fear wash over him when he drew close to her side.

Someone led her into the house and held her there. He felt Billie's fury boil as hot as his own. He knew what he had to do.

There were too many men for him to take on, so he watched and waited as they hauled away the rest of the plants. And just like the first time, they left a man behind. The man moved through the brush, his image flickering in Mike's sight, jumping like the frames of an old film. He couldn't make out a face, but he could see the cold iron of the gun on his hip.

This body, he wouldn't hide. This man would pay for what they'd done to Billie.

Mike called his dogs from across the field, bound their bones with vines and willed them to walk. He followed the trespasser until the man found the dead body Mike had left as a warning.

Absent the body, present with the Lord.

The dead man was just like the dogs, an earthly shell of a creature, the man's departed soul certainly destined for the fires of Hell. Mike wrapped his arms around the rotting flesh, gave it purpose and strength, curling around it with grasping briars that shifted at his command.

Mike stood from the brush pile, fighting the vegetation that held him. He moved toward the enemy, trying to remember how it felt to walk like a man. Hysterical, the man tried to run but the land—Mike's land—betrayed him, sending him sprawling to the ground. His cries of pain steeled Mike's resolve to see this man die.

Vengeance is mine, and retribution. In due time, their foot will slip; For the day of their calamity is near.

The pack closed in, tearing at the man's legs as he kicked at their sun-bleached bones and tried to pull his gun from its holster. When he finally drew it, one shot shattered a dog's skull. He turned the gun on Mike.

Mike tried to draw breath, tried to release the scream inside of him so the fool would know why he had to die, but all that came out was a wheeze of putrid air from dead lungs. The sharp cracks of the handgun meant nothing. The wounds were just another set of holes in an already-putrefied body.

Mike wrapped his hands around the man's throat, willing the thorny vines to twist and grow. Sharp tendrils pierced the skin, pushing through the man's flesh like soft spring soil. Mike poured his love for his wife into the briars sprouting from his borrowed hands, fed them with the pain and fear he'd felt on the day he died.

Take me, dear Lord, just let her get away.

The briars rooted in flesh, seeking blood like water, splitting up through the man's jaw, piercing his tongue and curling down this throat, his cries muted by a long roll of thunder.

Mike ripped his hands away, spraying bone and blood. The man twitched on the ground, then lay still. Mike pulled himself away, letting the borrowed body collapse in a squelching heap next to the dead man. The dogs fell where they stood, returning to piles of crumbling bones.

The thought of Billie, home and safe, pulled Mike through the field. He passed over the sunflowers like the approaching storm, rustling the trees all the way up the dirt road to the house. The sight of the house and the bright light of Billie's spirit calmed him.

Please, Lord, let her be safe.

He found Billie in the kitchen. She gripped the phone to her ear, her frantic voice shouting about gunshots. Another figure, perhaps a woman, hovered nearby.

Mike wanted to wrap his arms around Billie and soothe her fears. He stayed close, just over her shoulder, his words drifting like the scent of vitex trees on the humid, storm-touched air.

You're going to be all right, Darlin.' Come and see. Come and see how much I love you.

Critical Mass

By Bryce Wilson

Colin couldn't believe what he saw. It took him a few moments to process the image. He was an easygoing fellow and people's potential for being complete assholes never ceased to astonish him.

What he saw as he crested the low hill at the end of Martin Luther King Jr. Boulevard—gateway to the student neighborhood of West Campus where high rises and row houses sat side by side—was a car stopped at a red light. It was heavy, black and low to the ground. It was vintage, but Colin wasn't a gearhead and couldn't tell exactly what model. It didn't look like most of the cars that car culture guys liked to show off. It wasn't from the fifties, and wasn't an old jalopy or a Rolls-Royce. It just came from THE PAST. It gleamed black like it was coated in enamel. It looked like it weighed about three tons, a relic from the days when cars were made of steel. Its long nose housed an engine that growled like a big cat pent up in a small cage. The windshield was entirely opaque. The thing seemed to suck in the light—even the headlights, bright as they were, seemed to cast shadows. The only glints of light came from the car's white wall tires and the luminous hood ornament that decorated the end of its engine block, a grinning chrome skull.

But none of this was what caught Colin's attention. What stopped him were the stencils on the side of the car.

If he had thought about it for a while, Colin would probably have found the cheap white paint odd. After all, this was obviously a car that had been cared for to the point of fetish; the gearheads Colin knew would sooner shit on an open Bible than deface the object of their affection. Yet here he was confronted with ugly cheap white paint that had been stenciled onto the side of the car. Mint condition be damned.

The stencil was the white outline of a bicycle, repeated three times, the way fighter pilots stenciled the silhouettes of Luftwaffe and MIGS they had shot down on the side of their planes. The paint was obviously new, and bled slightly at the edges. Three cyclists had been run down in Austin in the past week. A girl on Burnet coming home from her grocery shopping, hit from behind, her brains dashed out among carrots and melting ice cream. A guy on Manor who had been sideswiped. He had crashed so hard into a food truck he had left a dent. The final victim had been a guy on South 1st who had been practically split in half. None of the offending drivers had been identified. There had been no witnesses to what the police were optimistically referring to as accidents.

The prevailing attitude among the citizenry and the officials seemed to be, 'Well, you take your chances.'

But this shit went too far. This was gloating.

You came on the receiving end of a lot of weird unfocused hate when you were a cyclist. People flipping you the bird out their window as they passed. Chucking empty coffee cups at you in the morning, and empty bottles at night. Guys swerving into you to give you a scare. Chicks screaming indecipherable obscenities as they sped past. Sure, some cyclists rode with dickish entitlement, but that didn't seem to be the motivating factor for a lot of these folks. They just hated cyclists because they were cyclists. Hated them just because they existed.

They had both stopped at the light, where Guadalupe bisected Martin Luther King. Colin stared at the symbols and then tried to look into the cab. He couldn't make out so much as a silhouette; the windows were illegally tinted.

It took Colin about two seconds to decide that this aggression would not stand. He slid his Kryptonite lock from the handlebars and gave it a gentle toss, catching it by the u-bend. He tensed his foot on the peddle and then leaped into action.

He swung his left arm, cracking the heavy straight bar of the u-lock into the passenger side mirror as he launched into traffic. He expected to hear curses of fury, the revving of an engine, or at least the blare of a horn, that universally recognized symbol of "pissed off." But there was only the purr of the motor. That disquieted him somehow but he couldn't spare it too much thought as he weaved through the traffic, drawing horns and curses from other sources. Soon he was through, two streams of competing traffic between him and the old car. Peddling madly, he darted into the first alley he came to. Colin spent every waking moment possible on the streets. He knew every secret path that flowed through the city. He slipped from one to the next, going a mile and a half without touching a street that was named by a sign.

He was just allowing himself a chuckle of satisfaction at his impromptu act of vigilante karma correction when he saw the headlights in front of him.

The police would later tell his loved ones that if it came as any consolation he couldn't have seen what was coming. The police lied. The alley was narrow, but not so narrow that Colin didn't try to swerve out of the way as those headlights lurched toward him out of the dark, the sound of screeching rubber echoing off the tight walls. The gleaming chrome skull was the only thing visible on the front of the dark hulking shape, the smile etched onto it letting him know that he had fucked up.

Colin swerved to miss the car and collided with a green dumpster. The crash knocked him off his bike and sent him sprawling, but even with his head swimming he knew he had gotten off light. He pushed himself up on all fours and climbed back onto his bike. The world teetered like someone had put the horizon on a seesaw, but he kept his balance. He had to get out of this alley to somewhere where there were people, lots of people. If this was the guy who had killed the other three, he didn't like doing his business in front of others.

He had dropped into a low gear and was peddling hard when the car took him from behind. The low purr of its engine sounded like a cackle. Colin had just enough time to register how impossible it would have been for a car of that size to make a u-turn in an alley this narrow when gravity brought him back to Earth, ass over tits. He landed with a crunch that told him his left shoulder was trashed. The sound of this, more than the pain, finally brought it home to him that he could die here in the alley. That, even though he was the lead in The Colin Show, 24 years running with all signs pointing toward renewal. He might finally have found a situation that he wasn't clever enough, strong enough or lucky enough to survive. A kind of fear he'd never known swept through him. Jesus Christ, he thought, it was just a fucking mirror. Not worth this. Surely, not worth this.

He rolled onto his back with a gasp. The pain was still a faraway thing but Colin had an intimation it wouldn't be so for long. He clutched his wounded shoulder and screamed. He couldn't quite believe it wasn't over when the headlights pinned him again. He lifted his head as high as he could and saw the twin headlights of the hulk considering him. That's when he noticed the mirror he had broken had grown back. He held up his right hand in the universal sign of supplication, "enough please, I submit." The only response he got was the revving of all that metal, the sound of pistons churning. The car lurched forward, halving the distance between itself and Colin. Then quartering it. It was right on top of him, and suddenly Colin knew, not feared, but knew that he would not be leaving this alley alive. He said a quick apology to his family, and did his best to make his peace. His life didn't flash before his eyes, but he was able to run through some of the good times in his head. There had been a lot of them. Enough of them anyway. He was sorry he wouldn't be able to share more of them with Georgette, but as far as regrets went that was about it.

He flipped the bird to the driver's side of the windshield and even managed a chuckle before the car leaped forward and reduced his testicles to a bloody corned beef hash beneath its grinding rubber. Colin began to scream, and he didn't stop for much longer than he would have thought possible.

Georgette was near the front of the pack, which wasn't where she usually found herself. Georgette wasn't used to being noticed, period. She had a quiet personality, more guarded than shy, coupled with the kind of athletic build that went past tomboy and reached plain old boy—slim hips, gym teacher calves, breasts that had shrunk to nothing more than place holders due to her constant burning of calories. She was quiet in the company of those she knew any less than intimately. Masked behind glasses, black jeans, and a black Gaslight Anthem shirt, her black hair worn in a chopped butch cut. It wasn't that she shied away from attention, but she found loud notions expressed for the benefit of others to be tiresome. She knew who she was, no need to try and convince anyone else.

Yet here she was, at the head of the pack. A leader, if just this once. Behind her was the entire cycling community of Austin, among the most dedicated in the country, ready to put on the mother of critical masses. The way she had found herself there was an accident. Her boyfriend had died, run down in an alley in West Campus, probably by some drunken fratboy who had managed to slip away unnoticed in the aftermath. Normally, this would be nothing to inspire a movement of this size, but Colin happened to be the fourth cyclist to die that week and two more had followed him. Something had to be done.

The call went out. She'd been recruited. Organizers had approached her, telling her she was a needed voice. She felt a little odd stepping up. Georgette didn't know if what she and Colin had was love. But it was nice. He appreciated her, made her feel happy and six months in showed no signs of being a tool or looking to fuck her over. He'd shared her bed, and for a brief time, her life, and if that wasn't love it was still something that was worth enough to raise a fight when someone ran him down like a stray cat.

The call had gone out and the people had answered. They were behind her now, a swollen, still-growing tumor clogging one of Austin's main arteries. They grouped at Lamar just south of where the 183 Freeway bisected central Austin. The plan was simple; fuck shit up, swell down Lamar all the way into Austin's Business district. They'd cut across Sixth and clog Austin's downtown until they hit Congress, made the requisite storm on the Capitol, and then u-turn and pour across the bridge into the hipster stronghold of SoCo, where the cops would be too scared to retaliate lest they scare away the tourist dollars.

And it looked as though things were going extremely well; there were thousands behind her, literally thousands. Hipsters straddled on neon-colored fixies with garish color tires to match, black tires being considered the mark of a plebeian. For some that wasn't esoteric enough; they perched on top of trick unicycles like absurd birds or oversized tricycles looking like fashion-conscious preschoolers. Georgette saw a genuine antique; a giant front wheel, a small back one and a demure-looking, leather saddle ten feet off the ground. A slim girl sat sidesaddle on it, a top hat cocked on her head. These riders' biking gear consisting of waistcoats, handlebar mustaches and pocket watches. Others wore shorts and wife beaters, while some wore tank tops; all the better to show off their colorful sleeves of pop culture tattoos that wound up their limbs like lysergic-colored carp. Girls in jorts wearing pink-framed glasses that matched their sleek flamingo-colored bikes and feathered boas drew dour stares from the zealot faces of the serious cyclists, the kind that still wanted to be Lance Armstong. These were clad in bumblebee-colored lycra tops and tight black spandex that outlined their packages, topped with insectile helmets and finished with toeclips. The hipsters and the hardcore glared, each hating the other for their outlandish costumes. They were joined by fat secretaries on sleek city cruisers and retail veterans perched on battered mountain bikes whose worn tires spoke of a lot of hard miles ridden out of necessity rather than idealism or fashion. There were long-limbed bike messengers with willowy blond hair and faces like gelflings and suburban moms and old hippies with scraggly beards and long hair who rode old road bikes from the seventies with curled handlebars. Tough pedicab operators with bulging calves, canned ham thighs and Popeye forearms; they had esoteric facial hair, serious views on Marxism and packs of Gauloises rolled into their uniform black T-shirts. Another pedicab contingent dressed like anime magical girls in mesh, semi-ironic rainbow headbands and scripted their cabs and rigs with neon. Serious mountain bikers with beasts of gears sitting on fat tires, the fact that their flannel shirts were rolled up being their only concession to the high nineties weather. Journalists flitted around the edges, snapping pictures—this would not be a story lacking in human interest.

In the group, rivalries and taunts passed back and forth just underneath the surface, but they presented a united front to the rest of the world. Today, though they all belonged to different tribes, they also belonged to the same team. No matter what else they wore, all sported a black armband, filling Georgette with a true sense of pride she had not expected. An emotion powerful enough to blot out the grief for the first time in the week since Colin had died.

They were protesting for the things they always protested for. More bike lanes, stricter enforcement, or for that matter any enforcement of the three-foot rule. A general calling out of the bullshit attitude that cyclists took their chances just by going out on the street, and if their blood got spilled, it was just too damn bad.

Already they were being noticed. Four lanes of traffic were blocked. Horns gave out their staccato, atonal bleats. People catcalled and cursed, but they didn't get through. Georgette shot them the finger. She hated them with a pronounced vehemence.

For Georgette, cars had always been the opposite of bikes, their dark distorted reflection. Biking was fundamentally active. You wanted to go somewhere you made it happen. Driving was passive. When you drove, you fell into a kind of hypnotized daze until you arrived at your destination. In a car, you spent fuel. On a bike, you were fuel. A car made you a consumer, dependent in a very basic way, on roads, on gas, on others. A bike made you independent. You relied on your stamina, your will, your determination, your skill at mending your machine when necessary. On a bike, a machine became an extension of yourself. In a car, you buried yourself in one. It had always seemed to Georgette that she gave up part of herself when she slipped into a car. She became disconnected and anonymous. Indeed, that was part of the appeal. That was why people loved cars so much. They wanted to be identified with the sleek clear lines of classic design, with the efficiency and power of the best engines instead of all this fallible flesh. The aging guy with a pot belly and a bald spot could climb into a GTO and suddenly he was the GTO. In life, he might be ungainly and gawky but now he was graceful. Now he was cool. Maybe he couldn't kick ass like Steve McQueen or get women. But goddamnit he could drive like him. Why smell and let your muscles burn with lactic acid to sweat a crummy ten miles when you could slip into an automobile, be there in minutes and not feel a mile of it?

Georgette WANTED to feel it.

To Georgette, a bicycle was nothing less than white magic. Powerful white magic that transformed her from the girl with the awkward body, awkward manner and awkward name—into an avatar of grace and blessed blissful speed. She was no longer a duck-footed, slouch-shouldered, ungainly girl who knocked into tables, spilled drinks and dropped bottles on hardwood floors at parties. She left behind the girl who broke her nose three times over the course of her high school PE career and had never found a sport involving a ball or even her own two feet that she couldn't find new ways to suck at.

The way her rig became an extension of herself was what it was all about. It was a sleek black road bike with crimson highlights, narrow tires, a fixie frame and an Italian-style 20-gear system. The slightest shift of her weight, and the bike would respond with a graceful glide. A quick hit on the gears and a crouch, and suddenly she was hurtling down streets at thirty miles an hour, the bike under her feeling positively eager for the speed, weaving between cars. She would try to keep from grinning, aware that the only thing forestalling disaster was her own skill and luck.

The real world intruded on her thoughts, as it was want to do. Caddie pulled alongside her. She was peddling a fixie with a cool lime and silver paint job, completing the ensemble with a pair of steam punk goggles, and an old-fashioned leather pilot's cap that nearly swallowed her black mod bob, and a striped dress of a color matching her bike. Her grin was unseemly for a funeral procession, but Georgette couldn't blame her entirely. She was one of the organizers who had approached Georgette about joining the ride. Georgette was just a tourist, but this was Caddie's mission in life. The scene playing before her was a literal dream come true and she just couldn't keep the cost of it in her head. Georgette couldn't resent her for being excited.

"The natives are getting restless," she panted. All Georgette could see with the goggles was her own stoic reflection, but she had a feeling Caddie's eyes were positively shining. "Are you about ready to get started?"

Georgette pulled out her phone and glanced at the time. "I don't know, maybe we should allow a couple more minutes for stragglers. We might get a few more riders that way."

"A few more riders?" Caddie sputtered, "Who gives a fuck?! Do you see the crowd behind you? God, try to imagine doing this run with twenty, because I have! We couldn't dream of these numbers a month ago."

"Yeah, it's amazing what a motivator death can be," Georgette said.

She hadn't meant it to be harsh, but Caddie's pale skin turned a deep shade of crimson. Georgette was just making a genuine observation, but people often took the things she said wrong, and from past experience, she knew how useless it was to try and backpedal. Trying to explain that she hadn't meant it that way only made things even more awkward. "Right," Caddie said. "I'm sorry. I wasn't thinking. . ."

"No," Georgette said, "I think you're right, it's time. We got them together, let's see if they can do the rest."

A slightly more cautious smile returned to Caddie's face. She stuck two fingers in her mouth, blew a shrill whistle, and then followed it up with a surprisingly husky cry of, "Move 'em out."

On her cue, a guy with a patchy beard and curly brown hair pressed play on an iPod, and suddenly the theme from *Rawhide* was playing. Seeded riders started moving forward. And that was it. Two thousand riders of all shapes, sizes, races and rigs advanced, blocking all four lanes of the busiest street in Austin. And there was Georgette, at the front of it. She allowed herself a smile, not so wide as Caddie's, but a smile nonetheless. We pulled it off, she thought. You would have loved this, baby. And, as all revolutions do in their first crucial moment, it looked beautiful.

It went wrong almost immediately. The car waited just long enough to let the entire pack get into motion. By this time, the front of the group was about half a mile down the long sloping hill that made up Lamar. The last cyclists in the group pushed off, clearing the intersection and the hopeless snarl of traffic they left there. They made their way down the block when the black car pulled out of an adjoining parking lot and into the middle of the street. It straddled the double yellow line, half a dozen neat white stencils on its side, the last one still slightly wet. It revved up its engine, getting itself nice and limber.

And then it sprang.

About a quarter mile had opened up between the end of the pack and the car before it leapt forward. Just enough space to get up to speed.

It closed the distance in a matter of seconds. Late, far later than would be expected, some of the people at the back looked over their shoulders, their faces not even registering fear, but annoyance that someone would harass them like this. They assumed their safety. They assumed it was their right. That was what made them such easy prey.

The horn bleated for one vicious second over the squeal of its tires before it collided with them. And then the screaming covered the sounds of both.

First the car hit one of the pedicabs. The cab crumpled on impact, the rider pitched over his handlebars and was run over by his own rig. A loud "oof " burst from his lungs as the air was driven from them. The car slowed for just a moment before the left tire rolled over the rider's skull and popped it.

Some of the rider's brains sprayed the thighs of a girl next to him. She gave a wet shriek of disbelief. The car swerved left and it became a shriek of pain. She sprawled, knocked from her bike, briefly silhouetted against the sky. Landing on the sidewalk some twenty yards away, her neck snapped on impact.

One of the bikers tried desperately to get away, banking sharply into a screaming forest of metal and flesh. In his desperation, he knocked over a woman old enough to be his mother and didn't give her so much as a glance. She went under the rear right tire. There was a panicked look on his face, that of a badly shot deer, one who just wanted to get away. The car took him, braking to get behind him and then lunging forward. The rider was knocked to the asphalt, his helmet hitting the car's bumper, smacking his head back but not killing him. He was dragged underneath the car for fifty yards or so. By the time the car spat him out, what was left didn't look much like a person.

The waves of panic were rippling up the crowd, a game of telephone with lethal stakes. Already the participants on the edges were fleeing, trying for any side street that would give them sanctuary. The black car let them go. There were too many of them packed into too tight of a corridor for any kind of effective escape. There was still plenty of time to hunt.

The cyclists tried to fight back, beating futilely at its flanks with chains and u-locks. They left no dent. The hits that struck the windows bounced off, sometimes striking the riders in the face. Up ahead, people began to crash; in their desperation to get away, they rode recklessly, and each one who crashed brought down several other riders with them. They toppled like shrieking dominoes. The black car chose its course accordingly, but sometimes exceptions had to be made. Only once, when a girl pushing herself to her feet (glasses broken, nose bloodied) bore a look evidencing sheer disbelief that something like this could actually happen, did the black car appear to consider giving in to the temptation to reverse.

A man in one of the big bulky cabs, his body tightly roped with muscle, jumped from his bike to the hood of the car. For a second he began to slide off. His legs splayed over the left tire, the look of fear on his face its own reward. But he clung to his purchase, and eventually pulled himself onto the hood. He crawled across the long engine, pushing himself forward on the chrome skull hood ornament that was now slick with blood. He had wrapped a chain around his hand and he cocked back his fist to punch out the windshield. The car braked before he could complete the punch. The man flew from the hood like a missile, striking a pack of screaming fashionables in front of him. They went down in a tangle of limbs and gears that was quite gratifying to run down.

Now a cyclist was directly in front. The car roared forward into a space cleared by fleeing bikes. He sideswiped the bike, but the cyclist had tried to pull away at the last second, losing his balance for his trouble. He tumbled to his side. The toe clips on one of his shoes didn't detach, so when the cycle caught in the car's undercarriage, he was dragged along. His expensive low friction clothing was ripped against the road in a few seconds and his skin began to flay.

The cyclist screamed.

As fun as it was, the howling rider was dead weight and the black car sped up. For a minute the cycle wouldn't detach. Finally, the car accelerated savagely. The cyclist twisted and his leg gave way. It trailed behind the car for a while, sailing like a morbidly fresh foxtail that someone had tied too low. The ragged stump left punctuations of blood, like morbid musical notation, between the two red lines that the car had painted down Lamar for a full mile, like a trail leading back to hell.

It didn't take long for news of what was happening to filter up the ranks, though in the panicked thrust of information things were confused. It was a car, no, a semi-truck, no, a motorcycle gang. It was the cops. It was a shooter, it was a lone gunman and a pack. Some people from the back actually started calling people in the front, delivering sobbing, hysterical variants of information that were scarcely more accurate than the versions that had been filtered through twenty different panicked screaming matches.

Soon the rumors were drowned out by the fact of the thing. They had reached the part of Lamar that was a series of switch backs, so the fucking thing wasn't in sight yet, but it was loud. It sounded like half a dozen glass pack mufflers were buzzing in unison. It roared over the sound of screams, all the while its horn blurted out atonal, arrhythmic bleats that sounded to Georgette very much like laughter.

A look of panicked disbelief had latched itself on Caddie's face. Georgette couldn't blame her; part of her felt like she had discovered a rent in reality. A part of herself couldn't believe this was happening. But there was another part she was surprised to discover, and this part was not at all surprised. This part of herself had almost been expecting something like this. She had thought it herself, hadn't she, cycling was white magic? You couldn't use white magic without making the black powerfully jealous. That was one of the rules.

So, she was the one who had to make the call. "Break away!" she cried, "Get off the road." Some hadn't needed her advice; they were scattering toward the uphill side streets on their left, or down the hill to the strip of wooded park on their right. But there weren't enough of them. They were just shed hairs off a dog that was still running pretty much unheeded. She turned to Caddie, "If we can leave a core of about a hundred riders we can probably distract him long enough to let the others escape."

Her order snapped Caddie out of her fear. She dropped back to talk to her whips, and soon larger clumps of riders started to break away from the pack, led by determined lieutenants.

Georgette glanced at an upcoming street, one she knew well. There was a video store she liked to go to down there, a bakery and a small beer and wine store run out of a garage. She used to live in the neighborhood and she made it a point to visit this street often enough that they still knew her face. Exit stage left, she thought; but she didn't. She had a feeling that if she did, the thing in the car (because there was only one, and it was a car, she could see it in her mind, all the more brutal and ugly for affecting elegance) would follow her and run her down. And what was worse, it might not.

So, when another dozen broke away down the street she did not follow them. Instead she bent forward and pumped her legs.

A road block ahead had obviously been set up for them, to block their way downtown and divert them into the nearby suburban neighborhood where they would be less of a nuisance.

But now plans had changed. Frantic calls had gone out to 911, and though what they were facing was unclear—they hadn't even had time to set up tire strips—it had become clear that something had gone terribly wrong. A space had been made between two sawhorses, backed up by two black and white SUVs. Two cops flanked the hole, frantically waving the riders through, worry approaching panic on their broad faces. Four other cops leaned against the hoods of the cars, propping shotguns and AR-15's against them, clearly hoping for backup.

Georgette was among the first past the barricade. She made a sharp left out of the way, stopping just short of the sidewalk as other riders went whickering past her in a panic. The cops had too much on their hands to tell her to do the same. She craned forward on her pedals trying to get her first look at the thing over the moving sea of people in front of her.

All at once, the car rumbled into view, reeling its way around the blind corner of a wooded bluff. It ran down a frantically peddling woman, there one second and then gone under the car's tires, spit out on the other side out of sight.

"Holy fuck," one of the cops said.

"Don't fire," said the one with sergeant stripes in a panicked voice, visions of the five o'clock news dancing in his head. "There's no way we could hit it without injuring civilians."

The car was black, Georgette saw, but from the way it gleamed in the afternoon sun she knew it was covered in gore. It looked brutal, like something a caveman would paint on the wall if you gave him a model of a Studebaker. Already, she could see the highlight of silver at the end of its hood. A cackling bitch of a memento mori, its prophecy come true a hundred times over that day.

"Does this crazy son of a bitch think he can get away?" another of the cops asked, and Georgette thought she heard something like awe in his voice.

The car fifty yards away roared forward, splitting the crowd in two, eager to get at more challenging prey. Escaping riders poured off its flanks and the car showed no inclination to pursue. For the first time Georgette was able to see the grim red stripes it was painting down the road. She threw up, brushed the vomit off her chin and looked up again.

An empty corridor had appeared between the car and the roadblock. With a gore-covered bruiser of a car hurtling at them at seventy miles an hour, the cops apparently decided the potential rewards of semi-automatic weapons fire now outweighed the risks. All four guns fired at once. Georgette covered her ears and winced.

Sparks flew off the hood and bounced off the rubber of the tires with a dull thunk. But there was no screech of metal rims suddenly connecting with the unforgiving road, no jets of flame spurting from the ruptured hood, no long vicious spider webs in the windshield. Instead the car just roared forward, bleating a staccato burst of triumph with its horn.

"How?" Georgette heard one of the cops say in the moment before impact, but by then she was riding again, past the survivors, trying to retake her place at the head of the pack. Her thighs were burning with the effort, so much adrenaline pumping through her like fire ants were marching through her veins. That black car was no ordinary car. The doubters would talk later about reinforcements and new forms of bullet proof glass she was sure, but Georgette had never been one to disbelieve her own eyes. Whatever that fucking thing was, it had never rolled off of any assembly line in this world. It wasn't some psychotic gearhead's twisted custom job. This thing had emerged whole and black and smoking from some dark place, and it wasn't going anywhere until it had slaked its thirst. Or until someone made it go away.

As she peddled, she found her legs were churning to a rhythm, and it was one she recognized. It was a song from the Disney version of *The Legend of Sleepy Hollow*. She had worn out the library's VHS copy, watching it on her own or sandwiching it between late afternoon double features with her father, sitting on his lap while watching wide-eyed the hot rod horrors of *I Was a Teenage Werewolf* and *The Blob*. She remembered the advice delivered to poor old Ichabod by the townsfolk of Sleepy Hollow, who all seemed dedicated to the idea of scaring the shit out of him at the local

Halloween dance.

The bridge.

Getting to the other side of a bridge.

A plan began to form in Georgette's mind. Who's to say what had worked for old Ichabod wouldn't work for her?

But then again it hadn't worked that well for Ichabod in the end, had it?

She banished that thought from her head with the simple mnemonic chorus. It worked rather well.

The men with the guns were no problem for the black car. They were traitors and the car dealt with them with the glee that all loyal creatures take against punishing traitors.

Most of the victims had dispersed by the time the car was done with them. That did not matter. Whether or not they lived, it would be a long, long time before they rode. But not all had fled. The car sensed that there was a small clump of about thirty cyclists still riding just a mile away now. A perfect group for one last charge. The car relished the pop of a very expensive helmet and the very cheap skull beneath it splitting under its tires. It ground what remained into the pavement, turning its wheel back and forth. Its treads had become sluices of blood. It sped over the last policeman with a primal roar, its horn bleating a warning for the last of its prey.

By the time Caddie caught up to her a half mile down the road, tears were streaming down her face. There was a gash on her scalp and blood was pouring down from the leather cap across her forehead. "There are so many," she said through a wracking sob. "So fucking many. . ."

Georgette couldn't say anything to that. There was nothing to say. She was amazed that they'd gotten off as lightly as they had. Most of the crowd had managed to escape, and that was no small thing considering how very much like a shooting gallery it had been there for a while.

"Wanna make the fucker pay?" Georgette asked. Caddie looked at her like she had suggested punching out God.

"How?"

Georgette gave her the broad outline of the plan.

Caddie looked at her like she was crazy. "Georgette, it's just some guy. . ." she said slowly, the voice you use on a mental patient holding a chainsaw in one hand and a kitten in the other.

"It'll still work if it's just some guy." Georgette said.

Caddie gave a grim nod.

At Lamar's halfway point was a long four-lane bridge that crossed the Colorado River. The remaining riders went right for it, cutting out the trip downtown by mutual consent. The black car was thundering heavy behind them. And the blaring yips of its horn sounded like the baying of eager hounds. If it wasn't all downhill, and unusually clear thanks to the roadblock and the demonstration, they never would have made it. They passed other cop cars on the way there, setting up another road block that would hopefully buy them some more time. It was in the trunk of one of these cop cars, left open and unattended, that Georgette saw what she needed. She screeched to a stop, leapt off her bike and slung it over her shoulder. She didn't know if the cry she heard for her to stop was real or a consequence of her high-strung nerves, but she didn't wait around to find out. She just kept speeding until she reached the bridge. The others blew past her. Caddie stopped. Georgette unslung a circle of tire spikes and held it while Caddie pulled it out. It probably wouldn't have earned them a passing grade at the academy, but it covered all four lanes.

Caddie hesitated but Georgette waved her on. "Just try and block traffic from the other side, see if you can get the others to help you. I don't want to be facing this thing and then get killed by some asshole in a Volvo."

Caddie gave a grim nod, and then held out her hand. Georgette shook it.

Georgette could see the black car now. It fishtailed slightly as it roared toward her, all the blood covering its tires apparently played hell with their traction; but it was still coming at her fast.

Georgette was shocked by how little fear she felt. It was there, sure; but it was consigned to one of her mind's back rooms, locked in a cage with the version of herself that screamed over and over again that this couldn't be happening and it wasn't fair and other unhelpful thoughts.

What gripped her was a kind of insane calm—a feeling that she had heard combat veterans describe on particularly beery nights—the feeling that this was all predestined, and it was time to walk through her paces. What would happen had already happened, so there was no point fucking worrying about it.

The black car stopped less than a hundred feet from her. It revved its engine, the low purr of a jungle cat. She was sure that it would have leapt forward and ground her corpse into the pavement if not for one thing. Georgette was standing on the bridge.

Fifteen feet below her was the bank of the Colorado River. Five feet beyond that was the water, placid, polluted and running. And there she was right at its very edge.

The car was holding itself back, but only just. It revved its engine in anticipation. It would come for her, Georgette was sure. Now that she was as close to the car as anyone had been without being run down, she could feel it. A dark intelligence, but one underwritten by a hate that was even darker. Even hungrier. This thing had just fed on dozens, if not hundreds, of human sacrifices, and it still wasn't satisfied. It could have her and a thousand more like her and it still wouldn't be enough. It would always be angry, always be hungry. It ran on blood, and its mileage wasn't anything to write home about.

She gripped the handlebars and gritted her teeth. This would be decided in a matter of seconds, whether she was a hero or just another name for the body count. "Come on," she groaned, unsure who she was talking to.

The car surged and exploded ahead. It hit the spikes. The tires spun the rubber away and rims met the road and started shooting up sparks. It looked like it was riding on wheels of fire, and the high whistling of metal on metal whirred beneath the sounds of its engine and the final unbroken bleat of triumph the horn was making.

It was expecting her to run. And if she had, it would have had her, closed the distance between her and river and taken her apart.

Instead, she rode toward it. She took one second to apologize to her rig, and then leapt from it.

The black car plowed into it her bike going fifty miles an hour, dragging the bike under it, where it added to the sparks that were now coming up in sheets. As Georgette rolled, tearing long strips of skin off her shins, knees and elbows, she heard it trying to brake. But metal doesn't get the same traction as rubber. The car was carried farther and farther on.

It jumped the sidewalk and broke apart the crumbling masonry that made up the edge of the bridge. For a moment, it stopped midway off the bridge, tottering, its momentum undecided. Georgette held her breath.

It began to tilt back.

With a growl like the cry of a predator who was about to be cheated out of her prey, Georgette rushed forward, shoving her shoulder against the back of the car, pushing like she never had before. Every hour she had spent peddling, every afternoon of thirty-mile rides—it all came forth. She pushed against hard unyielding metal, but she was just as unyielding.

The black car tottered and then plunged.

It hit nose first in the shallow waters just off the bank. She might have imagined it but she thought she heard a scream.

She had landed on her belly when the car gave way, and now she dragged herself forward so she could peer over the edge to watch it die.

The long nose of the car had crumpled, so now the windshield was level with the water. The destroyed engine was leaking something that looked a little bit like oil but wasn't, something that had a darkness and a density that oil could never match. The water around it was foaming and churning, and then the whole thing was dissolving, coming apart in great shuddering chunks, like it was made of soap.

Georgette watched it until it was gone.

She rolled over onto her back and a wide grin split her face. Already she could hear sirens.

Soon the authorities would be there, along with other people who would demand explanations for things that couldn't be explained.

That was alright. It was still in the future.

The Black Thumb

By Bonnie Jo Stufflebeam

Dawn planted her potatoes with carefully gloved hands. In her cabinet the potatoes had sprouted the necessary eyes; she sliced them into quarters and shoved them deep underground. She stood back and peered over the rows of grave mounds. This garden would be a thing of beauty. She wanted more.

From the mess of cash in her money jar, Dawn pulled a hundred dollar bill. Her parents' death, four years ago, left Dawn with nothing but the memory of their money. Nineteen when it happened, she was not to blame. The inheritance they'd left her meant she wouldn't have to work for a good long while. She hid her money in her jar and spent it only on essentials: bills, food and plants.

Dawn slipped on her black outing gloves, climbed into her rusted white truck and drove to the nursery. Walking through the rows of marigolds, the lines of just-flowering lemon trees, she inhaled their lingering sweetness, nauseating, like apples too ripe to eat. When she found the vegetables, warmth spread up her arms. These were plants worth more than beauty. She picked through them until she located the best, chosen for how they spoke to her, the bend of their leaves rather than the strength of their spines. Three of each: zucchini, bell pepper, tomato, okra and a bag of onion bulbs to fill the bald spots.

The cashier at the counter took her money but didn't look her in the eye. Instead she stared at Dawn's cloaked fingers as they groped the cardboard trays. In town no one spoke to her with her black gloves and hair, ratty and long like a child's Halloween witch wig. As a little girl she'd been called striking. Now she was considered disquieting. The cashier handed Dawn her receipt.

When Dawn turned away from the counter, she was startled by the man before her. His hair was prematurely thinning in front and lay flat and thin upon his egg-shaped head. He wore a red vest and blue shorts; his name tag told her his name was "George."

"Hi," he said in his thick Texas twang. "My name is George."

"I see that," she said.

"Let me help you carry those." He reached for the tray.

"I've got it," she said. "But there's more on the counter. You can carry those."

He helped her load the truck bed. "Do I know you?" he asked.

"I doubt it." She heaved herself into the truck

"No, I'm sure—"

Dawn slammed the door and jammed her key in the ignition. His face wilted in the rearview mirror. Her stomach dropped—a twinge of pity—but she didn't want to talk. Sooner or later the conversation would turn to the same old shit: her parents, the gloves, why didn't she stop by the church sometime, take an interest in the Lord? Everyone in this town said the same old things.

George stepped out of the way as she popped the truck into reverse and sped from the parking lot, leaving the dust to settle across the top of his tennis shoes.

At home Dawn lined the plants beside the garden. She shoveled holes in the dirt and stuck her fist into them. Through the gloves she could barely feel the cold life of the earth and the warmth of the air around her.

Once the garden was littered with holes, she pried the peppers from their plastic containers, ripped the roots apart and placed them into the ground like a matching game: which plant to which hole? A city of plants began to be born. She imagined each newcomer as a neighbor.

Dawn hoped she would avoid an encounter with her human neighbor. She'd never met the man and tried to avoid the yard when she heard the creak of his chair on the porch or the growl of his mower. She had only seen him a couple of times from her window, raking leaves. Once he was walking to his car. She knew the pattern of his coming and going from the times of day she heard his car start in the morning and roll back into the driveway around sunset. She'd be okay for a few more hours.

She moved spider-like on her arms and legs, creeping from one side of the garden to the other, and by midday she had planted all but the tomatoes and the onions. She ripped open the bag of onion bulbs and began to fill the bare spots. The tomatoes would fill three large plastic pots she had set closer to the fence of her backyard. The bulbs' skin crackled as her fingers pressed them, a much better sound than the twitter of the blue jay in the tree above her or the buzz of bees in a patch of lavender beside her, sounds she could not control. When the bag was emptied, Dawn scooped the dirt back over the bulbs.

Then she saw the peppers. Where moments before the leaves had been green, they were now brown and brittle. She crawled to them. Her glove brushed one of the leaves, and it fell dead to the ground. All the plants were dead.

Her heart skipped a beat. It was eerie, being so close to the recently deceased, as if the plant's presence still lingered in the dirt. She scanned the garden for a culprit but saw nothing. With a sinking stomach, she examined her gloves. Sure enough, there was a hole right on the base of her middle finger. Her skin had touched the plants. They would all soon wither the way of the peppers, their roots trying to spit out the poison, the dirt tainted too. All that time, wasted. She had cared too much for a bunch of stupid plants.

Her stomach twisted and gurgled like she might throw up. She gripped a bell pepper by the throat and ripped it from the ground. It shuddered in her palm; its roots hung in thin, rotten strings. She tossed it aside and glared up at the blaring sun.

"Godamnit," she said. She pounded the dirt with her fists. She'd show the dirt how little it was worth if it couldn't even keep the things inside of it alive. By the time she unclenched her fists, she was weak as dead vegetables.

"Why, hello there," the man said. Dawn lay still in the dirt. She looked up, blinked dirt from her eyes. The man's squat form made him look like a frog. He wore a red vest and blue shorts. "Are you okay, ma'am?" When she didn't respond, he continued. "I knew I'd seen you. George, from the nursery. Remember?" He reached out his hand.

"Don't touch me," she said.

He folded his arms across his chest. "Well, all right. I didn't mean you no harm."

He paused as if waiting for her to apologize. The skin around his knuckles was scarred and red. Half of her didn't want him to go, didn't want to be alone. Suddenly she was aware of her heartbeat. She didn't like the tone it was taking with her. The only way she could think of to make it shut up was to say something.

"Just please don't touch me," she said.

He nodded. "You sure you're okay?"

"I fell," she said. "I'm sorry. I'm fine. I was just doing some gardening. I got tired."

He scanned the garden. Dawn hadn't quite realized that her garden was something others could see too. She felt protective, as if she should've put a cage around it. "Doesn't look like your garden's doing too well," he said.

"I know."

He reached his hand out to her again, palm open. She brought her nose closer, as if she were a cat and this his offering of peace, but she didn't take it. Instead she hoisted herself up.

"Guess you're that neighbor woman I never met." He chuckled. "Uncanny coincidence. I don't see you out here much."

"I keep to myself."

George kept smiling, peering into her eyes as though he wanted her to smile back. She couldn't make herself smile, but her gaze kept returning to those hands, how the skin rose and fell like a topographical map. She asked him if he'd like a cup of tea. There was a table in her back yard, and if he wanted she could pop inside, fix the tea, and bring it out. He accepted, and she left him at the table and went inside to the kitchen.

The teapot was dusty; she rinsed it off, put the water on to boil, went to the window and watched him at her table. Although she couldn't see the front of his face, she could tell he was still smiling from the bulbs of his cheeks. She still didn't know quite what to think of the man or the fact that he was on her small patch of land, seated in her lawn chair, about to touch her mug with his lips. It had been a while since she had entertained. Since the car crash, the funeral, when she'd been forced to accept visitors and their gifts of grief. She had made sure not to let them touch her, had even worn one of her mother's old hats with the veil across the face. It had been easier to hide in the shadow of tragedy.

The teapot whistled, and Dawn forced herself away from the window and fixed two mugs of blueberry tea. She set one mug in front of him, set one in front of the chair in which she would sit and muttered an insincere apology for the lack of sugar or honey. The breeze intruded on the silence that followed when she lifted the cup to her lips and drank, only to find it so hot it scorched the roof of her mouth. George didn't drink.

"What happened to your garden?"

Dawn tried to look as emotionless as possible. "It just died. I planted everything this morning, and then it all just died."

"This morning?" he said. "So those were the plants you bought?" A confused look passed over his face. "Well, maybe it's just the heat, or your soil, or maybe you were too rough with the roots. Did you water right after you transplanted?"

Dawn said she did, of course she did, though she hadn't actually had the chance. It didn't really matter. She knew what was wrong.

"It's me," Dawn said. "I'm not good with plants."

"I doubt that. That's the easy way out." He looked down into his tea like he was considering taking a sip. He didn't. "You know, I've always had great luck with gardens. I grew up on a farm. I could help you plant another, if you'd like."

"You grew up on a farm?"

"Yeah, but it wasn't for me, exactly. I like plants all right, but I wanted to be closer to people and farther from corn. I haven't had a chance this year, but usually I pot a couple tomatoes and cucs over on the other side of my fence. It would be real easy, between the two of us."

"No, I don't think so."

"Well, okay," George said. "Sometimes it's hard to start over." He looked at her hands, at the gloves. "You know what I mean?" He looked at his own hands, lifted the tea to his lips then set the cup down.

"What happened to your hands?" Dawn asked, surprised at the ease with which she found herself prying.

"Fire," he said. "The farm, it burned."

Dawn struggled to find something to say.

"Like I said, it wasn't for me," he said. He rose from his seat. "Welp, I best be headed in now. But I'm awful sorry about your vegetables." He held his hand out again, but Dawn didn't dare shake it. After a moment, he let it fall to his side, and he left her yard through the chain link gate, pausing only to take a final glance at the garden.

Even though the garden was dead, Dawn continued to water it. She woke early each morning for the next week and went out to her back yard, turned on the hose and aimed it over the upturned earth and let the water drench the dirt. She didn't bother planting the tomatoes; she left them in their little black containers, knowing full well that they would outgrow them and wither like the rest. She liked knowing that it was up to her whether they would live or die.

About a week after their first meeting, George again caught her by surprise in her garden. She was in the middle of watering, and he leaned over the fence and stared, making no move to speak. She dropped the hose. His left fist was closed beside him, and he unfolded his fist so she could see what was inside: a handful of seeds. "I brought you these," he said. He thrust his palm closer. "Go on, take them."

She didn't.

"They're for you," he said.

He was so eager, and she felt rude standing there, so she

opened her hand and let him drop the seeds into it. She closed her eyes as she felt the seeds fall against her uncovered skin, and the touch of his hand, however brief, made her wince.

Dawn opened her eyes. She knew what was about to happen. She would show him. She would scare him away. He would never come back. Her fingers closed around the seeds. There was a sizzle, barely audible. When she opened her fist again, most of the seeds were black.

George looked at them, eyebrows furrowed. "Guess they were bad seeds. I'm sorry."

He reached, but she flipped her palm upside down and let them fall. They scattered among the grass.

"I think it's time for me to go," she said.

"I'll get more for you. I didn't mean to—"

"You should go too." She marched through the overgrown grass to the door.

Once inside, collapsed on her bed, she heard George's car start down the road, then nothing. The silence closed in on her; she felt trapped by it. The secret she had wanted to tell him was lost: I'm poison. She buried her head in her pillow and breathed in the scent of fabric softener. Dawn had always wanted to make something beautiful, to put a seed into the earth with her bare hands and make something of it. At first she had hated hiding herself away in her musty old house, far from human touch. Then, after some time, she learned to accept the darkness and even to love it, to cradle it close to her and block out the sunlight. She hung thick black curtains in her bedroom and left the world alone.

Now, though, her body ached. She thought of George's hands, and the seeds, and the parched way he looked at her. It was dangerous to think of George. She tried to think only of her future, of the loneliness she'd grown accustomed to her whole life. There was something comforting in knowing she would never be able to lead a normal life. At least she knew which way she was headed. That was more than most people could say.

Evenings for Dawn were always the same, a routine she'd had

since childhood, left with a huge empty house, her parents out late working, her food prepared for her by a cook who paid her little mind. As Dawn sat down to her routine meal of plain chicken and plain potatoes, she heard a knock at her door. She peeked through the peephole, but all she saw was a blurry face behind the lens.

She let him in.

George looked worn; his hair stood straight up, as if electricity were surging through it, and there were bags below his eyes. His jeans were wrinkled, his shirt untucked.

One look at his droopy expression, the fallen features of his face, and Dawn's stomach sunk. She didn't know what she was doing. It was as if another person invited him inside. He slid into her house, and she crossed her arms. This was all so dangerous, she thought, just one lingering touch, and that would be the end of these knots in her stomach, the end of his goofy southern drawl.

"Please listen to me," George said. "Just give me a chance."

Dawn studied him with apprehension.

"You see, I think you're beautiful. And mysterious. I can't stop thinking about you, ever since I saw you collapsed, there in your garden, and, Dawn, well, you see, I get so lonely sometimes."

He took a step forward, arm outstretched. His fingers came close to her cheek, still streaked with dirt.

"No, wait," she said.

"I want to be with you." He grabbed hold of her arm and pulled her to him. Dawn struggled to keep her feet rooted in the carpet, but he was stronger than her, and she felt herself being ripped from her roots.

"I'm dangerous," she said. "Let go."

"We're outcasts, you and me. We belong together." He pushed her head to his chest; she couldn't move, couldn't breathe. "I know you're scared of letting people in. But I care about you."

The human half of her rattled the bars of its cage. She wished he could peel away her layers button by button, wished it were that simple, wished the world were as gentle as a garden in the morning light. But he was hurting her, and too many people had hurt her.

"I want you," he said. She heard his heart repeat it: *I want you, I want you, I want you.* She wanted to make it stop.

"I'm poison," she said, but it came out wrong, a breathless croak.

"Shut up," he said. He grabbed her chin and forced her face to look up into his. She stared into his broken bits of green, too much want there for one person to ever fill. Something else, too: hate. Did he hate her, as everyone else seemed to hate her?

She opened her lips to say it again, but he pushed his lips hard against hers and clutched the tangles of her hair in his fist. Dawn felt her eardrums pulse, and she could smell the faint stink of sweet summer air. Heat rose off of him and made her blush bright red. He fell with a great thud. She stared down at his limp body, the wilted arms and legs. She crawled beside him. His eyes were open, pupils wide, swallowing every last drop of color that only seconds before seemed so permanent.

Dawn let her hands trace the rough terrain of his hands. She put her ear to his naked chest to hear the sweet bump bump. All was quiet. She moved to kiss his lips. They were black as fertile soil.

A Drought Usually Ends with a Flood

By Stephen Patrick

Well-baked by the west Texas sun, the town of Prestige was not on Terry Milton's itinerary. Somewhere between El Paso and Odessa, he wasn't sure it was even on the map, but the faded green and yellow sign outside a roadside café promised the "last best cold drinks in Texas." A quick drink, maybe two, could give him one last bump before pushing home to Dallas. It might even give him a chance for one last sale on this trip. In a perfect world, he'd earn enough to buy Suzie that shiny ballerina dress, just in time for her birthday.

Sitting in his car in the dusty parking lot, he studied his face in the rear-view mirror, rehearsing his pitch one last time. His blue eyes were a bit bloodshot and surrounded by more wrinkles than he liked, but the crystalline money-makers still had the dazzle that made the girls swoon in high school. He practiced the intricate hand motions, voice inflections and even the slight eyebrow lift he had designed to mesmerize his marks and liberate them from their cash. "I don't sell magic," he announced, "I sell hope."

The Prestige diner was a simple shoebox design with cinder-block walls and a flat roof coated in tar that sizzled in the searing heat. A whitewashed wooden porch spanned the front, a throw-back to the Wild West, complete with broken boards and a few that twisted so hard, they looked designed to catch a cowboy's spurs. To the left of the diner, an old water tower silo lay on its side, rusting in the sun alongside a burned-out cinderblock structure whose only hint of its purpose or history lay in the shadows of the word "Auto" on the charred walls.

Terry grabbed a leather bag from the passenger seat and stepped into the west Texas heat. He stopped at the front bumper of his car, kneeling to pull the cuff of his slacks over his cowboy boots. Two pieces of white gravel caught his eye, gleaming amid the shades of gray. He grabbed both and tucked them into his pocket.

A brass chime announced his entrance into the diner. The place was long lost from time, forgotten rather than nostalgic, with none of the Route 66 memorabilia that adorned most roadside diners. Instead, the walls offered a dust-covered overview of the town's history, including a rail boom, the earthquake that sent the silo on its side and a series of fires that had eaten away the last vestiges of hope in the town. A yellowed newspaper clipping announcing the fifth straight year without water was also tacked to the wall.

A waitress leaned against the bar near the cash register, her thin hands mindlessly wiping the counter with a soiled rag. Her name tag read "Ida" and though she was dressed like a young woman, her eyes told Terry she was closer to fifty. A thin gold chain around her neck held a green plastic pendant and a very real diamond wedding ring. The pendant looked enough like a jewel to fool most people, but Terry could see the rough edges of a molded charm sold by mail to bring good fortune to "those who believe." A mis-sized wig completed a portrait of a woman committed to maintaining an appearance, but with few resources and skills to make the masquerade work.

Two old men sat at the end of the counter, slumped over plates of toast and eggs. Duke Ramirez and August Pogue were dressed like farmers, but their boots had seen more dust than soil. Sun-scorched faces revealed a lifetime of outdoor labor, although neither man had harvested a crop in nearly ten years. They were sharing a newspaper, both skimming the obituary pages for people they knew.

Terry took the stool beside them and turned toward Ida. "Can

I get something to drink?"

She grabbed a can of Pepsi from behind the counter and slide it in front of him. He instinctively popped it open and took a sip, quickly realizing that it was hot.

"No ice," said Ida, "On account we don't have any water." She wiped down the counter again, removing a wide arc of dust that had followed Terry into the diner.

Terry sipped slowly at the warm soda. The warm liquid sucked the life from him, but at least it was wet.

Duke spun his seat around to face Terry.

"So, what's your story, chief?" A thin trickle of tobacco juice navigated the creases down his chin. "Any time a stranger stops by, I figure he's here to sell me something. Am I right?"

"Good guess," answered Terry. He lifted his case onto the counter, draping his arm over it while sliding a business card toward the men. Shiny purple letters read: "Hope comes to those who believe! Terry Milton, purveyor of the supernatural."

"Bullshit," snorted Duke. "All bullshit. I don't need no more bullshit. You ain't trying to bullshit us, are ya, boy?"

Terry thought about opening the case, but the men seemed a bit too ornery and likely too light in the wallet to be worth his time. "Just hope," answered Terry, "that's it."

"Don't let him get to you," said August, leaning around Duke. "He hates strangers as much as he hates his friends."

August braced himself with a cane and staggered past Duke to the stool on the other side of Terry. He collapsed against it, holding his quivering right elbow. "Damn arthritis. The doctors can't do anything to help."

August ran his fingers over Terry's card. "Ain't no strangers come to town unless they're offering to help. Is that why you're here?"

"Help is what I do," Terry answered. "I give people hope."

"I'm seventy-five-years-old, my wife and sons are dead. I've got a bum arm so I can't even cut down my dead crops in this cursed hell hole. What hope should I have, Mr. Milton?"

"Hope can't be lost," said Terry, lifting his eyebrow just a little. "Sometimes, we just forget where we left it." He reached into his bag, keeping his eyes locked on the men. Deep in the shadows of the case, he opened a plastic box and palmed a small wad of cloth. He turned back to August, leaning across the dusty counter. "Do you want to hope again?"

"Mister, I'm no fool. I only trust what I can see and feel."

"Then find your hope in what you feel." Terry grabbed August's arm at the elbow, his fingers digging into the bulging mass of gnarled flesh. He gripped hard, pressing his palm flat against August's skin.

August screamed. "What the hell? You're burning my arm.!" He tried to pull away, but Terry held him tight.

"Do you believe?" Terry asked.

"My arm is on fire!" answered August.

"Do you believe?" Terry asked again, his eyes now locked on August's with the familiar dazzle he had used so many times.

Terry released him and August collapsed over the counter. The old man stared at his arm, feeling life return to the swollen tissue. He wiggled his arm, waving his hand around. He jabbed at the air like a boxer and chased Duke from his stool.

While Duke and August dueled in front of the bar, Terry slowly slid his hands into his lap and wiped the clear gel from his palm. The familiar numbness in his palm from the mixture of oleoresin capsicum and a mild opiate usually meant a sure sale.

August held out his right hand, wriggled his fingers and then snaked out his wallet from his back pocket. He plucked a twenty-dollar bill and slapped it on the counter. "This town's been desperate for a man like you."

Ida leaned across the counter, her rag removing a new arc of dust. "Desperate don't mean we're stupid. Parlor tricks ain't gonna save this town."

Terry turned toward her, his eyes catching the pendant hanging from her neck. "It's not about tricks. It's about hope. What are you hoping for? What dream lies just beyond your reach?"

"Leave this town alone," she hissed.

August and Duke made for the door, laughing like schoolboys during summer break. "Don't mind Ida," said August. "Ever since her boy disappeared, she's been trying to save us from ourselves. Thinks she can save this town by drowning it in her grief."

The door chimed as the men left. The diner fell silent, even the sands outside stopped swirling.

"I know why you're here," said Ida. "I know who sent you."

"Listen, I just came in for a drink. I don't want any trouble, but I did help that man."

"August Pogue's a fool, and Duke's no better." She stared at the rag in her hand. "This town is cursed. The whole thing's already taken one big step toward Hell. Five years ago, my boy disappeared and the water around here turned to blood. Then the crops turned to dust. We're just marking time, waiting for our turn with the reaper. We've no use for someone like you, trying to take advantage of us."

"You want to believe, don't you?" Terry grabbed his case. "That's why you wear the pendant? I've seen them before. I've even sold a few. Someone promised you it would let you talk to him again, didn't they?"

"Get out!" she screamed, stabbing her rag toward the door and filling the air with a fresh cloud of dust.

Terry grabbed his bag and walked toward the door. He stopped at the register, leaving a dollar on the counter. "It doesn't work, does it?" he asked. As he looked down at her pendant, he pulled two of the rocks from his pocket and set them on top of the dollar. "Armenian Soul Stones. Rub one between your hands and the answers you seek will appear on the smooth side. It only works once, so I'll leave you a spare."

As Terry's car pulled away from the diner, he rubbed his burning fingers against the steering wheel. He reached for a water bottle in the center console, forgetting it had been empty since El Paso. One more thing he forgot to do at the diner.

He was still an hour out of Odessa, which meant six hours to Dallas. Good traffic would put him at the door just after Suzie had finished saying her prayers. Andrea would be mad if he woke her up; he hadn't seen his wife or daughter in nearly two weeks.

As he settled in for the drive, a dust storm swept across the road. Terry's windshield wipers were no match for the swirling sand and his view turned into a thick mixture of white and tan. Terry's car began to sputter, the engine struggling as sand choked through the air intakes. He pulled to the side of the road and the engine died, stealing the fresh air when his air conditioner went silent. He cranked the engine, managing to score two coughs before it stopped. He tried again: *click, click, cough, sputter*—nothing. He didn't want to burn out the battery, so he reclined his seat, lay back, closed his eyes and waited on the storm to pass.

He began to drift off as the sand tickled the windows of his car, a staccato rattle that became soothing as the temperature slowly rose. He felt the sleep coming, but a tap at his driver's-side window pulled him from it. A shadow filled the window, including a long skinny finger that tapped again and made a circular motion. Terry rolled the window down a half inch, letting a tiny shower of sand fall into the car. Outside, the storm had stopped, but his car was coated in a thick layer of dust and sand. Terry blinked through the haze wafting into his car, but could make out a sheriff's badge on the man's chest. The man was tall and skinny, looking barely strong enough to stand upright beneath the badge. His sunken face was hidden behind a bushy moustache and a dirt-stained Stetson sat off-center on his head. He rested his left hand on the grip of the holstered pistol hanging low on his hips. "You Terry Milton?" the man asked.

"How did you know my name?"

The officer held Terry's business card in his hand. He looked Terry over, settling his gaze on Terry's bag. "Is that your bag of tricks, Mr. Milton?"

"I didn't mean any harm," said Terry. "I'm just heading for home."

"Ida said you gave her some sort of magic rock."

"Actually, it's an Armenian Soul Stone."

"Just like the others in her parking lot?"

"I paid for my drink, officer. I figured the stones made a nice tip. I didn't even charge the old man for helping his arm."

"I'm going to need you to come with me."

"I'd rather not. I'm running way behind schedule. Can you just write me a ticket or something, so I can get on my way?"

The officer leaned on Terry's door, his hand sending a new spray of sand down into Terry's window. "This sand out here can kill a man as fast as it kills an engine. It can take hours to get a tow truck out here."

"Am I under arrest?"

"We all have hard choices to make in life. Maybe I should put you in jail, maybe charge you with some petty crime. Or maybe I could leave you out here in the desert, where people get lost all the time, their bones worn away by the sand until there's nothing left."

"Are you threatening me?"

"I'm offering you an opportunity. Someone like you might call it 'hope'."

The brass bell at the Prestige chimed as Terry stepped inside. He stumbled forward, courtesy of a push from the sheriff, who then forced Terry onto the first stool and slammed his case down onto the counter. August and Duke looked up from a half-eaten plate of pickled okra.

"Is this him?" the sheriff asked.

"Yes!" screamed August. "That's the one!"

Duke stabbed a long slender finger at Terry, but said nothing. Ida, still standing at her counter, nodded, then returned to her duties. Four other men in overalls stood up from their tables and stepped closer, surrounding a woman in an ankle-length dress near the cash register. A frail-looking couple moved in front of them, holding hands beneath matching cowboy hats.

The sheriff unlatched Terry's bag and set it open on the floor in front of them. "Do it again, Mr. Milton! Amaze us! Sell us your hope!"

Terry knelt over his bag, running his hands over an assortment of glass vials, cardboard boxes and zip-loc bags filled with plastic stones.

The sheriff stepped back, letting the crowd move closer, encircling Terry. Instead of anger or fear, the faces around him were bright and smiling, shining despite the desolation etched into their eyes. Terry took a deep breath, feeling a calm come over him as he started his usual pitch. "What I offer," he continued, his voice resuming its polished cadence, "is hope. Hope for health and better times."

Terry pulled an assortment of crystals, gems and bottles from his bag. They shimmered in his hands as he twirled them. "Aches, pains, fortune, fame. I have something for everyone. You just have to believe."

Like an orchestra conductor, his hands moved in mesmerizing patterns, divining the pains of those around him and describing the "perfect cure" for each one. A balm for a bum knee. A tonic powder for marks on the skin, even an elixir that promised to solve halitosis and balding for women. As he worked, the door chimed and the crowd grew, until the two dozen residents of Prestige stood around him. The sheriff watched from the perimeter, and Terry waited for the law to come crashing down upon him.

Instead, Terry saw crooked men stand up straight. He watched moles and warts fall from skin with a swipe of a hand. Two women were amazed when their white hair sloughed off beneath their bonnets, forced out by the growing blonde locks beneath. Each person came demanding relief from an affliction and each left with a miracle, exchanged eagerly for the cash filling Terry's pockets.

The longer he talked, the higher the prices soared until Terry had sold everything in his bag, even the plastic packaging from a deck of cards that he re-christened as 'containers of good energy' that sent one man cartwheeling across the gravel lot.

As darkness fell on the diner, the sheriff cut through the crowd, drawing a chorus of groans from Terry's now-loyal followers. "We need to talk."

While the crowd slinked away, the sheriff escorted Terry behind the diner into a white-washed building with a star hanging from a single nail above the door. The sheriff directed Terry to a wooden bench facing a large tan desk, also etched with the sheriff's star. The lawman sat behind the desk, in front of a series of framed photos showing the past six sheriffs, three of which bore a striking resemblance to the man staring back at Terry. There was a soft creak, followed by the sound of boots hitting the hardwood floor. The sheriff stopped in front of Terry and leaned back against the front of the desk.

"Hope, Mr. Milton? Isn't that your trade?"

"I guess you've read my business card. What do you think?"

"From the look of your car, your case and what I found from calling the county, you're barely making a living. Divorced father of two, bankruptcy twice over. Your mailing address is a hotel."

"When you say it like that, I guess I'm on a roll," answered Terry.

"So, how do you explain it? Your 'roll'?"

"I'm not sure I can, but I won't look a gift horse in the mouth."

The sheriff scowled. "Do you believe in what you're selling?"

"I've learned that it doesn't matter if I do."

"Does that include the Armenian Soul Stones?"

"You saw it, same as me."

"Mr. Milton, the people of Prestige are a bit . . . simple. You might call us superstitious. We hang horseshoes from the doors and abide by old wives' tales, anything to keep from tempting fate. Doing so has kept us right by the forces of the world and kept our town alive."

"It doesn't look too alive to me."

"Five years ago, Ida's son fell into the well by the cemetery."

"She said he disappeared."

"We never found his body, but when we dredged the water, the water had turned as dark and vile as the stuff in the devil's veins. I called it in to the authorities, but the only response we got was from two men in suits carrying suitcases full of cash and a handful of contracts and documents. Kinda like you, they promised to save this town. They offered folks a new life, even offered to buy up "cursed" land. They said the cash was just incidental, a way to help out during the crisis. All they asked was a bit of silence about what was going on, "to keep the curse from spreading," Most folks took the money, but a few of the old timers won't ever leave. Ida wasn't gonna leave her home without her boy, and it didn't seem right to leave them without a lawman, so I stayed here, too. Soon as the suits left, the crops died and then the earth began to fall out from under us. Sinkholes popped up everywhere, sometimes more than one in a single day. A pair of them swallowed up Old Man Jenkins' prize cows and the worst ones tore open the cemetery.

"Water into blood, blight and pits down to Hell? You make it sound pretty biblical. What does that have to do with me?

"It's not about you, but about your magic. The town's full of foolish believers. Most will believe anything, but I trust what I see. We've been waiting for a savior. Someone to save us. What I saw out there tells me you're the one with the magic to make this right.

"Are you saying you believe?"

"It don't matter what I believe. I'm saying I need hope, and that's what you sell, right?"

"What's in it for me?"

"The satisfaction of saving a cursed town."

"And my fee?"

"If you can lift the curse, you can keep what you've taken so far, plus anything else these people want to give. Otherwise, you're spending the night in jail and I'm confiscating everything."

With Terry handcuffed in the back seat of the car, the sheriff picked up Ida from the diner. He drove away from the highway toward a blackened forest of dead mesquite trees. As they drove, Terry saw sinkholes dotting the land like fingerprints pressed into the dry soil and parched crops withered to dust. Beneath the trees, rows of cracked marble headstones stood up like jagged teeth, sunk in at odd angles and daring the wind to knock them over. The sheriff drove past the cemetery, and stopped at a small gray cylinder jutting up from the ground. It was a stone and mortar well, covered with weather-worn boards nailed haphazardly across the top.

"We boarded it up after the boy disappeared," said the sheriff, tugging at the ends of one board. It snapped in his hands and he tossed it aside. Another board cracked and splintered before tearing free from the well. Once the well was exposed, he motioned for Terry to come closer.

Terry looked over the edge, watching dust drift down and disappear into the darkness. "Now what?" he asked.

"Do your magic," said the sheriff, pointing down into the well.

Ida stepped between them, still wearing her apron from the diner. "How are you going to reverse the curse, Mr. Milton?"

Terry set his hands on the rim. "You say the water turned to blood?" A stone along the edge broke loose and fell into the darkness. "Most curses can be undone the way they were done."

"It's a blood curse," said Ida.

The sheriff reached over the edge, holding a bucket. "I figure you'll want to see this for yourself." He lowered the bucket, letting the rope slip quickly though his fingers into the darkness until it went slack in his hands. "That's the bottom."

"Pull it up!" said Ida. "Then he'll see."

The sheriff tugged at the rope, but it did not move. "It's stuck.

Maybe we should both try?"

The sheriff stepped back, handing the rope to Terry. Terry set both feet against the edge of the well and his shoes dug into the crumbling mortar between the stones. The sheriff grabbed the rope behind him, pulling it taut.

Moving to the opposite side of the well, Ida stared down into the darkness.

Terry pulled against the rope, but it did not move. He tugged again, straining more until he heard a crack beneath his feet. The edge of the well fractured beneath Terry's shoes, shattering the mortar between each stone. Terry let go of the rope, his legs churning as the stones fell forward out from under him and into the well. The earth gave way, the world falling out from under Terry. He turned and reached toward the sheriff, but he was too slow.

The walls of the well collapsed. Terry clawed at the stones and even the rope, but could not find a grip. His fingers scraped at the rough stones and dirt, still he felt everything give way beneath him.

He hit bottom with a dull splash. A bolt of pain raced up his left leg, and his momentum carried him forward, where he buried his face in a swirling dark muck.

Terry pushed himself up out of the water and wiped the mess from his bleeding face. The air was thick with the cloying odor of copper and rot. The ground moved around him, undulating like it was alive. Terry tasted copper with each new breath, and his left arm was numb from the shoulder down. The pain in his left leg told him it was broken.

"Mr. Milton?" asked the sheriff from above. "Are you okay?"

Terry rolled over to his right side, craning his neck up toward the tiny beam of light shining into the well. "I think my leg is busted." His voice wobbled from the pain. "Can you call for help?"

"Do you see the blood?" asked Ida.

"Yeah. Lots of it." Terry wiped a thick wad of fluid from his mouth, hoping to erase the acrid taste. "Some of it is mine."

He scooped some of the ooze with his good hand and held it to the thin shaft of light coming down from above. As it seeped through his fingers, he noticed the fluid was not thick like blood, but clear, leaving behind a grainy red sediment as it seeped from his fingers.

This isn't blood, he thought. It's just minerals, maybe chemicals, something seeping into the water.

"It's not blood. It's some sort of pollution, maybe a toxic spill or something."

Above him, stones continued to rain down, forcing him against the side of the well. The noxious water splashed up around him. He rolled to his left and then climbed up on the pile of stones gathering at the edge of the well bottom.

"Get me out of here before this thing collapses!" screamed Terry.

Ida leaned over the well. "How do you reverse a blood curse, Mr. Milton?" she asked, her voice barely audible above the creaking stone.

"There's no blood in this water," said Terry, hoping his voice could reach the surface. "That means there's no curse. It's just a plain, old-fashioned . . ."

Terry's words were drowned by the splash of a large stone falling into the well. The limestone wall around him shuddered and another large section of well fell in with him. He crawled over the wet stones, trying to stay above the fallen rocks and climb toward the light. Terry missed one grip and felt his foot slip painfully out from beneath him. He fell back into the mud, rolling quickly to his left as three more stones slammed into the water and sprayed him with copper ooze.

One of the stones was bright white. He dove his hand into the sticky goo and wrapped his fingers around a small sphere. He plucked it free from the mud and found he was holding a small human skull. Ida's boy.

"You want a damned curse? Here's your damned curse. On

the skull of your dead son." He wiped his hand over it a few times, wiping the red ooze from it. "Curse lifted."

The rumbling continued and a fissure appeared above him, spreading quickly across the stone surface, a jagged lightning bolt of cracks racing toward the surface.

"Now, hurry up and get me out of here!" Terry screamed

"A blood curse has to be broken with blood," Ida answered.

"Why did you try to trick us, Mr. Milton?" the sheriff asked. *"Where is your magic now?"*

Another rock splashed into the wetness, spraying Terry with red. He wiped his eyes clean just in time to see the light above him disappear. The last two curved stone edges of the top of the well came loose and fell toward him.

Two months later, Ida was back at the diner, wiping a wide arc on the linoleum counter with a clean white rag. A thin layer of condensation covered the windows, courtesy of the twin air conditioning units mounted behind the diner. A refrigerated cabinet was stuffed with water bottles and a frost-covered cabinet beside the cash register offered homemade pies, complete with a scoop of vanilla Blue Bell ice cream. A wooden board hung above the register with the hand-painted word "Hope." On the wall behind the counter was a photo showing two men in suits shaking hands with Ida and the sheriff. It was mounted beneath a framed check for two million dollars and a series of new photos detailing the construction of the new water tower beside the diner.

The tables were full of tourists and travelers, even the bar was crowded. August and Duke, forced from their usual spots, sat in a booth reading the obituary pages from the newspaper.

"More iced tea, boys?" asked Ida, leaning over the table with a pitcher. Her other hand held a carafe of ice. "Maybe just a few new cubes to keep it cool?"

August waved her away and returned to the paper. Opposite the obits was a notice that listed a missing person from Dallas, a family man, last seen two months earlier.

While Duke sipped his warm tea, August flexed his right elbow, gritting his teeth to fight the pain that had returned. His left hand held a small grey stone. His fingers rubbed slowly across the surface, wondering why his arm had started hurting again.

El Sacoman

By Crystal Brinkerhoff

Israel's shirt clung to his back with sweat. Camilla flitted around the party with no signs of perspiration, but then she was the lucky one. *Abuela* had always said so.

Across the yard David laughed. Well-wishers and loved ones surrounded him, soaking up every last minute they had with him before he left for college next week. Israel was struck by how much better David was at relationships. That was Camilla's influence. Everything about today was Camilla's doing. And yet Israel still felt a real and tangible pride.

Camilla collapsed in the chair next to Israel with a cold drink in one hand. "That's one of David's teachers." She gestured discreetly to an attractive middle-aged woman among David's well-wishers. "She's single."

Israel shot his sister a look.

She laughed. "You should go say something to her. You're his dad. It wouldn't be weird."

He had noticed her.

Her light brown hair was pulled back to emphasize the slope of her neck. He'd noticed the way she held back, not quite comfortable drawing attention to herself in the group of younger people, but enjoying the gathering enough to stay on the fringes. It would be easy to go over and say something to her. He'd probably even like it. But he'd never admit that to Camilla. That part of his heart was locked down and closed off.

He was married.

David bounded over. "Mom, we're talking about going to see a movie later tonight. So, I won't be in until late."

Israel still bristled a little at the title for Camilla though David had used it for nearly fifteen years. She'd certainly earned it, he couldn't deny that. She'd taken David in and raised him in a caring and loving environment. She'd watched over his studies and taught him to embrace life. Israel was the first to admit it. But a part of him took satisfaction in the fact that David's eyes carried the mark of his Asian mother. His real mother.

A neighborhood cat jumped up on the food table. Camilla thrust her drink into Israel's hand to take care of the intruder.

Israel took a mouthful of the cold, soothing drink. "I'm heading over to the Millers' tomorrow if you want to come," he said to David. You could see Sam before you take off."

David hesitated. "I'm not sure how late I'm going to be out tonight."

Israel nodded. He'd tried to teach David the business for years. But David had decided that cleaning pools for Houston's rich and elite wasn't for him.

David wandered back over to his friends and Israel was left to watch from a distance. To Israel's terror and delight, the reserved teacher worked her way over to him. "Do you mind?" she asked, claiming the seat where Camilla had just been.

"Not at all." And he found that he really didn't.

"I'm Tabitha, David's English teacher." She held out a hand. He took it. It was soft and warm. His was just sweaty. "I couldn't stay over there. They're telling ghost stories now."

"You don't like ghost stories?"

She shook her head emphatically.

Israel was intrigued. "Are you a believer or a skeptic?"

Most white people he knew didn't acknowledge the paranormal. Not if they wanted to be taken seriously. It was different for Mexicans. Discussing your dead cousin's spirit was considered appropriate Sunday dinner discussion.

"In the light of day, I am not a believer," Tabitha offered. "But at night, when it's dark outside and I'm alone in the house, I believe in all sorts of things."

Israel laughed. "Which demon are they resurrecting now?"

"Sack man? Sack of man? Something that will give me nightmares."

"Ah, *El Sacoman!"*

"That's it. As soon as they mentioned a man who carries children away in bags, I was out."

"Yeah, he's scary. My *abuela* used *El Sacoman* to keep me in line. Don't fight with your sister or *El Sacoman* will steal you from your room. You won't brush your teeth? *El Sacoman's* bag is awfully light tonight. I think he's looking for naughty little boys."

"Your *abuela* told you that? It's like a terrifying version of Santa Claus." She looked as though she were trying to decide if she should laugh or be frightened.

"Yeah, her parenting skills weren't so warm and cozy. Her cooking was, but not her way with children."

Tabitha did laugh now. Israel liked her laugh. It was full of life.

He went on. "The most terrifying thing about *El Sacoman* is that he's not a monster that hides under the bed. He's a normal person that everyone accepts as one of their own. A psychopath. He could be anyone. The old man down the street. The mail carrier. He lives in your neighborhood. Your parents know him and trust him. When the kids go missing nobody suspects him."

"What does he do with the children?"

"Some people say he eats them. My *abuela* was more about suffering. She told us he'd turn us into slaves and make us work for him."

"Now I am definitely going to have nightmares. Maybe I need a dog. A really vicious one. Like a Rottweiler. Not that I'd know what to do with one. What would protect me from the Rottweiler?"

He grinned as she laughed at herself.

That night, when Israel walked through the front door, the house had an oppressive, earthy musk that was hard to escape. He flipped on the light and three large cockroaches scurried along the baseboard. He'd have to call Rafael in the morning.

The bed springs creaked as Israel sat on the edge. He usually talked to his wife in the evenings, sharing the details of his day, enduring her criticism and eventually finding wisdom in her words. But something about tonight felt wrong. He'd enjoyed talking to Tabitha. Really enjoyed it. As she left the party she'd asked if he'd like to get coffee sometime. The yes was on the tip of his tongue and he was stunned by how badly he wanted to toss it out there into the open. But he'd hesitated too long.

She'd said an awkward goodbye and left.

The stained-glass lamp on the bedside table sat dark and cold. He reached to push the switch, but his hand hesitated. His wife always seemed to know when he was hiding something from her, and he didn't have the energy for her jealousy tonight. He pulled his hand away from the lamp and lay down gently. She would be angry, but he pushed that thought away. Plenty of time to deal with it later.

Israel's response to the familiar trill of his phone was automatic. The time on the dash of the truck read 10 a.m. Without even looking at the screen he knew it was Harriet, his next appointment. With a swipe of the thumb he answered the call.

"Hello."

"Israel? Is that you?"

"Yes, ma'am."

"Are you coming today?"

His mouth twitched at the predictability.

"Of course, ma'am. I'm just stuck in a little bit of traffic right now. I should be there in a few minutes."

"I just wanted to be sure you were still coming today."

"Yes, ma'am."

"I'll see you in a few minutes then."

"Yes, ma'am."

Harriet was in her eighties and made that phone call every Monday morning.

When he pulled up in front of the brick rambler he was surprised to see a familiar white truck out front. The tailgate was open and paint tools lay piled on the grass. Big red letters on the side announced that Bob the Painter was here. Again.

Israel gathered up the long pole with the wide net and his water testing supplies out of the back of the truck, stuffing two packaged chlorine discs into his pockets.

Harriet waited for Israel by the pool in a wicker chair. She sipped at something in a mug, one leg crossed over the other. A loose, cotton dress hung to her ankles and a straw hat sat on her white hair to cover her face from the glaring sun. Israel wondered why she bothered. The years of sun exposure had already done their worst on her leathery face.

"Oh Israel, you came." Her face broke into wrinkled smiles.

He suppressed a chuckle. "Yes ma'am. You have painters?"

She waved her hand at the house. "They're just starting. I've been needing that guest room painted for some time now. It's such a relief to have it taken care of."

He wondered if he should remind her that Bob had just painted the guest room a few weeks ago, but he didn't want to make her feel foolish. So, he kept quiet and listened to her talk about paint colors while he emptied the skimmers and checked the chemical levels.

"I'm just gonna grab my hose," he said and walked around to the front of the house to grab his equipment. Bob was at the back of his truck stepping into his paint coveralls. Maybe he should say something. But was it really his place?

Bob waved hello, but Israel did not return the greeting. He was perturbed that Bob would take advantage of Harriet's failing memory. He pretended to be occupied with his phone.

Rafael had sent several texts.

-At the house now.

-Not good.

-You have termites.

-Might need a tent treatment.

Israel touched the green phone icon and his cousin answered in a stream of Spanish before he could even say hello.

"The cockroaches shouldn't be a problem anymore, man. I went ahead and sprayed for them. But you've got termites. Have you noticed a dirt smell in your house? That's the termites. It's bad. I found them in three of your walls."

"And you can't just do a spray?"

Israel pulled the hose out the back of the truck while they talked. He threw it over his arm and made for the back of the house, unloading it onto the deck by the pool. He stood there rubbing his chin, trying to sort through the bad news.

Rafael had a possible lead. "Let me talk to someone. I've got a guy who might be able to just do a regular treatment. But you might need to find somewhere to stay."

Israel exhaled a long breath. "Who's going to put me up on such short notice?" And what about his wife?

"I'd offer my couch, but it's already occupied."

Israel didn't ask details. Probably another cousin crashing there.

"How soon can we treat it?"

Rafael made a drawn-out "Uhhh," while he considered. "I could start tomorrow. I've got a job in Huntsville, but I can come over tomorrow afternoon."

Israel groaned. "Ok, yeah. Let me know what your guy says. I don't want to tent if we don't have to."

"Ok."

Israel stuffed his phone back in his pocket, and bent over to pick up the vacuum hose. A movement startled him. Harriet was sitting nearby still nursing her drink. He thought she'd gone inside.

Her tongue smacked as she swallowed her drink. "You need a place to stay?"

He mentally cursed. He hadn't realized Harriet spoke Spanish.

"My place is being treated for termites." He'd found over the years that he had to be careful what he said around Harriet. If he openly admired the flowers in her yard he'd wind up going home with a vase full of them as well as a description of the species and how to care for them.

"It will smell like fresh paint, but I've got a guest room available."

Israel suppressed a smile. Harriet's generous nature was as predictable as her 10 a.m. phone calls every Monday.

"Oh, I'm not sure I'm even going to need to vacate," Israel said.

"Well, if you need a place you know where I live."

"Thank you, ma'am."

As he pulled away from Harriet's house Israel tried to work out why he was surprised that she'd understood his conversation. Plenty of white people spoke Spanish. Most of them were pretty upfront about it, even eager to practice their language skills on him. But in all the time he'd been cleaning Harriet's pool she'd never once given any sign that she spoke Spanish.

Israel followed the bend in the road to Tracy's, a handsome two-story brick house with large trees in front. Referrals in the same neighborhood were great. Less travel time meant more work and more money.

Tracy's grown son Evan and his girlfriend, whose name Israel had never caught, were lounging poolside when Israel let himself in through the back gate. Evan had moved back home in the past year and Tracy found more and more excuses to travel. She still paid the bills, but it seemed Tracy had been chased from her own home.

Israel nodded politely when Evan opened his eyes to look his way. "Everything working ok?"

Evan pointed to the Polaris on the deck. "Something's wrong with the robot. So I pulled it out."

Israel examined the little cleaning machine on wheels. He connected the hose back to the wall and watched it move around the floor of the pool, picking up debris. Everything seemed in order. He called over to Evan, "It's hooked up. I'll keep an eye on it while I'm here."

Evan didn't even bother opening his eyes, but simply raised a thumb up in the air.

Israel's thumb tapped the steering wheel while he waited in line behind two other cars. A uniformed guard took note of license plate numbers on his clipboard while a second guard chatted with the driver at the front of the line. Israel hated trying to get through the gated communities in The Woodlands, and Carlton Hills was the ritziest that he serviced. What did the ultra-rich think they were hiding from?

In addition to the checkpoint at the entrance to Carlton Hills, the Millers' house had its own private security. Israel didn't mind this as much. Mark Miller requested cleaning twice a week for his massive pool, so the private security guard knew Israel on sight. He barely glanced at him as he opened the iron gates.

Israel drove his small gray pickup along the expansive park-like grounds. The main drive pulled up to a glistening fountain in front of the massive French-style mansion. But Israel circled around to the back where he pushed a security button. With a metallic whir, the wrought iron gate leading to the back of the house rolled open.

The seven-acre property was rumored to be worth four million dollars, though Israel suspected it was more. The Millers' pool was the largest Israel maintained, and he took a certain amount of pride in keeping it crystal clear. With seven pumps and three filters, the Millers' pool required much of his attention. Not that he minded. He enjoyed being one of many parts that made the estate run.

Hauling the vacuum hose over his shoulder, Israel passed a robed woman with long blonde hair and tan legs stretched out in her lounge chair. Ruth must be out of town. That's usually when the young, attractive girls showed up at the house.

"Hi, Israel," the woman said behind dark glasses.

Israel was taken aback. Mark's girlfriends didn't usually pay attention to him. He waved casually as if beautiful women spoke to him regularly while he cleaned pools.

He went about his work, checking on the equipment, testing the chemical levels of the water, and cleaning the filters. He was on his knees cleaning leaves and debris out of one of the skimmers by the side of the pool when Mark emerged from the house. Mark often came out to chat with Israel, even offering him a cold drink on occasion. One of the reasons Israel liked working on Mark's pool was that even though the man had a lot of money he always treated Israel as if his opinions mattered. Sometimes they'd sit on the porch and share a drink before Israel moved on to his next job.

A broad, dazzling smile usually filled Mark's face. But not today. Today he walked toward Israel with great purpose.

"Look at this," Mark said. He thrust a paper into Israel's hands.

Israel wasn't sure what he was looking at.

"Seventeen thousand dollars. That moron spent seventeen thousand dollars to turn himself into a woman. *A woman!"*

The credit card statement made Israel squirm. Cleaning pools over the years had taught him something. The back yard is where you learn the truth about people. Something clicked. The tall blonde who'd known his name. That hadn't been one of Mark's girlfriends.

Sam.

The chair on the porch was now empty.

"Wow," was all Israel could muster. He was reminded of the biggest drawback to the Miller family: having to step delicately through family drama.

When Israel pulled around to the front of the estate he was surprised to see Sam waiting out front for him. He slowed to a stop. Even from a distance Israel could tell Sam was crying. Sam had been an awkward preteen when Israel first brought David to help with the pool. The boys got along well, but it was hard not to compare the two over the years. While David had thrived under Camilla's care, Sam had withered under his father's constant criticism.

"You think I'm an idiot too, don't you?" Sam spoke in a more effeminate voice than Israel had ever heard him use. Softer and a little higher than usual.

"Seventeen thousand dollars is a lot of money." Israel shrugged. What would he do with that kind of money? He had to be careful not to think like that when he was at the Millers'.

"He can't stand what I am."

It was strange at first, but behind the long hair and the dress and effected voice it was still Sam. Israel found himself feeling sorry for . . . *her.* He'd always had a soft spot for Sam.

"He's kicking me out and cutting me off." Sam drew long red nails awkwardly through his blond strands. Clearly not a move he'd practiced much.

Israel scratched at his chin. "Is your mom out of town?" If Ruth were around she'd help Sam.

"She gets back tomorrow. Dad told me he wants me out by this afternoon. Israel, I don't have anywhere to go. Can I—can I stay with you?"

Israel thought of his wife. What would she say? And then there was David's bedroom that sat waiting for him to come home at a moment's notice though he hadn't used it in months.

"My house is pretty small, Sam. I don't really have the room."

Sam's chin quivered and he burst into tears. Horrified, Israel found a napkin in the glove box and thrust it at Sam.

"I'm sorry," Sam sniffled. "I've been a wreck all day."

Israel sighed. "Give me your number. I might know someone

you can stay with. She's old and kind of forgetful though."

"Oh, that would be wonderful."

"She'll charge you rent."

"That's ok. Mom will be home tomorrow. Oh, thank you!"

"I'm not making promises. I'll text you later and let you know."

As Israel waited in the security line to return his visitor tag he texted David.

-So, Sam is a girl now.

-What???

-You should have come. You missed drama.

-Thank goodness.

His phone dinged again, but it wasn't David. It was Rafael.

-My guy can spray. No tent!

Israel sighed with relief. The old lady was sweet, but he didn't want to share a house with her. And now he had a place for Sam. Strange how different David and Sam were. David would never ask Israel for help finding a place to stay.

Israel dialed Harriet's number.

"Yello," she said.

"Miss Harriet, it's Israel. Do you still have that guest room available?"

"You bet."

"My friend, Sam needs a place to stay for a little bit. Cost won't be an issue."

Harriet sounded thrilled. "Bring him on by."

Him. Should he tell her about Sam's sex change? Sam certainly didn't look like a him. Israel decided against it. Sam was an adult and could figure it out.

"Yes, ma'am. Thank you."

Israel shot a quick text off to Sam.

-Found a room for you to rent until you figure out what to do next.

-Can you give me a ride?

-Yup. When can you be ready?

They agreed to meet at the Chipotle in a shopping center near the gated community so Israel didn't have to go through security. He really didn't want a record of this visit.

The parking lot was busy with customers coming and going. Sam was nowhere to be seen. A row of trees offered shade and Israel took refuge, not knowing how long he'd have to wait. Thirty minutes later a tall blonde stumbled across the parking lot in heels, tugging at a mid-thigh red dress with one hand and carrying an oversized hand bag in the other.

Israel rolled down his window. "What are you wearing?"

Sam fiddled with a knot of pearls and looked down at the red dress. "It's new."

Not exactly running away attire.

They pulled up to Harriet's house. For the millionth time Israel warned Sam. "Harriet is kind of forgetful. Don't be surprised if you have to tell her your name more than once."

The humidity was stifling as they walked up to the house.

Harriet threw open the door before they reached it, a blast of cold air welcoming them and offering relief from the heat. "You must be Sam. Come in. Come in. I'll show you your room."

With a rush of emotion, Sam threw long arms around Israel. Israel was so much shorter than Sam and it was awkward for him to return the embrace.

"You've been so nice to me," Sam's voice quivered. "You're more of a father to me than my own dad."

Israel cleared his throat and clapped Sam on the arm. "Text me if you need anything. A ride or whatever."

Back in the truck Israel flipped on the radio. The strong beat of salsa music filled the cab, drowning out the echo of words bouncing around his head.

You're more of a father to me than my own dad.

At home, Israel rifled through a pile of neglected mail when a knock at the door interrupted him. He left envelopes and papers strewn on the counter to answer the door.

Camilla stood there, her dark hair pulled back into a ponytail and a small pan in her hands. She held up the pan and Israel let her in.

Her smile disappeared. "Ugh! Israel, it smells! Are you running your air?"

"It's better than it was. Rafael says the smell just has to work itself out."

She wrinkled her nose at him as if she doubted him. "So? What did you think of the party?"

"Fine. It was good to see David."

"He said you didn't talk much," Camilla chastised.

"I talked when there was something to say," Israel shrugged. He doubted David cared all that much if he'd talked or not.

"I'm glad you came."

Camilla made her way to the kitchen and Israel pushed the pile of mail over to make room for the pan.

"I did my baking today and thought you could use something that doesn't come from the freezer." She put a hand on her hip. "You and Tabitha seemed to hit it off."

He threw a glance to the bedroom door. "You mean at the party? No. I was just being nice."

"You looked like you were having a good time."

"How did David like the movie?" Israel asked.

Camilla didn't let him distract her. "I don't understand. It's been fifteen years."

"And yet you won't give up."

"No, I won't. You deserve to be happy too, Israel. So." She dug through her purse and handed him a slip of paper. "Tabitha said I could give this to you. I've got to go. David needs a few more boxes for packing."

Israel pulled out his wallet and handed her some cash. "Let me take care of that."

She pecked him on the cheek and left him to consider Tabitha's digits on the slip of paper.

The smell of Camilla's fresh baking drew Israel to the pan. It was full of stacks of flour tortillas and corn tortillas and *torta* bread and *sopapillas.* He inhaled and savored the aroma. He could almost forgive Camilla for mentioning Tabitha where his wife might hear.

He grabbed a single bit of *sopapilla* and popped it into his mouth. The taste instantly transported him back to *Abuela's* kitchen, a place of a thousand memories—some good, some painful.

Like that traumatizing day the family dog, a small poodle, got into chicken scraps from the trash. Trash that Israel had neglected to secure tightly. The dog whimpered as it squirmed and stretched, trying to expel the painful bone shards cutting him from the inside. The kitchen floor was hard and unforgiving, but Israel stayed by the dog's side. Any comfort he tried to offer was futile because the dog snapped at him whenever he tried to touch him. "Please be ok. Please forgive me."

The dog gave one last whimpering shudder and then went still. *Abuela's* bony finger shook at Israel. "This is your doing. The devil has cursed you."

That's how it was anytime something went wrong.

The devil has cursed you.

Abuela never offered a solution to breaking the curse. It was only an explanation, a fact of life.

The *sopapilla* in his mouth felt too solid. Like a lump that he couldn't chew through. Israel's eyes fell on the bedroom door. He'd already waited too long. Throwing back a glass of water, he swallowed the lump of *sopapilla* down. It was time to face his wife.

He slipped into the bedroom and eased himself onto the side of the bed, never taking his eyes off the lamp. The shade was made from real stained glass, not the fake plastic panes he often saw in the stores. His fingers reached out and touched the grooved switch. He trembled like an alcoholic about to drink from the smooth lip of the bottle.

With a gentle push, the lamp clicked on.

The bulb glowed hot and pulsed in rapid flashes. He'd known

she would be angry.

The words came to him clearly, an internal voice that both soothed and terrified him.

You're avoiding me.

"No."

Are you seeing someone? Is she pretty?

"I'm not seeing anyone."

You don't need to find a new mother for David. If you'd let me see him, let me show him what I can do, I'd be mother enough for him.

Israel shook his head. "That's not true. David doesn't need more mothers. I tell him about you all the time. And Camilla has been a great help."

David only knows the stories you tell him. He doesn't know me like this. Let me see him.

Her words almost made sense, but Israel knew the danger. She was addicting, the way her soothing voice filled him and made the world a little less lonely for just a moment. But that's all she ever was. Just a voice. It was maddening how he couldn't leave her alone.

He knew he was right to leave David out of it.

"David is going off to school. You are all I have."

And you are all I have.

Israel was asleep when the ringer on his phone went off. He reached over and checked the time. It was after midnight. He didn't recognize the number. Clearing his throat, he swiped the screen to answer.

"Hello?"

"Is this the pool guy?" A male voice talked too loud in his ear.

"Yes."

"Man, I need you to come over here right away. Something's majorly wrong with the pool. Someone stole our water."

He's drunk. "Who is this?"

"Evan. Tracy's my mom. My girlfriend and I are watching the

place while she's out of town."

Tracy. An I-don't-care-what-it-costs-fix-it kind of client. Israel sighed.

"I'll be there in a bit."

Evan hung up without another word.

Israel dragged himself from bed, slipped on his jeans and shoes and fumbled his way in the dark to find his keys.

He drove to the familiar neighborhood in The Woodlands and parked in the driveway that he normally only saw by the light of day.

Outdoor lights flooded the backyard. The pool, now a hollow cavity, only had a foot of water in the bottom. Israel tapped on the glass to the back door to alert Evan that he was there and used a flashlight to guide his way around the corner where the pool equipment sat hidden from view. The strong scent of chlorine hung in the humid night air. Several inches of water covered the ground around the pad where the pool equipment sat. The fiberglass filter, which normally stood chest high, was dented and broken and water gushed from slashes and holes. This wasn't a malfunction of equipment.

Evan splashed in the water to get a closer look. "Can you fix it?"

"I'll have to get a new filter. I don't know what would do that kind of damage. Did you see anything?"

"No. But Steph said she heard something a while ago. We usually go for a late swim, but she wouldn't even step outside. Said we should call the cops, but I mean . . . *it's The Woodlands.*"

"Well I'll pick up a filter in the morning and install it tomorrow. But there isn't much I can do about it tonight. All the damage is already done."

The flashlight scanned the ground, revealing white shards of fiberglass. Israel bent down and picked up a broken piece of fiberglass with a clump of black hair on one end. It was soggy and coarse between his fingers.

What would drive an animal to do this kind of damage?

Evan called to Israel as he left. "Hey be careful. There's weird juju out there, man."

Israel waved in acknowledgment. A ding announced a new message from his phone as he got inside his truck. A text from Sam. Why did Sam think he'd be awake this time of night? Twenty-somethings don't realize forty-somethings aren't twenty-somethings.

-Miz H is a terrible sleeper.

-Her new tenant probably snores.

-I snore ballads. She's really loud. She's in and out and slams doors and I swear she puts on heavy boots to stomp around right outside my door.

When Israel pulled around the bend he saw Harriet's garage lights on. She'd probably left them on when she was taking out the trash or something.

He shot off a quick, one-handed text to Sam.

-H's garage lights are on.

-Are you a stalker? What are you doing here???

Israel laughed.

-Pool call around the corner.

-You clean pools this late at night?

-Only for the rich.

Israel chuckled to himself, knowing the joke might have fallen a little flat on Sam. This neighborhood was barely scraping by compared to the grand Miller estate.

-I haven't told you about the dolls H has. She loves them. They are super creepy.

-My abuela collected dolls. We weren't allowed to touch them.

-I feel like they're judging me.

-Or waiting until you fall asleep...

-Jerk.

An animal darted out in the road in front of him. Israel slammed on the brakes, and pulled hard on the wheel to swerve. With a sickening thunk, the front end of his bumper clipped it before he could come to a full stop.

He swore. He really was cursed. He jumped from the car praying the creature wasn't dead.

But the asphalt was empty.

A disturbance in the bushes came from the nearby walking trail.

A single street lamp around the bend in the road cast a shallow orange glow that failed to penetrate the shadows of the trail. Israel reached for his phone to use as a light, and realized too late that he'd lost it somewhere in the car. He approached anyway. The thrashing intensified and Israel hesitated.

Using a low, soothing voice he spoke to the creature in the bushes. "Come here, I'm not going to hurt you." As he talked a massive shadow moved along the ground toward him. "That's right. Good. Let's get a look at you."

A large, limping dog emerged, bushy tail pinned between the hind legs. But as it drew closer Israel's voice trailed off. The dog had no face. Instead it was a mess of raw, open flesh that glistened in the dim orange light. Israel recoiled in horror and the dog let out a pitiful scream, a noise unlike anything Israel had ever heard before. Fear shivered down his back and he scrambled for the truck.

Trembling with adrenaline, Israel managed to drive the rest of the way home. He went straight to his bedroom and turned on the lamp. The light cast looming shadows that stretched across the ceiling. He paced, running his finger over the rough edge of a freshly ripped-off fingernail.

"I hit something with my car tonight. A dog. Its face was all messed up. It was gone. No eyes, no nose, no fur. No face."

He knew he was babbling, rattling his thoughts off out loud.

Something is out there.

"Who could stomach that?"

El Sacoman.

Israel stopped pacing. "That's just a superstition. He's not real."

He's very real.

He rushed to her side and glared into the lamp's leaded glass panes. "Why can't the dead just leave us alone? You had your chance at life!"

You think I want this? To live this way? You want to be rid of me? Go to a priest. Explain to him how you want to absolve our marriage vows. This is a gift, Israel.

When she talked like this it always confused him.

Besides, El Sacoman isn't like me. He isn't a remnant of someone's life. He is just as alive as you are. You're upset and you're tired. Lie down. You need sleep.

He obeyed while she dimmed her setting, and his anxious breathing filled the quiet room. She started to whisper a tale about dogs, cute and fluffy and happy. Israel switched the lamp off and the sound of silence filled his bedroom.

No dogs tonight.

Israel felt calmer as he ate day-old *sopapillas* for breakfast the next morning. He pulled up Camilla's name on his phone while he ate.

-Thanks for the food. It reminds me of Abuela.

-I hope that's a good thing.

-A little bit. So, I saw the freakiest thing last night. I hit a dog while I was driving.

-Are you ok? How is the dog?

-I'm fine. Here's the weird thing. It was seriously mangled. Someone hurt it bad.

-It was hurt because you hit it.

-Not just that. I got out to check on it and something was really wrong with its face.

-You got out of your car in the middle of the night? On a dark road? Alone???

-I had to check on it.

-That's how people get murdered. Or picked up by El Sacoman.

Israel chuckled. For some reason, her overreaction made him feel better.

He didn't have to go clear down to The Woodlands today. He stuck closer to home cleaning for families in his own area. There was something noble about cleaning for families with kids. Like he was responsible for providing a space for them to create happy memories.

He got a text around lunchtime from Sam.

-I went to turn off the garage light last night. H was in there. She was throwing stuff around and talking to herself. It was super weird. I left her alone.

-She's 82. She's getting old. Keep an eye on her so she doesn't hurt herself.

His phone dinged again and he was surprised when it wasn't Sam, but Mark.

-Can you come over?

-Yes. When?

-As soon as you can.

-Give me thirty minutes.

When he got to the Miller estate he pulled into his usual spot by the tool shed. He walked to the back porch and found Mark sitting in the shade of the outdoor kitchen.

"You hungry?" Mark was holding two iced teas and handed one to Israel.

Israel accepted the cold drink gratefully. "Thanks, I'm good."

"You sure? I can make us up a little something."

"It's ok. I've already had lunch. Do you need me to clean the pool or something?"

Mark waved a hand. "The pool's fine." He indicated an empty chair next to him and Israel sat down. "I know Sam came to you."

Israel simply nodded.

Mark crossed a foot to rest on his knee. "I figured it was you. The security feed shows him talking to you."

"I tried—" but Mark cut Israel off.

"It's ok. I'm glad he came to you." Mark took a drink. "Is he ok?"

"I haven't seen him since yesterday, but we've texted a little. I think he's fine."

"He's safe?"

Israel nodded.

"When you talk to him next, will you let him know he can come home? If he wants to, I mean."

Israel leaned back in the chair. "I think he's just trying to figure out what comes next."

Mark nodded and drew a hand down his face. The easy smile was gone and Mark looked old. "This is new to all of us, you know? It's not what we wanted for him."

Israel knew what he meant. His life was full of disappointed expectations.

"Just let him know he can come home, okay?"

"I will."

Mark sipped at his drink. "Ruth gave him a credit card. She's been tracking it. She doesn't know that I know." He gave a wry chuckle.

Israel texted Sam before he left the driveway.

-Just got done talking to your dad.

When Sam finally responded several hours had passed.

-I was out in the garage helping H straighten up. I know I'm not a gardener, but she has a lot of weird tools. What did my dad say?

-He says you can come home if you want to. And he wanted to know you were safe.

-I'm fine. H is feeding me and making me tons of iced tea.

-Let your Dad know where you are when you get a chance.

-I'll text him right now. Then I'm going to lie down. The garage was hot and that last iced tea didn't settle well.

The next day the sun bore down on Israel and his clothes stuck to him each time he got out of the truck. He sent David a text.

-It's so hot. You might be onto something with this college business.

David responded with a laughing emoji.

It was with relief when he finally sank onto the couch in his air-conditioned home.

He flipped on the TV and his phone dinged. It was Mark.

-Have you heard from Sam?

-Not today.

-Can I get that lady's address where he's staying? I was going to pick him up for breakfast this morning but I never heard from him.

-Strange. I haven't heard from him.

Israel looked up Harriet's address on his phone and shot it over to Mark in a text.

After a cool shower and a hot plate of dinner, Israel was alarmed to see another text from Mark.

-You still haven't heard from Sam?

-No. He wasn't at Harriet's?

-She said he didn't come home last night.

-She doesn't have the best memory.

-Would you check in with her? Since you know her? I'm about to go to the police.

Israel sent a quick message to David.

-Heading over to Harriet's to check on Sam. Want a break from packing?

-Yes!

-Leaving the house right now.

Harriet answered the door with a smile and an embrace for David. "Look how you've grown! You're so handsome. Your dad says you're heading off to college."

David grinned at the attention. "Yes, ma'am."

"Did you come to clean my pool today?"

Israel shook his head. "No, ma'am. I come on Mondays. We're looking for Sam."

An odd look crossed her face. Confusion. "Sam? Well come in.

Let me get you some iced tea."

They followed her in. Israel had never been in the house before. They passed a formal sitting room on the right and followed the flow of the grand entrance to the living room, where a large kitchen opened up. Harriet chattered at them while she pulled two glasses from the cupboard.

A wall of windows looked out onto the back yard. Another wall was lined with shelves of dolls. Israel examined them. They were ugly and he couldn't resist reaching out to touch the hand of one. It wasn't made of porcelain like his *abuela's* doll collection. Instead it was the softest, smoothest leather Israel had ever felt.

David whispered to Israel while Harriet prattled on. "Look at the eyes."

The eyes were the most disturbing part. The nearest doll to Israel had fine black hair and the same strange leather skin. But the eyes looked remarkably real. A reflection of his face looked back at him in the pupil.

"You almost expect them to blink or something," David whispered. "Creepy."

Harriet came in with two glasses of iced tea. The glass was already sweating even though they were inside an air-conditioned house.

Israel took a drink. "Thank you, ma'am. Is Sam around?"

"Sam?"

"Yes, Sam. Tall, blonde, living in your guest room."

"Honey, I don't have anyone in my guest room. It's not fit for company. I need to get it painted."

Ugh. Not again. How could he get her to remember? Maybe that was too much to expect.

"Could I take a look at your guest room?"

"Suit yourself. Up the stairs, first door on the right." She opened her arm in a welcoming gesture. Israel put his glass on a coaster on the coffee table and left David and Harriet chatting in the living room.

The smell of fresh paint assaulted his senses. A black handbag sat open on the foot of the tidy bed, the same over-sized bag Sam had worn over his shoulder when Israel dropped him off at Harriet's. Sam's cell phone sat on the bedside table. Israel picked it up, a feeling of unease settling in. Who went anywhere without their phone?

The window on the far wall overlooked the backyard and gave Israel a straight view into the garage. The door was closed, and the windows were dark.

Harriet's laugh sounded from downstairs and Israel couldn't shake the feeling that something was wrong.

Bob the painter had been here two days ago. The smell of paint shouldn't be this strong. Israel reached out and touched the wall where a drip had been neglected. A small chunk of wet paint came away on his thumb. He tested the tackiness between his fingers, the white color contrasting sharply with his brown skin.

This paint couldn't be more than a few hours old.

He needed to get inside that garage.

At the bottom of the stairs Israel could see into the living room. David laughed at something Harriet said and took a drink from his glass of iced tea. A cold feeling of dread gripped Israel at the sight. But he couldn't identify why.

Forcing a bright smile Israel marched into the room. "While I'm here I'm just going to check out your equipment. You'd be amazed the stuff that's been happening in this neighborhood recently."

"Oh, that's not necessary." Harriet waved his concern away.

"I'd feel better if I could just make sure."

Outside, the heat sweltered and he broke into a sweat. He made a big show of examining the edge of the pool in case Harriet was watching through the window. After a few minutes, he wandered over to the garage. With a quick twist of the knob the door creaked open. He glanced over his shoulder as he entered.

Daylight lit the room through the windows revealing two

work tables in the middle of the garage. An empty garbage can sat at the end of one table, and a pile of leather strips at the other end. One of the tables had dark stains on it. Oil? Or something more nefarious, like blood? The silver gleam of a large blade winked at him on the table farthest from him.

Across the garage a sturdy sewing machine was plugged into one wall. The walls on either side of the machine were lined with doll forms of different sizes.

Near the sewing machine, a string of pearls caught Israel's eye. An image of Sam clutching a string of pearls in the parking lot at Chipotle flashed in his mind. A noise from outside startled him and he stuffed the pearls in his pocket.

He peered out the windows and seeing the coast was clear, exited Harriet's doll-making shop.

Israel called Mark the next morning.

"Mark. Any word on Sam?"

"Yes." His response was empty and Israel's heart sank.

"Is he okay?" Please let him be okay. Let this be another stupid incident that Mark will be mad about for a day or two before he gets over it.

"He's dead."

Israel closed his eyes. No. "Dead?"

"They found him by one of the walking trails. They wouldn't let us see him. I guess his face—it's—well there isn't much left to it."

A chill shot down Israel's spine. "What do you mean?"

"It's been chewed off."

"Chewed off?" Israel knew what that looked like. Raw. Wet.

"One of the mowing crews found him face down in the ditch." Mark's voice was hollow as he described the gruesome scene. "They think there must have been water in it at the time and he drowned. That raccoons or maybe rats did the rest."

"I'm so sorry. What can I do for you and Ruth?"

"I don't—I don't know. I don't know."

He hung up with Mark and buried his face in his hands.

When was he going to learn to leave things alone? The devil had cursed him and he destroyed everything he touched.

Israel held the phone to his ear, praying David would pick up. David definitely preferred texting.

"Hey Dad."

"Hey, can you come over?"

"Sure."

He paced around the house, cleaning and tidying up with a nervous energy.

David let himself in and Israel was unsure of how to break the news. When *Abuela* had died his uncle had been very matter of fact about it. Israel had hated him for it, but he didn't know a better way.

"They found Sam this morning. He's dead."

"Dead? How?"

"They think maybe he was drunk or something and wandered into a ditch by accident. It must have had water in it and he drowned."

Tell him everything.

His wife's voice filled him and he could tell from the way David looked around him that he'd heard her voice too. Israel could kick himself. He'd left the lamp on. How could he have been so careless? How? This was why he'd asked Camilla to take care of David. She didn't make mistakes like this.

David looked at Israel. "What was that?"

Israel shook his head and acted confused. It had worked for Harriet. "What was what?" He had to get David out of the house.

David shook his head. "Nothing."

"You know what? Maybe right now isn't a good time."

"Dad, you got me over here. Tell me what you know about Sam. What else do they know? Are they doing a funeral?"

Israel licked his lips and eyed the front door. "Let's go for a drive. He grabbed his keys and pushed David to the front door. "I'll tell you in the truck."

The voice sunk into his insides and he felt both a dread and a thrill at the same time. He should really get David out of here. But he longed to hear her speak to him again.

Quit lying to him, Israel.

Israel noticed David's raised eyebrows. "Dad? What is that?" David's eyes looked around as if he were afraid to make any sudden moves.

Israel sighed with defeat. "It's your mother."

Show me to him.

He had to explain to David first.

"The lamp in the bedroom? Your mother bought it when she was in college. Around the time we met. When your mother died your grandfather wanted to bring her home. He wanted us to go and live with him in Hong Kong. But I couldn't leave Texas. I wanted to raise you here. He begged me to at least let him have the funeral in Hong Kong. I didn't know what to do. Your mother was so young and there were so many details to sort through. I've never felt so helpless. One night I don't know if I was talking to God or your mom, but I just kind of said, 'Tell me what to do.'"

David looked concerned. Israel rushed on, the weight of his wife's demand to share her with David pressing in on him. David had to understand.

"And there was an answer." Israel pointed to the bedroom. "Your mother's lamp, it flickered. That voice you just felt? That happened to me too. It was like it was inside of me. *Let them take me home*. So, I did. Your mother's body is in Hong Kong, but a piece of her stayed here with me. With us."

"Dad—" David said.

"Look, I know what this sounds like, but I can show you." Israel brought the lamp out into the living room and plugged it in. "She can only hear and communicate when she has power." He clicked the lamp on and his wife glowed with joy. He beamed at

David.

David reached over and unplugged the lamp from the wall. "Dad, this is crazy. Surely you see that, right? You were just trying to get me out of here and away from that thing. And now you want me to be friends with it. Does Mom know?"

Israel laughed. "If I told Camilla that your mother talks to me through a lamp she'd go nuts. It's not that I don't think she'd believe me."

David nodded. "No, she'd completely believe you. And she'd have a priest bless and cleanse your house."

Israel chuckled.

"Dad." David looked at Israel with sincerity and real concern. It was a look Israel often reserved for Harriet. "I'm not so sure she'd be wrong. The dead shouldn't live our lives for us.

"Your mother is not living my life."

"You're not living your life."

Israel hesitated. He had protected David from his wife for so long. But David was an adult now. He was getting ready to head off to college. He wouldn't even be around to be influenced by her. One demonstration couldn't hurt that much.

Israel found himself needing to show David. He reached over and plugged the lamp back into the wall.

She erupted into warnings.

It's coming. The lamp flashed urgently. Something is coming. Really bad. Run. Hide.

"What's coming?"

It's coming for you Israel. You've brought it to David. You took the pearls. Why did you take the pearls?

Israel scrambled for the locks on the front door. "Lock the back door!"

"What pearls? What is she talking about?" David asked.

"The locks. Go!"

David ran through the kitchen and Israel heard the locks click.

The lamp continued to pulse in the living room, pounding

along with his heart.

It's coming. It's coming.

Israel peered through the blinds outside and David joined him at the window. The dark street in front of the house was empty.

A knock at the door made them both jump.

It's here. El Sacoman.

"Israel? It's Harriet. You left something at my house and I thought it might be important."

David shot Israel a look of exasperation. "You see what I mean? That thing got us all worked up for nothing. Turn off that lamp."

Israel watched to make sure it really wasn't a bogeyman in disguise. But when David opened the door, Harriet stood on the steps with a plate of cookies in one hand and a cell phone in another.

"Is this your phone Israel?" She offered it to him.

"No. I think that's Sam's"

"Well I brought you some cookies anyway. Try them. They're best fresh. I like to bake. It helps me clear my head. But I don't need all these calories."

Israel and David both obliged.

Israel accepted the plate and took it into the kitchen. When he returned David was bent over on the couch, Harriet next to him patting his back in a comforting gesture. Israel's stomach cramped up in incredible pain and he doubled over.

"You have such a handsome face," Harriet told David. "It deserves to be admired."

"Harriet," Israel groaned.

Harriet shushed him and Israel collapsed onto the floor unable to move.

"Israel, you took my beads. I was saving those for a project I'm working on."

He watched helplessly as she lay David back onto the couch. "I know this hurts, but I had to. This way you won't be able to move a muscle. Take comfort in the fact that you will live on display forever on my shelf."

Throw me. Throw me at her. You can move. Just pick me up and throw me at her.

Israel tried to move for his wife. His muscles were useless and he couldn't control them.

Try. You're not trying hard enough. You brought this woman into this house. You took the pearls. You brought her to our son. Move.

His foot kicked out and hit the leg of the table, knocking the lamp forward onto the couch.

Not good enough. Do it again. Throw me. Reach for me. Hurry.

Harriet removed something from the bag at her hip. The glint of a blade shone in the glass panels of the lamp. Israel strained with every muscle, but couldn't move. He watched Harriet's reflection finger the blade and heard her whisper, "You will be a great joy to recreate."

Do it. Throw me. Throw me. She's going to hurt him.

Harriet drew the blade down the side of David's face and Israel screamed, though no sound emerged. Instead his hand reached the edge of the couch for the lamp and he threw with all his might. It was a pathetic toss. The lamp didn't go far and crashed, the glass panes breaking into millions of tiny shards. The base of the lamp simply rolled across the floor and stopped at Harriet's foot.

Israel roared internally at his failure. *Worthless. Useless.*

But a pool of ethereal light poured from the broken pieces of the lamp base and gathered itself together. His precious wife. She slipped up Harriet's leg and wrapped herself firmly around the old woman's heaving chest in thick bands of light. She pulsed with hot white energy.

Harriet dropped the knife and swatted at the light. She snarled and whimpered in pain and the light grew brighter. The light intensified and Harriet's shrieks grew with it until both consumed the room in a blinding, deafening roar. With a burst, the light broke and Harriet's screams were silenced. Harriet was nowhere to be found.

It took several agonizing minutes for movement to return to Israel's limbs. When he could move again he dragged himself through his wife's scattered remains to David who was stirring on the couch.

The gash on his face would need stitches, but David was alive. That's all Israel cared about.

After a trip to the hospital David crashed in his childhood bedroom. Too restless to sleep, Israel cleaned up the living room. The glass shards from the lamp shade glinted at him as he swept them up and tossed them in the garbage. It was a strangely liberating feeling to see them sitting in the trash.

He picked up the base to the lamp, but hovered over the can. *Just dump it and be done with it.*

Why couldn't he bring himself to do it?

Instead a wild thought seized him and he searched for the duct tape. By early morning he had an unrecognizable version of what his wife had bought years ago, a crooked stump of splintered wood and duct tape.

He reshaped the bent socket, inserted a new bulb and pushed the switch. Nothing. She really was gone.

He glanced over at the TV stand where a familiar slip of paper sat. He reached for it.

Tabitha's number.

Maybe it was the lack of sleep, or maybe it was that he'd just fought an old woman in his house. Maybe it was that the oppressive voice of his wife had been lifted and he felt free to dare. But Israel imagined what it might be like to take Tabitha up on the invitation for coffee. To sit and talk to a real breathing woman whose laugh he could hear with his ears, whose skin he could touch.

And a faint glow lit up the room. The weight settled back into place. Israel reached for his phone to text David.

-She's here.

Hunger Creek

By Hayden Gilbert

When he heard the phone ring that summer night, Opie Stokes didn't even pick it up. When you were as old as he and had no immediate family left, people only called that late for one reason.

The call could have been about any number of people, really. Opie had lived his life in a very friendly manner and liked to say he never met a stranger, so for an old loner in Northern Idaho he still kept up with quite a few people. The voice on the other end of the phone could have been anyone, but Opie knew it was Frank Baird.

The face he hadn't seen since young adulthood came to his mind before he even heard the first ring. Memories of himself and the boys of Loeb buzzed in the night air like electricity, and when the chime rang out again, a little later from inside the cabin, he knew it was Frank. That static knowledge came like a whisper on the wind off the mountains as he sat looking at them across the Moyie River. The water had been rising since spring and what was once a faint trickle a few months back now sounded violent and hungry.

There wasn't any definable reason he should have but he knew it was Frank, and goddamn if he didn't know it was about Cat Bluell.

Opie sighed into the wind as the ring carried across the river and into the woods below the mountains. Those mountains spelled Canada and they spelled about as far away from Loeb as one could get. For Opie it hadn't been far enough.

The phone rang and rang and then went silent. Some kind of worry settled on his chest like a rock and made a home for the night. From somewhere in the darkness a loon sang. Nothing answered.

A tear came to Opie's eye. He let it fall and the phone rang again. That same cognition brought to mind Tuffy White. He figured it was the kind of electricity you naturally build between yourself and someone you have known your entire life. The way you can finish a friend's story before they're even halfway through it. The way you can feel when your ex-wife is in the same room as you before you've ever met eyes. And the way you can know that she's the one before you've ever spoken. That kind of electricity of souls.

"Jesus," he said, "Jesus Christ, Cat."

The river carried on and the stars danced in its ever-beating throe.

Just like that Opie Stokes knew Cat Bluell was dead.

After a lifetime of running and trying to forget, Opie knew it was time to go back to Loeb, Texas.

In the twenty years of the quiet life Opie Stokes had led in northern Idaho, he had come to miss many things about Texas. Nearly all of them were the food and nearly not a one was the weather. The southeast Texas summer saw the men at the visitation in their nicest blue jeans, dress shirts and ties. The coat hangers of the Gatlin Funeral Home were adorned with black suit jackets aplenty, and it would be a minor miracle if everyone got their own coat back.

The worrisome rock had not lifted from Opie's chest in the days following the night of the two phone calls, and it pressed a little heavier when he saw the sheer amount of people gathered to mourn Cat Bluell. One of the perks of never leaving your hometown, he supposed.

Cat had built quite the family. Opie shook hands and exchanged pleasantries with the three kids, Virginia, Lynne and Hank, and their spouses, and he waved to the eight grandchildren and finally came to Cat's wife, Susan. She looked just as beautiful as the day he convinced Cat to ask her to dance at the Senior's Ball in high school. He gave her a big hug. She kissed his cheek and the two said everything they needed to say with their eyes.

The crowd was a mirage of faces he remembered, but names he couldn't, and Christ did they make him feel old. He shook more hands and then went off and stood by himself. He saw the coffin, beautiful in a sleek, morbid way, in his periphery. He wanted to walk over, peer in, and look at his friend but his feet were made of lead.

"Opie!" he heard called from the archway by the foyer. He recognized the voice. His beard hairs prickled.

It was Frank Baird and his wife, Laura. Opie was surprised to see the moustache had survived the last two decades and Frank still wore it proudly, along with a very pronounced beer belly. He scuttled across the carpet and clapped hands with his friend from long ago.

Frank rubbed Opie's bald head, winking at Laura. "Good luck," he said.

Laura shook her head and Opie forced a smile, faking a punch into Frank's gut.

Frank gave a great big laugh, locking his hands around Opie. "Good to see you."

"You too," he said.

They cut up and talked for hours; but Opie never looked into the casket.

The sun had set over the town of Loeb, but the humidity hung in the air as heavy as ever. The family thanked everyone for coming to the visitation and saw them out of the funeral home, whose director let everyone know the time of the next morning's services.

Opie felt his shirt cling to his back like a second skin, and the sweat dripped from his brow as he and Frank walked to their cars.

"I don't know about you," Frank said, "but I could use a cold one."

"I couldn't possibly turn that down,"

"How 'bout Gus's?"

Opie stopped in his tracks, "You mean to tell me Gus's is still in business?"

"As I live and breathe," Frank said with his right hand to the sky.

"Gus isn't still?" Opie began a ridiculous question.

"No, *Ope,*" Frank said snorting, "Gus would be over a hundred now if that were true. His son runs the place."

"Yeah? What's his name?"

"Gus," Frank said and they laughed.

Frank turned and saw Laura walking with Cat's family. "Laura, darling," he called. "We're going to Gus's."

Laura made a face as if to say, *At this hour?* but didn't protest. Frank shrugged.

Hank broke from the group and caught up with Frank and Opie. "I don't mean to intrude, but would it be okay if I came along?"

Opie looked at Frank, who seemed a little taken aback. "Sure, son. As long as you don't mind being seen with a couple of old-timers like us."

"I don't mind at all," Hank said, running back and kissing his wife and kids.

"Think he can keep up?" Opie asked.

"Not a chance."

Gus's place was still there all right. It seemed to be the only business in Loeb that hadn't changed at all. Opie, who had gotten lost trying to find the funeral home earlier in the day, felt a little comfort sitting in the same booth he had been in on the last night he slept in Loeb, Texas.

There was still one TV and the same shitty radio. As with most holes-in-the-wall, there was a collection of autographed photos, only the display in Gus's consisted of pictures of locals and one of Bruce Springsteen that Gus had bought at a garage sale. Gus Jr. looked the spitting image of his dad.

Hank returned with another pitcher of beer and filled their glasses. He was already walking funny and resting his swimming head in his hand.

"I guess I knew him about as well as you can know your dad," Hank said. "But not as much as I wanted to know him."

"We all feel that, son," Frank said, "Your dad was a hell of a man. One I can say I always looked up to."

Opie raised his glass.

"Growing up in a small town like Loeb, it's all stories," Hank said, watching the beer swirl in his glass. "Stories from when you're a kid all the way up, and you never know how much of them are true. All I ever heard growing up was about you and dad and Tuffy. But there's still so much I don't know."

"Like what?" Frank said pouring himself another glass.

"Well, like how'd he even get the name 'Cat?'" Hank asked, and they laughed. He laughed with them.

"He liked to tell people different things," Opie said, and wiped at his cheek. "Always had a different answer."

"The two big ones were," Frank said counting on his fingers, "because he always landed on his feet and because he had nine lives."

Hank was in suspense. "And the real reason was?"

Frank and Opie looked at one another, and Opie gave Frank the floor.

"When we would go hunting or camping," he said, leaning in, "he would always bury his shit in the leaves."

The answer hung in the air for a while and Hank's face turned to a confused frown. Opie and Frank laughed at him.

"That's it?" he asked. "That's what I've been wondering about my whole life?"

"The thing about stories is, son," Opie said, "they give you the chance to make it mean a little something. When you find out the truth, most times it's a little stupid or disappointing. Might not mean anything."

"Disappointing is right," Hank slurred. "Where is Tuffy anyway? I haven't seen him since I was little."

"He'll be in tomorrow morning," Frank said, "with the new girlfriend in tow."

"Good to know some things never change," Opie said, finishing his drink and pouring another.

Hank looked at him. "It was really nice to finally meet you, Mr. Stokes. My dad always said the nicest things about you."

Opie smiled at him and clinked their glasses.

"How'd you all meet each other?" Hank asked, his eyes fluttering.

Opie and Frank both thought for a second.

"Not much story behind that one," Opie said.

"We followed the girls," Frank smiled, "and here we are."

"And why'd you all leave?" Hank asked, but he was out before he got his answer.

Opie looked out the window and Frank tapped the boy on his head. "Like a light."

"Had my first and last drink in Loeb in this place," Opie said looking at the Christmas lights hanging from the ceiling.

"I remember the first," Frank said, "Homecoming, sophomore year."

They both smiled.

"Susan?" Frank asked.

Opie didn't speak, but his smile said enough.

"Ol' Gus let us get away with a lot, didn't he?" Frank smiled.

"Murder," Opie said and they chuckled.

"Was I here for your last drink?" he asked.

"No."

An oldie played on the radio. Something by the Stones.

"You ended up in Idaho, right?" Frank said finally.

Opie cracked a smile and said through it, "Yeah."

"Jesus H. Christ, *Ope*," Frank guffed, "Why the potato state?"

"It's beautiful up there, Frank. Really." He thought for a while. "I had to get out of here."

Frank filled his glass again, getting the last from the pitcher.

"Shit, we all did, *Ope*," he said, avoiding his eyes, "except Cat."

Some kids entered the place. They were loud and one of them walked over to the juke and played something new, something neither Frank nor Opie recognized.

"I've been thinking about it a lot," Opie said. "The day at the creek."

Frank finished the glass in front of him.

"Have you?"

"Not a day goes by I don't think about it," Frank said, his eyes red in the Christmas lights. "When I got away from here, it was to 'Nam. Me and Cat both. People called it 'the Shit' and it's like a joke now, calling it 'the Shit.' But to be honest with you, Ope, that's the best way to say what we did. All the shit I seen there and I still think about the creek."

The perspiration from the pitcher had run off in the heat from the night. The water now ran down the table and onto the floor in a stream. Opie felt cold all over.

"You know that's where they found him, right?" Frank added.

A glass broke by the counter and Opie nearly leapt from his skin. He knocked the table with this knee and saw that one of the loud kids had dropped their beer and was laughing. Hank continued to sleep.

"What?" Opie asked through the searing pain in his knee.

"At the creek," Frank said, taking Hank's flat glass of beer. "They said he drowned."

"Jesus," Opie said under his breath.

"Yeah. Honest to God. I'm buddies with the coroner, Al Boudreaux. He did great work on our boy today. They said by the time they pulled him out of the water, gars must have got to him."

Opie had nearly gotten lost again driving Hank home but the street signs were all he needed. Without the light of day, he wasn't distracted by how the woods were all gone and how many new houses and fast food places there were. This late they were all dark, and there were only those green signs on every corner. Hank slept soundly in the passenger seat.

With the windows down he could feel the oppressive choke of the humid air, but a night breeze had come in. He passed a deer on the road and it looked at him with unblinking eyes.

When he finally came to East Ashbury Street, he found his way easily to the stone house at the end. Cat's and Susan's home stood in the dark where Cat's parents' house had been.

Opie tucked his arm under Hank's shoulder and helped the young man to the door. He was fumbling for Hank's keys when the door came open and Susan stood there, clutching her robe about her.

"Sorry, Sue, I didn't mean to wake you," Opie said.

"You know I'm up at any little noise," she forced a smile.

"I know he and the kids are staying at their aunt's in town," Opie said. "But I don't know where they live, so I figured he could crash on his mom's couch."

Susan shook her head and ushered them in.

They made their way into the living room and he plopped Hank onto the sofa. He and the couch both grunted. This was the same spot where his family had come to watch the Apollo 11 on the Bluells' TV.

"Where are you staying tonight?" she asked.

Opie blew through his beard, "I just figured I'd find a room somewhere in Beaumont and drive back in the morning."

Susan shook her head. "No, don't be silly, Ope. Come on. You can sleep in Hank's old room."

"You're telling me to take the boy's room and leave him on the couch?"

"Does he look like he minds?" she asked.

Hank didn't mind at all.

That night, in the dark, Opie was thinking about everything Frank had said when he heard the branch of a tree scrape against the window.

Suddenly restless, Opie got up. He crossed the room and pulled down the vinyl blinds. He didn't want to be woken up too early by the sun peeking into the window.

At least that's the reason he told himself for getting out of bed.

He was sure it was just fatigue that had him on edge, but he was very glad for the dark.

He had spent many days and nights of his life at this house and he knew it as well as his own.

And Opie knew there wasn't a tree outside the window of that bedroom.

What woke Opie in the morning wasn't the sun, but it might as well have been. Susan stood over him with a cup of hot coffee in one hand and a plate of eggs and waffles in the other.

"Sue," he said, "you shouldn't have."

"Oh, please," she huffed and walked over to the window, "it's only eggs and Eggos. It took five minutes."

Opie felt a stupid, childlike fear, like a spider crawling in his stomach, as she pulled up the blind. All that was outside was the day that lay ahead of them.

The air inside the Gatlin Funeral Home got a little stuffy, so Frank and Opie stood outside. Frank lit a cigarette and offered the pack to Opie who waved it away.

"What, you never started?" he asked.

"Tried once," Opie said, "didn't take."

Frank grinned. "Always the Boy Scout."

A silver Bimmer pulled around the drive and parked across

the road. The jet-black hair and movie star face that emerged surprised neither Opie nor Frank. Tuffy White was the kind of person that would always look as good as he did in his young adulthood. Tuffy walked around the side of the car and escorted his new girlfriend (this year's looked Middle Eastern) across the lawn. He kissed her for what seemed like a long time and told her he would join her in a minute. She smiled at them and went inside.

Frank just shook his head and laughed. "Don't you beat all."

Tuffy, always humble, just smiled. He regarded Opie with a look the last man on earth would give a picture of his family.

"Opie, I—" he tried and failed.

Opie met him and hugged him.

Tuffy tucked his face into his friend's shoulder and his own shoulders bounced as he cried. Frank came forward and put his arm around them, and when Tuffy brought him into the circle even Frank began to cry.

"I've missed you boys, but God," Tuffy said. "I didn't want this to be the way."

The first wind of the morning blew through the trees outside Gatlin Funeral Home. A cat snaked across the lawn behind them but it didn't look their way.

The service was officiated by a man named Reece Tanner, who looked about twenty years old. Susan had told Opie he was new to Loeb and, despite what people had feared, the old Baptists of the parish took to him quite well. Times had certainly changed, Opie thought.

In the crowd he saw many of the faces from the day before, and many more that hadn't made it. He saw Hank, clearly nursing a hangover, and Susan.

The mourners sang "Amazing Grace" and listened as Betsy Thurston, valedictorian of the class two years Opie's younger, sang a hymnal.

The pews creaked as everyone came to sit, and Opie felt that worrisome stone settle once again when he saw Tuffy remain standing. Tuffy took his girlfriend's hand, squeezed it gently, and walked before the congregation.

"I wanted to do something special today, on account of," his throat clicked with dryness, and he cleared it. "On account of the best friend we ever had."

He looked at Frank, who stood and came to his side. Then he looked to Opie. It seemed like the eyes of the world bore down on Opie and he felt his face burning. He bit his lower lip and shook his head just enough, but Tuffy just looked at him with those green eyes and smiled. With all the strength he could muster, Opie stood as if his legs were made of wood, and made his way out of the row.

When he came to Tuffy's other side, Tuffy patted both of their shoulders and squeezed.

"We're going to sing Cat's favorite song," he said and looked at them. "Well, I'm going to sing it anyway. Frank and Ope are going to play it. You all know I was never good at much, just pretty."

Everyone laughed.

"These boys always had the talent."

Frank went straight to the two acoustic guitars sitting beside the piano, next to the casket.

Opie could see he was smiling a little and he knew that the son of a bitch had known about this all along. He knew exactly what song it was. It was the song Cat had on the record player every day. The song they learned to play on.

Frank held one of the guitars out to Opie, who took it and finally, without meaning to, looked at the body inside the box. It resembled Cat a little, if he'd just been a familiar store mannequin with a chalky face.

Opie must have been standing there for a while because he felt the silence around him and saw that Frank and Tuffy were looking at him, and they seemed to say, *It's okay.* Opie made those wooden legs and stiff feet of his move and felt the guitar, remembering the weight one of these things had. He put his back to the casket.

"I remember listening to this one so many times," Tuffy said.

"And Cat's dad, Walter, getting righteously pissed that we were listening to 'hippy crap.'"

Everyone laughed again. "But he put up with it and even bought Cat a guitar so we could all learn to play crap of our own." Tuffy's eyes met his girlfriend's and they shared a long look.

Opie brushed his calloused fingers over the strings delicately and looked to Frank who nodded. He strummed a G.

The note reverberated throughout the room and no one made a sound.

Opie chanced another look over his shoulder at the man in the box. He could still vaguely see the boy whose living room they had spent nearly every day in as children, talking about girls and music and, later in life, about girls and everything else. He could see a little of Cat in the box and he seemed to be smiling.

Opie played the opening chords and Tuffy began singing. The tune was "Homeward Bound."

The funeral went about as well as a funeral can go. The man went in the box and the box went in the ground. Everyone felt like they should smile, but they cried. Everyone felt like it should be a celebration of life, but it was really an unwelcome meditation on death.

The wives and Tuffy's girlfriend were gathered around pictures at Susan's house. The kids and grandkids milled about the front yard and back. Opie waved to Hank who lifted one of the little ones on his shoulder and bounced him about.

"How are Kay and the kids?" Frank asked Tuffy.

"They're good," he said. "Hadn't heard from them for a while, but they called to check up on me when they heard about Cat. The bastards."

They laughed.

"Yours?" he asked Frank.

"Oh, you know," he said, waving at the air. "Hunter's in Chicago, Katie's in France."

Opie smirked and they both felt sorry for asking in front of him. Then, Opie broke with the pleasantries. "I've been thinking I may go out to the creek while I'm in town."

Frank bit the inside of his cheek and Tuffy scratched at his chin.

"Yeah?" Tuffy asked through a cotton mouth.

Opie looked into the sun. "Just a lot of memories around that place."

"Opie," Frank began.

"Frank," Opie said.

Their eyes met, cold and hard.

"I'm going up there today, stay the night in the old fishing camp," Opie told them. "My plane leaves tomorrow evening."

Tuffy chewed on it, and Frank wanted to scoff but didn't.

"I think I'll join you, Ope," Tuffy said.

They both looked at Frank who, without saying anything at all, agreed just the same.

They had a cooler of beer and three rods and reels in the back of Frank's pickup when they pulled up to the fishing camp. The cooler they planned to use, the rods and reels were a maybe.

The camp was really just one large open floor building with cots, a cleaning station and a generator. There was an outhouse and shower under the large light outside and a plank that extended out over the creek.

The men pulled up a few hours shy of sundown and cracked a few, building a fire and roasting hot dogs over the flames.

"Holy shit," Tuffy said and shot up from his chair.

"What?" Frank asked, poking the fire with his stick.

"If it's still here," Tuffy said walking to the live oak where a tire swing once hung, "it'll be a miracle."

"There's absolutely no way," Opie said.

"Oh my," Tuffy shouted in disbelief, "there is a God!"

From the twisted knot at the oak's roots, Tuffy held aloft an ancient mason jar. In it sloshed liquid nirvana or damnation, depending on where you stood.

"*Ho-Lee* shit," Frank said, laughing and clapping his hands, "that is something else."

Tuffy turned it over in his hand and nothing leaked out. He raised it to his face and wrenched at the cap.

"Tuff, no," Opie protested, "put the shine down."

With some effort the cap came off and Tuffy's jet black hair seemed to prickle from the escaping fumes. He held it at arm's distance and coughed violently.

"Oh, boys," he nearly hurled, "it's still kickin', bubba."

He came back to the fire, returned the cap and tossed the jar to Frank.

"Ol' Henry's moonshine," he said, "hot damn."

They looked back and forth at one another.

"I mean," Opie said, "we have to, right?"

"I'd say it's been written in the stars," Tuffy said brushing the dirt from his palms.

Frank popped it open once more, winced at the scent and raised the jar. "To Cat."

He swigged and his eyes shot open and nostrils flared. Frank nearly fell backward, swinging his arms wide and finally caught his breath.

"I believe that is actual hellfire," he choked.

They laughed and Tuffy took it from him. "To Cat."

Tuffy's swig was brief, but much to the same effect. He nearly dropped the jar.

"No," he yelled, catching it between fingertips and coughs, "The nectar of life."

He handed it to Opie who cracked it open and tried not to sniff, but it was impossible. His eyes began watering, so he closed them and said, "To Cat."

They had spent many summers out here as boys. This waswhere they had tried acid together, with Connie Briggs, Charlotte Smalley,

Betsy Thurston and even Susan.

"Remember when we got Betsy to buy acid from her brother?" Opie asked.

"I wish I could forget," Frank said.

"I don't," Tuffy said, and they all laughed.

"Shit was a nightmare," Frank said, putting his beer aside. "I don't see how anyone thinks it's fun."

"I didn't even feel it," Tuffy said.

"That's because you're the devil himself," Frank answered, squinting one eye and giving Tuffy finger-horns.

"All I remember is skinny dipping with Connie Lou," Tuffy said. "I know I have three kids, but I can easily say that was the best night of my life."

"That's pretty sad," Opie said.

"I'm kidding, Opie," Tuffy said, "'Course I love my kids."

"No," Opie said, crushing his can. "I mean it's sad the best night of your life was when you swam naked with Frank Baird."

Frank and Tuffy howled with laughter.

They looked into the fire a while, then Tuffy stood up.

"Shit, man," he said.

Frank sneered, "What?"

Tuffy stripped his shirt away and ran toward the water.

Opie slapped his knee, "Tuff, get your ass back here."

Tuffy's jeans were gone and in a second he flung himself into the creek.

"Gar's gonna bite off your pecker," Frank called after him.

"Not a chance," his voice was shrill. "It's summer, but holy hell it's cold."

The two at the fireside laughed.

"Aw hell," Frank said and held his beer in one hand and began unbuttoning his shirt.

Opie would have protested but there was no point.

The two shed their clothes and waded into the water.

Up to his knees, Opie hollered as the icy water stung his skin.

"Just gotta jump, fellas," Tuffy said, "Feels mighty fine already."

Frank threw himself forward and broke the surface, swinging his arms like he had after drinking from the moonshine. Opie followed.

They were up to their shoulders, but the creek's swell was far from the full power of the Moyie this time of year. The creek simply nudged you along, almost as a suggestion rather than a force.

The men laughed and splashed and talked about that night with the girls. Tuffy loved talking about Connie. He seemed to be looking for her in every woman he met. Frank kept nervously mentioning gar and Opie just looked at the stars.

They had not noticed where the current had taken them when suddenly Tuffy's smiling face went grave. His body stood like a rock in the middle of the creek. The other two planted as well and looked to where his eyes were.

They saw at once where they had drifted and Tuffy dryly said, "Come on guys, let's get the fuck out of here."

The walk back along the bank was sobering. Not just because they were naked, but also because the light from the stars and moon shone on all the memories they had of the creek. Especially the one that brought them there.

They had gathered their clothes and taken turns in the shower, though Tuffy just soaped up by the creek's edge. Frank killed the fire with what was left of his beer and, with a belch, retired to a cot inside.

Frank had always been a snorer, and it had only gotten worse with age. Opie turned over in his cot and was never so glad that there were no windows in the place. He heard something shuffling around outside and tried to tell himself it was only some kind of animal. But the electricity that links souls also speaks to the part of you that recognizes something that shouldn't be. The charge was coursing through Opie now, as strong as the night of the phone calls; and it was telling him that *she* was outside.

"You hear it, too?" Tuffy whispered.

Opie didn't jump. He wasn't startled. He merely nodded.

"It isn't a deer," he said.

"I know."

"Do you know what it is?" Tuffy asked.

"I think so."

They listened for a long time. Both of them wanted to get up and out of their cots but they didn't. Perhaps if one of them had, the other may have had the courage to follow. But neither budged.

They listened as whatever it was slithered outside until it finally came to a stop at the door.

In the morning light Frank went about collecting the cans and debris from the night before. Neither Tuffy nor Opie mentioned what they heard, nor did they particularly want to. They knew Frank. He would laugh them off and say it was something they knew it wasn't. He would point to the tracks outside and say they were "from us acting like dumb as shit kids last night" and he wouldn't listen to them when they told him that the footprints weren't theirs. That they couldn't be because they were too small.

Opie followed their tracks in the mud along the bank to where they had gotten out the creek the night before. He didn't want to go back, but he had to. It was foolish to come all the way from Idaho to Texas, to Loeb, to the creek, then to turn back before returning to where it happened.

His legs were wooden again, and his feet made of lead. He swore to himself that with every breath and every inch gained, the bend seemed to stretch even farther away. But he pressed on.

The air was thicker than ever, like soup, and the mosquitoes buzzed around his eyes and mouth. Opie swatted at them and dug them out of his ears.

As he got closer to the bend, he was remembering back to that summer day. Before the night of skinny dipping. Before Homecoming their sophomore year. When he and Frank, Tuffy and Cat had snaked around the bend, carrying their rods and reels and a pack of cigarettes they had stolen from Frank's older brother.

Opie kept moving. He could feel his feet sinking deeper into the mud with each step.

The four of them had come around the bend to a grove of willows, their skirts skating on the surface of the creek. A huge pine snag stuck out of the water and onto the bank. There was no wind, and no mosquitoes. They had all been blown away by Hurricane Lee a few days before. The storm had torn apart their little township and left the houses along the creek in shambles.

Opie jerked his feet free as he went and began to cry. Then the ground was solid and the mosquitoes were gone. The sky went dark and a hush settled over the creek.

Opie was following himself and the other three boys, a lifetime ago now, as they heard the choked coughing from the pine snag. Opie watched as the boys stopped in their tracks and listened.

They heard it again. It was soft. They approached the snag carefully, stepping over the trunk and its jutting branches.

"Oh Christ, boys," Opie said.

There was a girl, probably one of the people lost in the flood. Probably teenaged, but maybe not.

She was half submerged in the brackish creek water and a steady flow of black-red blood pooled around her head and dissipated into the stream. She whispered something but no one could hear what it was. Her eyes just stared up at the sky. She didn't blink. And as the boys looked on, they didn't blink either.

"I'm sorry," Opie said, through fresh tears and a mouthful of spit. "I'm so sorry."

"Opie," Tuffy called from behind. "Opie, please. Let's go."

"I will," he said, not startled by Tuffy's presence. Opie knew Tuffy had been behind him all along. He just wondered if the walk was as hard for him. "Just give me a moment."

Tuffy knelt beside his friend in the mud and put a hand on his shoulder.

At the fishing camp, Frank fell to his knees beside his pickup truck and began to weep. For the first time since he was a young boy, he cried ugly.

Opie turned to Tuffy.

"What did we do to that poor girl?"

"I don't remember."

"Uncle Sam called your number, huh?" Opie said, "Bum deal, man."

"Yeah," Cat said, lighting a cigarette, "Dad's proud. Worried, but proud."

Gus came by and slipped them their drinks. He gave them a wink and went back to the counter.

Opie looked into his drink for a while, "I'm leaving this summer, too."

"Yeah?" Cat said with a drag. "Where to?"

"Canada maybe."

"Canada?" Cat laughed, "You're no draft dodger. And even if you was, Mexico is a hell of a lot closer than Canada."

"I don't speak Spanish."

"You don't speak French either, buddy," Cat said.

Opie smiled and rested his chin on his arms. "I like the cold."

"You be likely to fit in more up there, Opie Taylor," Cat reached across the table and ruffled Opie's red hair. "You really leaving?"

"Think so."

Cat understood. It was the same reason why Cat wasn't running for the border when he learned he was drafted. It was a ticket out.

"I still see her," Opie said and looked around nervously.

Cat nodded and gave him a cigarette.

Opie took it and lit it against Cat's.

"You're taking all of this really well," Opie said as the cigarette burned his throat.

"I'll see you again. Just got a feeling."

"Keep dreaming, because once I'm out I'm gone."

"I'll get you back one way or the other," Cat said with that grin.

"Yeah, yeah. Stay cool, Cat."

In one gulp, Opie drank his last beer in Loeb, Texas.

They drove home in total silence.

They didn't look at each other or even Loeb.

They only looked at the road.

When they got back to Frank's, Opie said his goodbyes and they drank one last beer to Cat. Opie watched Tuffy pull away in his Bimmer and saw Frank back into his house. He got into his own rental car and cancelled his flight.

He drove back to the house on East Ashbury where he had seen the Beatles play on the Ed Sullivan Show and Cat's sister had nearly lost her mind.

There were more cars parked outside still, but not as many as had been yesterday. A few of the kids were passed out on the lawn. One of them waved and he waved back.

He knocked on the door and Susan answered it. She smiled.

"What a pleasant surprise," she said, ushering him in.

The day grew later and the two talked a bit but mostly sat in silence. Very warm, comfortable silence. Mourners came and went and Susan saw everyone off. Opie shook Hank's hand, and patted him on the shoulder and told him that Cat was the man he always wished he had been. Even if it wasn't true, it was what he had to say.

At night the big grandfather clock bonged and on the twelfth they knew it was another day.

"Opie, I hope you don't mind but," she began.

"Sue," Opie said, "You know I would never mind."

"It's just that, out of the four of you," she continued, "you were always the most put together. The most stable one of the bunch. It wasn't an accident that I went with you to that disgusting bar you boys all loved on Homecoming." She searched for how to ask.

Opie didn't like where the conversation was heading.

"And yet you are the only one who never started a family," Sue said. She held her hands in front of her and smiled. "I'm not about to preach to you and say children are the answer to everything. I've just always wondered why you didn't settle down"

Opie had half-expected worse. It was a fair question, but one he had never thought he would have to answer because he had no one who cared enough to ask.

The words came to his mouth but he held onto them.

"Because, Susan, I've always thought if I had a baby," he said, "If I had a little girl . . . "

He trailed off.

The face of the girl lingered in Opie's mind, eyes unblinking and mouth popping silently, her face like marble set against the blood pooling around her head.

"How could I bring a poor little thing into this world?" he said, his lower lip trembling.

Opie would not sleep that night. And it wasn't just the face that he couldn't get out of his mind or the scratching at the window. There wasn't any scratching. There weren't any shuffling footsteps. He was waiting for them and they were not there.

Opie sat up in bed and looked to the window. There was no moon and no stars. It was a black pool beyond the glass.

He could feel something out there just beyond that pane. It was watching him.

He slid his legs over until his feet felt the floor. He adjusted himself, feeling every muscle and tendon pull in the action of standing. He equaled his weight in order to stop the bed frame from creaking.

As he rose his joints popped and he felt each one. He shuffled that long, long walk to the window, to lower the vinyl blind. The floor then seemed very much like the mud of a creek bed. He could almost feel the breath, the heat, even the weight of whatever was just on the other side of the glass and he was terribly sure he knew what it would be.

At the window his hand felt the blind, but he did not pull it down. Something was out there, just beyond his vision. Something was looking at him in the dark. Something was watching him.

At the tree line he saw a soft white glow popping in and out, flickering like a lightning bug, like the unblinking girl's lips. *Pop pop pop.* It pulsed with a brilliant flourish, soft white and then a hundred different colors. It seemed to float across the back yard, welcoming, beckoning, like an outstretched hand.

Opie couldn't move. His feet no longer felt like lead, but instead roots reaching deep into the ground and he was stuck at the window, one arm raised, face pressed against the glass.

The figure that came into view at first looked like a blurry photograph of the girl from the creek. As she came closer he could see it looked like something else entirely. The eyes became blank and endless orbs. The mouth became a hideous pit of teeth and all at once it looked like something pulled from the sea.

Her mouth still pop pop popped, just as silent as the day they met, and Opie realized she had been searching for him all his life, and he had been searching for her.

It was a scream that woke him. He shuddered and felt his knees give out and he fell. Opie found himself on the floor in front of the bedroom window, the blind in one hand torn from its sheath and the sunlight beaming down on him.

The police lights were faint in the morning light, but Opie recognized them for what they were. He stumbled outside to see Susan weeping silently, surrounded by family and neighbors. They were all bawling while the officers stood in front of them with grave faces and bad news.

Opie approached Susan, but she wouldn't look at him. "What's wrong?" he said, looking into the crowd. "Where is Hank?"

That night, Frank and Opie sat alone at Gus's once again.

"Can't believe a thing like this happening to poor Susan,"

Frank rasped around his beer. "What has she ever done to deserve such?"

Opie didn't say anything.

"He seemed fine to you, didn't he?" Frank asked. "The night he came here with us, and at the funeral? He seemed to be taking it pretty well, considering. Jesus, and we were just at that creek."

"Sure," Opie said, looking at his hands. "He seemed fine."

"What could have possessed him to go out there?" Frank ventured. "Was he keeping vigil for his dad, or . . ."

Frank didn't finish. He pinched the bridge of his nose, instead.

Neither of them said anything else for a long time.

"Jesus, I know it's awful and I shouldn't be saying it at a time like this," Frank said. "But Jesus God we were lucky the other night. From what they were able to pull from the creek, Al says the gars must be some kind of bad down there."

"I don't know," Opie replied finally, through his teeth. "I don't know."

Frank suddenly shuddered.

The perspiration from Opie's beer had begun to pool again and drip off the table. He jerked his leg out of the way to make sure his jeans didn't get wet.

Bios

Jacklyn Baker

Jacklyn Baker is a member of the SMU Writers Path living in the Dallas area and currently working on her first novel.

Summer Baker

Born in Oregon and raised in Texas, Summer Baker has spent her entire life on the eerie High Plains around Amarillo. She graduated from West Texas A&M University with a degree in English and has had two stories published in *The Legacy*. When she's not feigning adulthood, she likes to write and read fantasy and horror, play tabletop RPGs (like Dungeons & Dragons, Deadlands and Delta Green) and take road trips with her friends to hunt cryptids and old bookstores.

E.R. Bills

E.R. Bills was born in Fort Worth and raised in Aledo, Texas. He received a Bachelor of Arts in Journalism from Texas State University and started freelance writing for local newspapers, magazines and weeklies in 2006. He is the author of *Texas Obscurities: Stories of the Peculiar, Exceptional and Nefarious* (The History Press, 2013), *The 1910 Slocum Massacre: An Act of Genocide in East Texas* (The History Press, 2014), *Black Holocaust: The Paris Horror and a Legacy of Texas Terror* (Eakin Press, 2015), *Texas Dissident: Dispatches from a Diminished State, 2006-2016* (Eakin Press, 2017) and *Texas Far and Wide: The Tornado with Eyes, Gettysburg's Last Casualty, the Celestial Skipping Stone and Other Tales* (The History Press, 2017). Bills co-created the Texas horror *Road Kill* book series with writer and legendary schlock filmmaker Bret McCormick in 2016 and co-edited volume one.

Crystal Brinkerhoff

Crystal Brinkerhoff is a resident of Spring, Texas. "El Sacoman" is her first short story in the *Road Kill* series. When not writing she can be found trail running, exploring ghost towns and watching *The Twilight Zone* with her husband and five kids.

Hayden Gilbert

Hayden Gilbert is an amateur filmmaker from Lumberton, Texas. He has a degree in communication and film from Lamar University and has been involved in the creative arts since age ten. He currently resides in San Marcos, Texas, and this is his first published story.

Jeremy Hepler

Native to the Texas Panhandle, Jeremy Hepler lives with his wife Tricia and son Noah in a small rural community in the heart of Texas. He has had twenty-eight short stories published in small, professional, and online markets, and his debut novel, *The Boulevard Monster*, was published by Bloodshot Books in April 2017. Besides writing, he loves to read, garden, draw and repurpose old furniture. For more information, contact him on Facebook, Twitter (@jeremyhepler), or Goodreads.

R.J. Joseph

R.J. Joseph is a Texas-based writer and professor who must exorcise the demons of her imagination so they don't haunt her being. A life-long horror fan and author of many things, she has recently discovered the joys of writing in the academic arena about two important aspects of her life: horror and black femininity. When Joseph isn't writing, teaching or reading, she enjoys spending time with her family.

Andrew Kozma

Andrew Kozma's fiction has been published in *Albedo One, Escape Pod, Interzone* and *Daily Science Fiction*. His book of poems, *City of Regret* (Zone 3 Press, 2007), won the Zone 3 First Book Award.

James H. Longmore

James H. Longmore originally hails from Yorkshire, England. He relocated with his family to Houston, Texas, in 2010. Longmore has an honors degree in Zoology and a background in sales, marketing and business. He is an affiliate member of the Horror Writer's Association and has five novels in print: '*Pede, Tenebrion, Flanagan, And Then You Die* and *The Erotic Odyssey of Colton Forshay*–plus *Blood and Kisses,* his definitive short story collection. Longmore also writes screenplays and currently has three under option (a spine-chilling horror, a Tarantino-esque crime caper and an animated family movie). In 2014 he was commissioned by Spectra Records to write a biopic feature on the early life of Bob Marley. In 2015 he was a writer for hire on the Kenyan sitcom 'The Samaritans'. Longmore has also written and directed several movie shorts, which have won awards at Splatterfest and the Remi awards at Houston's Worldfest Film Festival. Go to www.jameslongmore.com for additional information on Longmore's work.

Mario E. Martinez

Mario E. Martinez draws his inspiration from the landscape of the South Texas border, a place where busy roads cut through ranchlands and dark mysteries of the natural world sit beside shopping plazas and new neighborhoods. His works have been featured in *Nothing. No One. Nowhere., left hand of the father, Collective Exile, Deadman's Tome, Pulp Modern* and *Robbed of Sleep Vol. 5*. He recently published his third book, *A Pig Named Orrenius & Other Strange Tales.*

Bret McCormick

Bret McCormick is a writer, artist and film maker living in Bedford, Texas. From 1984 through 1996 he produced and directed a slew of indie movies for international distribution. His novels, *Hellfire* and *Headhunters from Outer Space,* are available in Kindle, paperback and audiobook formats on Amazon. McCormick co-created the Texas horror *Road Kill* book series with writer E. R. Bills in 2016 and co-edited volume one.

Ralph Robert Moore

Ralph Robert Moore has been nominated twice for Best Story of the Year by The British Fantasy Society. His books include the novels *Father Figure, As Dead as Me* and *Ghosters,* and the story collections *Remove the Eyes, I Smell Blood* and *You Can Never Spit It All Out*. SENTENCE at www.ralphrobertmoore.com features a broad selection of his stories, essays and other writings. He and his wife Mary live in Cedar Hill, Texas.

S. Kay Nash

S. Kay Nash grew up in the desert southwest, raised by a cabal of university professors, anthropologists and librarians. A copy editor by day, she also writes short fiction and book reviews. She uses her university degrees as magical wards to prevent her from being hauled back into the Ivory Tower. She lives in Texas with a mad scientist and a peaceful contingent of cats and dogs. Find her on Twitter @Gnashchick or visit pulleditouttamyass.com

Stephen Patrick

North Texas writer Stephen Patrick never tires of the diverse literary palette that ranges through his home state and enjoys contributing to that oeuvre when he can. His work has appeared in various publications, (including *Road Kill: Texas Horror by Texas Writers Vol. 1*) and he is a frequent panel guest and contest judge for DFW's own FENCON and ConDFW. He lives in the DFW area with his family.

Dennis Pitts

Dennis Pitts is a science fiction and fantasy writer living in Richardson, Texas. He is currently working on a series of short stories that revolve around a private investigator in post-WWII Fort Worth.

Bonnie Jo Stufflebeam

Bonnie Jo Stufflebeam's fiction and poetry has appeared in more than forty magazines such as *Clarkesworld, Hobart* and *Lightspeed.* She has been a finalist for the Nebula Award and the Selected Shorts' Stella Kupferberg Memorial Prize. Her audio fiction-jazz collaborative album *Strange Monsters* was released from Easy Brew Studio in April 2016. You can find her online at www.bonniejostufflebeam.com or on Twitter @BonnieJoStuffle.

Keith West

Keith West works in academia in west Texas and has been a fan of science fiction, fantasy, horror and mystery all his life. His stories have appeared in *Storyhack Issue 0* and the anthologies *Weird Menace, Vol. 1, Tales from the Otherverse* and *Rocket's Red Glare.* West's current projects include a hard-science sword and planet novel, a sword and sorcery series about an exiled prince cursed to kill his father, and a near-future space opera. He can be found online at www.adventuresfantastic.com.

Bryce Wilson

Bryce Wilson's work has been featured in the anthologies *State of Horror California, The Edge: Infinite Darkness* and *More Raw Material.* His film criticism has been published in *Paracinema, Art Decades and ScreenRant.* His books include *Son of Danse Macabre* and *The Unquiet Dead.* He currently lives in Austin, Texas.

Road Kill:
Texas Horror by Texas Writers
Volume 1

An ancient demon plays cowboy and takes on the Texas Rangers. Three teenage girls sneak into a "body farm." An aging African American couple defies the Grim Reaper. An FBI agent discovers an entire city that's gone to the "dogs." A handyman learns that the fixer-upper he's working on has a doorway to the past that's way out of square. And a pack of possums burrow into the body politic.

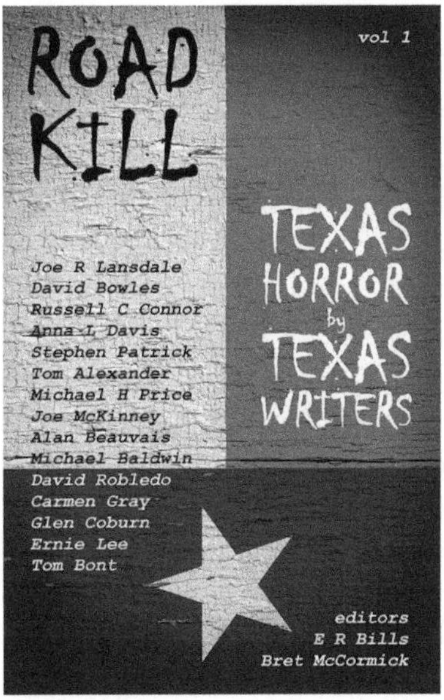

Join seventeen Texas authors for a harrowing spin on the twisting freeways and dark back roads that wind through the Lone Star State. Includes works from Joe R. Lansdale, David Bowles, Anna L. Davis, Stephen Patrick, Carmen Gray, Russell C. Connor, Michael H. Price, Tom Bont, Ernie Lee, David Robledo, Alan Beauvais, Michael Baldwin, Glen Coburn, Joe McKinney, Tom Alexander, Bret McCormick and E. R. Bills.

ISBN-13: 978-1681790794
Paperback • 238 pages • $17.95

Also Availableas an Ebook

CPSIA information can be obtained
at www.ICGtesting.com
Printed in the USA
LVHW01s2012181117
556825LV00003B/20/P

9 781681 790992